T0304864

The Berlin Agent

Stephen Ronson

HODDER &
STOUGHTON

First published in Great Britain in 2024 by Hodder & Stoughton Limited
An Hachette UK company

1

A CIP catalogue record for this title is available from the British Library

Hardback ISBN 978 1 399 72128 8
Trade Paperback ISBN 978 1 399 72129 5
ebook ISBN 978 1 399 72131 8

Typeset in Plantin Light by Manipal Technologies Limited

Printed and bound in Great Britain by Clays Ltd, Elcograf S.p.A.

Hodder & Stoughton policy is to use papers that are natural, renewable and recyclable products and made from wood grown in sustainable forests. The logging and manufacturing processes are expected to conform to the environmental regulations of the country of origin.

Hodder & Stoughton Limited
Carmelite House
50 Victoria Embankment
London EC4Y 0DZ

The authorised representative in the EEA is Hachette Ireland, 8 Castlecourt Centre, Castleknock Road, Castleknock, Dublin 15, D15 YF6A, Ireland

www.hodder.co.uk

For Bill, one of 'the few'

Never in the field of human conflict was so much owed by so many to so few.

Winston Churchill, 20 August 1940

I
Thursday, 6 June 1940

Every window of the idling train was crammed with soldiers, leaning out, holding tin cups and cheap church-hall plates. I worked my way along the platform, teapot lifted to shoulder-height, filling each cup. Mum followed close behind, adding a splash of milk, talking with the men, making them feel like conquering heroes. Behind Mum, volunteers from the Women's Institute passed out sandwiches. Every house in Uckfield had answered the call for food and drink to be delivered to the station, for our brave boys, back from Dunkirk.

German tanks had rolled through France without slowing, and our worst nightmare was realised. They'd reached the English Channel, encircling our men. Four hundred thousand men, along with every piece of artillery we possessed. We got most of the men away, a flotilla of boats shuttling them off the beaches under constant bombardment. They left the equipment behind, destroying some, abandoning the rest.

I caught the eye of a young soldier as I filled his mug. He looked away.

I didn't hold their defeat against them. I'd been there in my day, the man in the trenches, following orders of the strategic brains back in London, or more likely back in a comfortable country house where the tea is poured into bone china, and the sandwiches are cut into triangles. Blaming the man on the front line for the strategic failure that had led to our catastrophic withdrawal from the beaches of Dunkirk was like blaming a schoolboy for failing an exam set in a language he'd never been taught.

Only a month earlier I'd gone to London to sign up. If we were going to repeat the mistakes of the Great War, better me dying in a trench than a young man with a family. But the army told me they had different plans for me. Some of them, a small faction hidden deep inside the War Office, had predicted the speed of Hitler's sweep across France. I'd met with a curious man dressed in rumpled civvies who called himself Bunny, who told me to start preparing for the invasion. I was to form a unit of men like myself – ex-army, farmers and landowners, men who knew the countryside, who knew how to disappear into the woods. Men, and women, as it turned out. All of this was to be off the books. Hush hush.

The platform was a crush of people: volunteers shuttling trays of food and fresh teapots, carrying away empties; mothers and sweethearts, hoping against all odds to find out if their lad had made it back; soldiers hurrying to the toilets, or to post a letter, that nervous run from a train that had been idling for hours, but could leave without notice at any minute.

Further back down the line, another train waited. More blocked the line ahead. The biggest troop movement in England's history. We'd done the hard part, getting them off the beaches and across the Channel. Now it was all at risk if we couldn't get them out of harm's way. The Germans would be hot on their heels, expected any day. First the parachutists, dropped behind our lines. Then the invasion proper. The press said they'd start with artillery, firing from their battleships in the middle of the English Channel. And then, when we were appropriately softened up, the landing craft.

Everyone had a suitcase packed. If you had a car, you had the tank filled and the map ready. You didn't want to be around when the Panzers rolled through town, their steel tracks screaming on the tarmac.

My plans would be different. When the tanks arrived, I'd put Mum and Uncle Nob in the car with our two evacuees and point them towards Scotland. I'd walk away from my farm, meet up with my team. Lie low. Wait for the invaders to pass on. Then, when German High Command declared victory and returned to Berlin, we'd start our operations. Making trouble. A killing here. A train blown up there. Whatever we could do, until they caught us. Two weeks, they estimated, the predicted life expectancy in units like ours. Give a man a crate of TNT and a few guns and he could get a lot done in two weeks. Bunny had provided the weapons. We'd hidden them away, but not safely enough. The lion's share had been stolen by one of our number, a man I'd thought I could trust. He'd left us practically empty-handed, with barely enough to get the job done.

The bomber came out of the south, flying low. A speck in the sky, a deep rumble that was felt, rather than heard. It came out of the sun, following the train track up from the coast. Every head turned and watched, the crowd hushed. Then the first scream. An electric spark running through the crowd. A whistle, followed by shouted orders, barked by an efficient sergeant major.

'On the ground! Now!'

Crockery smashed in the scrum. Cutlery tinkled on the concrete platform, amid the growing roar of the bomber.

Only two of us were left standing. Me, and the sergeant major at the far end of the platform, perched on the raised step of the train. He looked down the track, at the bomber that now filled the sky, then he turned to me. I met his eye.

A moment of connection, perhaps the last of our lives. An understanding. Lying down on the ground was good for crowd control, for giving people something to do, but it wasn't going to help anyone if there was a direct hit.

The plane roared over us with a rush of wind. The bomb bay doors opened. But it wasn't our day to die. Instead of bombs, bundles of paper came tumbling from the plane on a diagonal path, the speed of the plane dictating their momentum. The wind pulled at the bundles, and they came apart in a flurry of newsprint, as the plane flew on, its roar dissipating.

There was a thump from next to me as a bundle landed intact, splitting open on impact with a slew of paper.

People got to their feet, grabbing papers, like trying to catch falling snow. I picked up a copy. It was a newspaper, although the typeface was wrong. Not one of ours. Strange how a little thing like that could look foreign.

'An Appeal to Reason', the headline stated politely. Not the catchiest introduction. Below, a dense block of text, uninviting to the eye. From Hitler himself, apparently. Lucky us. Appealing to the people of England. No need for war. That sort of thing.

'I'll take that lot,' a Tommy called to me from the train. He jumped down from his carriage and scooped up what he could from the remains of the bundle, checking with me as if it was my property. I nodded.

'Got to be a week's worth of bog roll there,' he said, as he lugged it onto the train.

The atmosphere on the platform had changed. Before, we'd been tense, fearing the worst. Now we'd faced our fears, it was like a holiday. Perhaps it wouldn't be so bad after all.

There was a crash several carriages back, and an ironic cheer from the boys closest to the action. I craned my neck to see what had happened. Shouts of concern. Calls for space. For air. For a doctor.

I pushed my way through the crowd, holding my teapot above my head, back past the boys I'd already served.

An elderly woman was on her knees, picking sandwiches off the platform, putting them back onto a large tray. Her cheeks were red, her eyes brimming with tears held back. Embarrassed to be the centre of attention. Angry with herself. I knelt down and helped clear the mess, throwing slices of grit-encrusted ham under the train, onto the tracks. She flashed a watery smile as we finished. As she picked up the tray, she winced.

'I'll take it,' I said, pulling the tray towards me.

'No,' she said, reaching for it, like a tug of war.

I recognised her from a lifetime ago, when I'd been a boy, before I'd gone to war. Before a lot of things. Mrs Leckie, my first teacher at the Saunders School on Church Street. It must have been thirty-five years and she looked the same as she had then.

As she pulled the tray, the sleeve of her cardigan rode up her arm and I caught a glimpse of purple. A livid bruise. She winced again.

'There's enough sandwiches being handed out here to feed a division,' I said to her. 'I could do with a cup of tea. Come and help me find one.' Slightly absurd, with an over-size teapot on the platform by my side, but she didn't seem to notice.

If I'd suggested she take a break she would have refused. It would have been a sign of weakness. My asking for help gave her cover. Not to onlookers, to herself. A lifetime of bringing tea to a man when he asked, or even when he didn't.

We sat in the waiting room as the chaos of the station continued around us. The usual smell of coal smoke and cigarettes mixed with a new smell, already familiar, wool uniforms and leather, soaked in sea water and engine oil, permeated with sweat. And underneath all of it, the smell of war, the smell of fear. If I closed my eyes I could have been back on the Western Front, or huddled in a cave in Afghanistan, where I'd learnt my craft after the Armistice. But I wasn't at the front. I was in Uckfield, my sleepy, unremarkable home town in sleepy, unremarkable Sussex.

She gulped down her tea, in a hurry. She winced as she raised her arm.

'I shouldn't have come,' she said, 'Stan'll be missing me.'

I presumed it was Stan who'd put the bruise on her wrist.

'Where do you live?' I asked.

'Palehouse Lane, there'll be a bus along in a minute.'

'I'll drive you,' I said. 'Got to get back myself.'

The volunteers on the platform would cope without me. Mum would make her own way home. I wanted to meet Stan. I wanted to find out more about the bruises. Have a quiet word.

2

Palehouse Lane was three miles north of town. One of those turn-offs from the London road before it climbed up to the high, open expanse of Ashdown Forest. I'd driven past it a thousand times and never taken it. We took the turning and the lane dipped, around a sharp bend, and then over a ford, where a stream bubbled across the road.

'What happens when the water's higher?' I asked, as we splashed through the ford.

'We stay at home.'

It was the most she'd said for the whole ten-minute journey. I'd tried my silent treatment, known to work on surly farm labourers and Tommies alike. Most people don't like silence. Keep quiet long enough and they'll start talking to fill the void. Tell you what's on their mind. Seemed Mrs Leckie was made of sterner stuff. Probably knew what I was up to. Probably planning a quick thank you and goodbye at the garden gate, before scurrying into the house, back to Stan. Planning her apology for leaving him alone. Fetch his tea and his paper.

We left the ford behind and headed on, through thicker woodland, around winding turns. Through the open window I heard the roar of an engine and slowed, forcing my aging delivery van onto the grass verge. Lucky I did. A large lorry roared around the corner in the middle of the road. He swerved when he saw me but didn't slow, roaring past me with inches to spare, a slew of sand and earth thrown onto the road and clattering against my van.

The lorry was gone in an instant, hurtling around the bends I'd navigated, the driver obviously familiar with the contours of the road.

'Maniacs,' she said, anticipating my question. 'Night and day, back and forth.'

The lane ran on for another mile. Longer than I'd imagined, taking us deeper into a wooded valley I'd never known existed. I kept an eye out for her house. I predicted a short terrace of farmworkers' cottages. Two up, two down, dark brick, damp.

We took a sharp right-hand turn, and the road headed upwards, like running straight up a cliff. The engine in the old van complained and I had to drop down through the gears, all the way to first. Trees crowded the road and then suddenly we were clear of them, like surfacing from the sea, onto an island of heath. The sky was vast and blue, with only a few contrails. The day's dog-fighting hadn't kicked off.

Mrs Leckie nodded towards a small cottage as we approached, at the apex of the hill. Black timbers and white plaster. Laburnum blooming around the door. And all around it, the huge blue sky, like a massive dome covering slopes of purple heather and distant clumps of trees that looked like toys on a child's train set.

There was a sandy layby across the road from the house, and I pulled into it, the engine running fast after its exertion getting up the hill. Mrs Leckie tensed as we slowed, checking the surroundings with quick, darting looks. Like somebody about to go into battle, doing their reconnaissance, assessing likely sources of danger. She gripped the door handle, ready for a quick exit.

'I'll walk you to the door,' I said.

'No need,' she said, opening the door before I'd stopped the van. I stood on the brakes, didn't want her killing herself jumping out of a moving vehicle after I'd been so gallant about bringing her home. The van slid on the white sand, then she was out.

I climbed out and caught up.

'You've got to go,' she said, looking up and down the road as if she were crossing a city street, rather than an empty country lane at the top of a forgotten hill in the middle of nowhere.

'I want to make sure you're going to be OK. Don't want you getting any more bruises.'

She slipped through the garden gate and pulled it closed behind her, putting a barrier between us.

'Please,' she said.

She left me there and hurried to the front door, fumbling in her bag.

I watched her at the door, scratching at the lock with her key. Not a practised manoeuvre. Not the way you'd do it if you'd unlocked the door every day of a long life. I looked around. Good visibility in every direction. Probably one or two houses further along the lane, or wherever the lorry had come from, then a dead end. No strangers. Probably lived here for decades without locking the door. Never needed to. Until now.

Put the locked door together with her nervous threat assessment as we'd approached the house, and I had to consider I'd been wrong. Perhaps Stan wasn't the problem.

I opened the gate and strode to the front door. She got it open and hurried inside, but I got my boot in before she could slam it shut.

'What's going on?' I asked.

She looked at me, blocking her door. She was terrified, her eyes darting past me to the lane.

She thought she had a decision to make. Ask me to help, or turn me away. But there was no decision required. She needed my help, so she was going to get it.

3

I heard the gun being cocked as I followed her into the dark hallway. The click of a well-oiled ratchet, pulled past its setting point, then resting. Ready for release. Waiting for the trigger. The sequence repeated. Two clicks. A double-barrelled shotgun, well maintained by its owner.

Not too late for me to dart backwards, out of the door. But that would leave Mrs Leckie alone with the gunman. I could drop to the floor, use the second gained to look for the source of the noise, but my eyes were still adjusting to the gloom of the hallway after the bright summer morning outside. The sound had come from my right, through the doorway that presumably led to a snug. So I stepped forwards, between Mrs Leckie and the doorway, into harm's way. I'd come here to protect her. Time to live up to my ideals.

'Put the bloody gun away, Stan,' Mrs Leckie snapped. 'It's Johnny Cook, he's given me a lift home.'

'Cook?' came a voice from the snug.

'You remember,' she said. 'Bess and George's lad. Always had a cricket ball in his hand.'

Mrs Leckie hung up her coat and hurried forwards into the kitchen.

'Now you're here, you may as well make yourself useful,' she called back to me. 'You can get my sterilising pans down from the top shelf. Still time to get the jam made before the Boche get here. Waste not, want not.'

It was brave talk, but the tension in her voice was audible. I heard her opening drawers in the kitchen, making noise, warding off the fear.

Stan was sitting in an armchair, a blanket over his knees. His thin neck and small head disappeared into the starched collar of his shirt, like a tortoise poking its head out for a quick look around. The shotgun extended towards me, long and heavy, wobbling as he struggled to keep it aimed. He looked at me carefully.

'They said you died at the Somme.'

He uncocked the gun and carefully leant it against the side of the chair, his hands shaking with the effort.

'That was my dad,' I said.

'What happened to your brother? Nob, wasn't it?'

'My uncle. He came back, just about. Shell-shock.'

Stan grunted. 'Sounds about right,' he said, as if returning from the war irreparably damaged was a character defect.

As my eyes adjusted to the gloom, I got a better look at Stan. The left side of his face was swollen, bruises extended down his neck. The way he was sitting, it looked like he was in pain, holding himself still.

'What happened?' I asked.

His eyes flicked towards the kitchen, then back to me.

'You'll be wanting to get on your way,' he said, loud enough for his voice to carry.

The room stank of dog shit and mould. Every surface was covered with stacks of *Wisden* magazines and newspapers. Not much evidence of a woman's touch. Division of territory perhaps. I take the kitchen, you take the snug. One way to get through the years together at the end of a country lane where you're trapped every time it rains.

'Where are the dogs?' I asked.

'Back garden,' he said, nodding that way. 'Put them down last year. In case of gas attacks.'

They'd told us to expect gas the first day of the war. The country had been in a panic. There'd been a fuss about gas masks for pets, but the government said they couldn't spare the raw materials. People had their animals put down to spare them the unspeakable death that gas would deliver.

A car slowed as it drove past the house. Stan reached for his gun.

'What's going on?' I asked.

We heard the car crunch on stones as it turned off the road, pulling in behind my van on the sandy layby. The engine cut off with a shudder, the fuel mix too rich.

Stan picked up the gun and recocked it. Both chambers.

'It's the person who hurt you both,' I said. 'They threatened you. Hurt your wife. Thumped you around. But they didn't get what they wanted. So now they're back. Am I warm?'

'A tactical error on their part,' Stan said. 'They've misjudged the situation.'

A car door slammed, then another. Two people. The garden gate slammed shut.

'Wait in the kitchen,' Stan said. 'Don't let them hurt her.'

A fist pounded on the front door.

Mrs Leckie opened a connecting door from the kitchen to the snug.

'They're back,' she said.

'Take Johnny,' he said. 'Lock yourselves in the kitchen and don't come out until I give the all clear.'

I followed Mrs Leckie into the kitchen. Better to stay with the unarmed person, see what I could do.

The pounding on the front door repeated.

'Are you going to tell me what's going on?' I asked her.

'It's too late now. Keep quiet and you'll be all right.'

She thought I was scared. She was protecting me. Her and her husband, sitting in the snug with his shotgun, fighting their own fight.

'I can help,' I said.

She shushed me, putting her finger to her lips for emphasis. We listened. A third knock.

'It's not locked,' Stan shouted.

The door creaked. Footsteps. Two men, stepping into the hall. Waiting. Eyes adjusting to the darkness.

'In here,' Stan said.

I pictured them looking right, as I had, through the door into the snug. Seeing an old man, wrapped up in his blankets. The long barrel of an antique shotgun wavering through the darkness towards them.

Mrs Leckie whispered to herself. I strained to hear.

'Shoot,' she said.

She did it again.

'Shoot, you old bugger,' louder this time. I got the feeling she wasn't entirely happy with the division of labour – her hiding in the kitchen while her husband took point. If it had been her in the armchair with the shotgun, the intruders would be dead by now.

'That's the plan?' I asked.

She nodded.

'Stay here,' I said.

I opened the door to the snug and stepped through, back into Stan's domain, dog shit and mould.

4

I took stock. Stan in his chair. A man in the doorway, another behind him in the hall.

'I told you not to come back,' Stan said to the man in the doorway.

'Who's that?' the intruder said, noticing me.

Stan looked at me. A mistake. The intruder took his chance. Quick. Decisive. Rush the man with the gun, jam up his decision-making process. He kicked the gun before Stan had a chance to react.

Stan's shotgun clattered away, lost behind a pile of newspapers. Stan sat, frozen, eyes wide. The fear that immobilises you when your plan fails utterly and your enemy stands before you. He looked wildly for the gun, but it was gone.

It didn't matter. He didn't need it. Stan had another weapon.

Me.

The two intruders were only one threat. The second intruder was out of play, behind his partner, bottled up in the hall. As long as Mrs Leckie kept the kitchen door locked he was out of the picture unless his partner ducked forwards, letting him in. Job one for me was to keep him out of play. Divide and conquer, as my old CO would have said.

Added to that, I was worried about Stan. He was vulnerable. Probably immobile. Close enough for the intruder to finish him off with a fist or a boot. As long as that situation persisted I had little power in the situation. Job two was to take Stan out of the equation.

I strode forwards, putting myself between Stan and the intruder, getting in his face. He took a step back before he realised what he was doing, blocking the access to the room for his nervous partner. Now Stan was behind me, taken out of the geometry. I'd turned a triangle into a straight line, and if the intruder wanted to get along that line to Stan he'd have to go through me.

'Who the fuck are you?' the intruder said, trying to establish some dominance after I'd forced him onto the back foot.

I didn't answer. There's no rule that says you have to answer every question a stranger puts to you. Especially not such an impolite question. Instead, I took the time to look the intruder up and down, gathering intelligence.

He was younger than me, and shorter. Five foot seven, compared to my six three. Possibly heavier, but softer. My weight was muscle from a life in the army and on the farm. His bulk was from long evenings sinking pints in his local. He wore brown overalls with a notepad and pencil in the breast pocket. He looked like the foreman for a removals company, or a warehouse, keeping track of things, assigning tasks, his own days of lifting and carrying already behind him. He would have been a bully at school, the strongest one in the playground, but now his childhood strength was turning to fat. He was on his way to being old, he just didn't know it yet.

'You're not welcome here,' I said. 'The gun should have been a giveaway.'

'They're being evicted,' the intruder said. 'It's all above board.'

Mrs Leckie hurried in, piles of yellowing papers in her hand.

'Your grandfather said we could live here the rest of our lives. We've paid our rent every month on the dot.'

'Grandad's dead,' the intruder said. 'We're in charge now.'

'We're not leaving,' Mrs Leckie said.

'You agreed,' the man in the hallway said. 'Twenty pounds to help you get set up by the sea.'

'We changed our mind,' Mrs Leckie said. 'The money's on the console, by the telephone. It's all there.'

'Sounds like the deal's off,' I said. 'What's your plan? Beat them up some more? How did that work for you last time?'

'It's not up to me,' the intruder said, the refrain of the working man. It's not me, it's my boss. I'm just following orders.

'Who's it up to?' I asked. 'Let's go and talk to him. We can take him the money and explain the situation's changed. No harm done.'

I could see him thinking. He looked up, to the left, imagining. He'd be seeing pictures of me walking into a trap. Him and his boss teaching me a lesson. Serve me right.

'It's the best offer you're going to get,' I said.

He turned back to his partner, wanting to check. Curious. Clearly there was a pecking order, and clearly the man in front of me was at the top of that order. Didn't seem like he'd seek approval from his mate, or even advice. Probably a misdirection.

His right arm whipped back towards me, and he pivoted his shoulders in the same direction. A solid backhand. A good move. A flash of metal. I was right, his show of consulting with his partner was for my benefit. Put me off guard, masking the set-up for his attack, focusing my attention on the conversation rather than what he was doing with his hand.

The knife flashed towards me. A bold move on his part. This wasn't a polite schoolyard punch-up. He meant business.

The problem with a move like that – it's all or nothing. You put all your hopes on the knife. If it does its job, you've won. If it doesn't, your arm's overextended, at the end of its swing, your face and body undefended.

I leant back, keeping my feet planted firmly, swaying from my hips enough that the knife flashed in front of my face, a miss. I grabbed his arm as it swung past my face, but instead of trying to stop it, I helped it on its way, completing the arc, smashing his forearm into the door frame. A long bone, smashed across a narrow, immovable object. Only one way for that to end. A loud crack as his bone snapped. A clatter of metal as he dropped the knife.

His face blanched as the pain hit him. He'd be going into shock in seconds, but until that happened, he'd have adrenaline on his side. No telling what he'd try next. So I put my knee into his groin, not holding back. Long-term damage, not the kind of thing you walk off. He sank to his knees. Not very sporting on my part, but we weren't playing cricket. He'd put the bruises on Stan and Mrs Leckie. Now he'd come back to finish the job. He was lucky he was alive.

As he crumpled to the floor, gasping for air, I turned my attention to his friend.

'Let's go and talk to your boss,' I said. 'What do you think?'

5

I let them go ahead, following behind in my van, wondering what Mrs Leckie and Stan would make of it all. Probably put the kettle on and go back to their routine.

We dropped down from the Leckies' private hilltop, took the sharp left at the bottom of the hill, then followed the lane back out, across the ford.

The men in the car in front would be trying to invent a story that would be least damaging to them. A large group of assailants. A posse whipped up by the Leckies. Young relatives. Grandsons, neighbours, soldiers.

The man with the broken arm was going to be a problem, for their story and for me. He'd clearly been in a fight and he'd clearly lost. Whatever happened with his boss, he'd end up nursing a grudge against me. He'd be telling himself I got lucky. Working himself up to instigate a repeat confrontation. I wasn't worried for my own safety, I could fight him a hundred times in a row and win every time, but I'd seen how easily he took to violence against the weak and defenceless. If he didn't know who I was now, he would soon. The downside of small-town life – nobody's a stranger. I'd have to keep an eye on Mum and Uncle Nob, not to mention our two evacuees. It would reduce my own effectiveness. I was meant to be readying our defences for the upcoming invasion. Harder to do if you've got half an eye on protecting your own home front.

They stopped at the Uckfield-to-London road. I imagined them arguing, aware of my van behind them. Trying to decide. After a long minute, they took a right turn, back towards Uckfield, then quickly took the next left, towards Fairwarp. I'd cycled around here as a boy, but that was a long time ago. Still, I found myself anticipating the corners, and each new stretch of road looked like I'd expected it to. Like listening to a song you knew as a child, each line unlocking the following line in your memory.

They slowed as we came to another junction. A tiny triangle of grass signifying a choice. A white finger-post in the triangle looked sorry for itself, its arms freshly amputated to confuse invading Germans. I didn't need directions. A right would take me back to Uckfield, three miles. Left was a narrow lane with one house at the end.

They took the left, and I followed, along a sunken lane, carved into the surrounding fields by centuries of traffic. Horses, carts and cattle, churning up the mud, rain washing it away, eating into the ground year after year, sinking the roadway deeper and deeper. As we headed uphill, trees closed in overhead, forming a green tunnel.

We came out into daylight at the top of the slope, and the lane ended with two pillars, stone lions defending the entrance to a driveway. My pulse rose as we passed them, a residual effect of the last time I'd been here.

The gravel driveway led us to the front of a large villa. Double oak doors, herringbone brickwork details, leaded glass. A handsome house, built to order at the turn of the century for a London barrister looking to raise his family in the country. The car in front of me carried on, round to the back of the house, to the garages and the servants' entrance. I didn't follow them. I stopped by the front door.

The last time I'd come here I'd been a boy, here to ask a girl out, heart pounding and mouth dry and painfully aware I was out of my league.

Kate had been the quiet one at school. Everyone knew who she was, but nobody knew her. Clothes immaculate, a cut above the rest of us wearing hand-me-downs a couple of owners into their useful life, she sat quietly, and worked hard. When the rest of us ran out of the classroom as soon as the bell was sounded, Kate was likely to linger behind. She didn't join in any of the playground games. She didn't even play stoolball, which at our school was practically a religion, overseen by the headmaster who insisted we play every day, right through winter.

Kate had intrigued me. Her father was the closest thing to a rich man any of us were likely to get, and that made Kate like royalty. But most of it was her quiet intelligence, evident every time she opened her mouth to answer a teacher's question.

One summer day, when I was thirteen, I'd got up my courage and cycled out to Kate's house. I made it halfway down the driveway, my bike wheels sinking into the deep and luxurious gravel. I'd looked around at the manicured lawn and the topiary. I'd been a fool, I realised. Farm boys didn't ride up to the front door of a mansion and ask the girl of the house if she wanted to go to the pictures. I saw the servants laughing in my face. Worse, I saw Kate, politely declining, running back to tell her parents so they could laugh at me over dinner.

I'd turned my bike and headed home. As I did, I'd noticed Kate at the upstairs window, looking out. I'd interpreted her expression as one of pity, but as I cycled home I'd realised she'd looked disappointed. The next time I saw Kate at school, we both pretended it hadn't happened. That was our last year at school. I'd left to work on the farm, then off to war, and Kate had been sent away, to be finished, whatever that had involved.

6

I reached for the heavy iron knocker, memories of the young boy who'd turned back, knowing he wasn't welcome. I stopped myself. This was different. The young boy was long gone. Since that day, I'd faced a lot worse than the impropriety of walking into a house unannounced. I tried the handle and the door opened. Unlocked. Like the Leckies' cottage, like my farm, far enough from any big bad town.

I walked through the house. There was a dark study to my left, smelling of leather and the remnants of long-gone cigar smoke. 'Grandad's dead,' one of the men had said. Kate's father, presumably, which would make the men her sons. There was a drawing room to my right, musty furniture from the glory days of Victoria's reign. The house was grander than the Leckies', but just as neglected.

'Are they gone?' A woman's voice came from upstairs, followed by a tread on the upper step.

'No,' I said. 'They're not gone, and they're not going. We need to talk.'

The owner of the voice paused, then the footsteps resumed, down the stairs.

'What are you doing here?' she asked, when she was half-way down the scuffed oak staircase. It was Kate, but it wasn't. I'd been expecting a young girl, but instead I met an aging woman, dressed for outdoor work, a pair of leather gloves in one hand. She must have been going through the same thought process. How much of the thirteen-year-old boy was left in me?

We stared at each other.

'Kate,' I said.

She took another few stairs, and stopped again, keeping the high ground.

'Cook,' she said.

My adversaries appeared. They stopped in the doorway, like dogs that weren't allowed past a threshold.

'There's a problem,' the injured man said.

Kate sighed and looked at me.

'I presume you're the problem?'

'He was waiting for us,' the man said. 'He had a gun.'

I admired his use of the English language. He hadn't lied, just hadn't specified who 'he' was. He was afraid of Kate. Didn't want to be caught out in a lie. Needed some way of backing out of it.

'Lucky I was there,' I said.

'Apparently we've got some catching up to do,' she said, finishing her descent of the stairs and brushing past me. She shouted to the injured man.

'Get that arm looked at. You're no use to me like that.'

I followed her into the drawing room and stood awkwardly, unsure of how to regain the initiative. I'd come here expecting a fight, now I was being received. The drawing room smelt of coal from the fireplace. Too many years without having the chimney swept. I studied rows of untouched books on the shelves, thick with dust.

'Sit,' Kate said, as she herself sat on a couch in front of the fireplace. I studied the books for another minute, for form's sake.

Kate rang a bell on a side table, and a uniformed girl appeared.

'Tea,' Kate said. A statement. Not a request to the servant, or a question to me. A woman who knew what she wanted and was used to getting it.

I sat. Opposite sides of the fireplace, a settee each, like two great nations facing off over a piece of disputed territory. She looked at me, not hiding her curiosity.

She was the same age as me. Forty. I'd always imagined she'd been living a refined life, the wife of a minor aristocrat. A success story for the daughter of a self-made solicitor, having clawed her way out of the middle class. I'd been wrong. The woman who sat in front of me hadn't lived a life of ease. Her face was lined from years of outdoor work. Her hair was greying, pulled back in a functional ponytail.

'I heard you're a big landowner now,' she said. 'Riding to hounds with the local gentry.'

I shook my head. 'Just a farmer, trying to make ends meet like everyone else.'

'I don't think you know the first thing about making ends meet.'

'Is that what you're doing with the Leckies?' I asked.

'I'm not doing anything wrong,' she said.

The servant came in with tea. She pulled out a table and put it in the middle of no-man's-land, leaving the tray on it.

I waited for her to leave. 'Your sons beat two defenceless old people to within an inch of their lives, left them terrified, then came back today to finish the job.'

Kate poured. Handed me a cup and took one herself.

'The Leckies were paying rent that was fixed during the last war. They've got a son in Wales. They said they'd go and stay with him. Get out of harm's way for when the tanks arrive. Lots of people are leaving.'

'From what I saw, there was some arm-twisting involved.'

She sipped her tea.

'I give Victor autonomy to run things as he sees fit.'

'He's pretty handy with a knife,' I said.

'It puts me in a sticky situation, though,' she said. 'The property's not mine. I'm just the agent. The owner pays me to do a job. In this case, the job is clearing out the house for new tenants.'

'Who's the owner?' I asked.

Kate smiled but didn't answer.

She finished her tea, put the cup gently on the saucer, back on the tray. Back in no-man's land. The détente unbroken.

'Your father used to own the property,' I said.

'Used to.'

'What's going to happen when you tell your boss you failed to get rid of the Leckies?'

'I imagine there'll be some disappointment expressed,' she said. 'But that's my problem, not yours.'

She rang the bell for the maid. We waited in silence. It wouldn't do to argue in front of the staff. Once the tea things had been taken, Kate stood up, brushing non-existent crumbs from her dress, memories of a time when tea would have been cakes and sandwiches.

She held out her hand and I took it.

'Thanks for visiting,' she said.

★

Victor was standing by my van, nursing his broken arm. There was broken glass on the gravel. He'd kicked in all of the lights, front and back. A child who hadn't got his way, lashing out.

'You should quit while you're ahead,' I said, walking directly towards him. 'One arm out of action's an inconvenience, but you can still get by. You'll have to use your left hand. It'll feel like you've got a girlfriend.'

He scuttled back, out of range, as I reached the van. I kicked the broken glass out of the way of the tyres.

The gravel crunched behind me and the maid appeared, a shawl round her thin shoulders and a basket in her hand.

'Going into town?' I asked.

She looked at me cautiously, and flicked her eyes to Victor.

'I'll give you a lift,' I said.

Victor grabbed the maid's arm and pulled her to him.

'Mabel likes the walk,' he said. 'Gives her more time away from the old dragon.'

He draped his left arm over Mabel's shoulder. She froze. His hand covered her breast, and squeezed. She ignored it, keeping her eyes fixed on the horizon, her face flushing red.

'Come on,' I said. 'I could use the company.'

She pulled away from Victor and I held out my hand, helping her up into the passenger seat.

She was quiet as we pulled out of the driveway, back down the sunken lane. I didn't know what to say, so we both sat with our thoughts. She couldn't have been older than fifteen. Her first job, working in the big house for minimal pay and a straw mattress at the end of the long day. She was gaunt. She'd grown up hungry. A common enough story. Going into service was more about finding somewhere warm and dry to sleep, where the meals were provided, than the pay.

'He'll take it out on me later,' she said.

'Tell him he'd better not, if he wants to keep the other arm available for use.'

'You and whose army?' she said.

I dropped her by a row of dark cottages in Snatt's Road.

'You could find another job,' I said.

'She's all right,' she said. 'Doesn't pay too much attention.'

She climbed out of the van, and I handed her the basket. The cloth covering slipped. A grey pork chop, presumably stolen from Kate's kitchen. I replaced the cloth.

'Don't come back,' she said. 'Better for everyone.'

I waited in the van as the front door opened. An old woman looked out, left and right, cautious. She grabbed the basket and pulled it in, along with the girl. The door slammed shut. Not such a crime, taking a bit of food from the big house, back to your mum.

7

The air-raid siren carried across the fields.

'One raider, south by south-east.'

The watcher replaced the handset on her field telephone. She was a young woman, barely out of school, but she seemed to know what she was doing. Her partner, another efficient young woman, put down her mug of tea and scanned the sky to the south.

I'd written to the War Office during winter and offered a corner of my land for an anti-aircraft emplacement. An un-workable corner, filled with sandstone outcrops. There'd been months of silence after my letter, and I'd forgotten about it. Then, out of the blue, a ten-tonne lorry had rumbled down the lane, towing a 40 mm Bofors gun, its seven-foot barrel still glistening with packing grease. State of the art for bringing down enemy planes. The only problem was, the Germans had as many as we did. Bofors, the Swedish manufacturer, was doing a roaring trade selling them to both sides.

'You should go,' the watcher said. 'Take care of your people.' She picked up her binoculars. There was enough light left in the sky for her to scan the southern horizon, where the South Downs loomed. Her partner, the gunner, hefted a four-round clip of shells and loaded them into the gun. She took her seat and powered up the sighting mechanism.

'It's going to be a full moon,' I said. 'I doubt the Germans will want to drop their best and brightest on a night when any idiot with a gun can pick them off. If I were them I'd wait for a dark night.'

'Would you want a clear sky or clouds?' the watcher asked. 'If you were going in?'

'I'd go by boat for a start,' I said. 'I'm too old to start throwing myself out of an aeroplane.'

'Clouds would be better for the safety of the pilot and the plane,' she said. 'Not much chance of being shot down if they don't know you're there. But it would be useless if you wanted to drop your people in a specific place. You wouldn't be able to navigate unless you had incredibly accurate bearing and distance. Even then, you'd probably drop them miles from where you wanted them.

'I'd do it on a clear night, but no moon,' she continued. 'You'd want someone on the ground with some kind of signal so you could drop your men in the right place.'

It sounded like she'd been thinking it through. Strange times, when a young woman was sent out to watch for invaders, and even to contemplate mounting a counter-attack.

'Maisie, I'm sure Mr Cook's got places to be,' her partner said. Quite right. We'd let our guard down.

We listened to the noises of the evening. An owl. A rustle in the dry leaves. The siren wailed again, still the standard warning, no indication of whether a plane had actually been sighted.

The watcher unclipped her handbag and took out a pistol. She broke it open and checked the chamber. She closed it and put it back into her bag. A nervous ritual.

'If it's one or two, I'd let them land and give them a chance to surrender,' I said. 'Doesn't seem particularly sporting to pick them off when they're floating down out of the sky.'

'What if it's thousands of them?'

'If it's the invasion, ditch the uniforms,' I said. 'Come to the house. We'll find you some farmworkers' clothes you can change into. They won't shoot farmers if they're thinking straight.'

The siren changed to a short series of pips. Enemy sighted.

*

I hurried into the kitchen, not bothering to take off my boots. A loaf of bread cooled on the rack, and the oven was still warm.

Feet clattered down the wooden stairs, unmistakably Frankie, the young boy with his enthusiasm for war not yet dimmed by reality.

Frankie had come to us a month earlier as part of the evacuation scheme, one of the great waves of children sent out of the cities before the bombers arrived. All through '38 and '39 the perceived wisdom had been that the day the war started, England's great cities would be levelled. 'The bomber will always get through' the headlines had screamed. Frankie hadn't taken to country life at first. He was warming to it slowly, but I could tell he was counting down the days until he could get back to the slums of London, back to his family.

Frankie burst into the kitchen, going for the shotgun. It was our agreement. On nights when I was gone, in the event of an air raid he was to take the shotgun down to the cellar and keep it trained on the door. If a German opened the cellar door it was up to him to defend the family. He took the responsibility seriously, but it was still an adventure. He was disappointed to see me.

Elizabeth slipped into the kitchen behind Frankie. She stood with her back to the counter, her eyes wide with fear, watching Frankie as he took the shotgun down from the shelf.

Elizabeth was an evacuee, like Frankie. But her evacuation hadn't gone as planned. Instead of a safe berth in the country, she'd ended up a prisoner of men who saw the chaotic rush of children as a gift, a way to satisfy their perverted desires. She'd been held captive and put through a hell that no child should have to experience. By the time I carried her out of her bombed-out cell, she was pregnant, and orphaned, her mother killed by the same men who'd tormented her. She'd lost the baby, barely surviving the trauma of being buried alive in a bombed house, and we'd taken her in.

'Take the gun,' I said to Frankie. 'Make sure Elizabeth gets down there safely and don't leave her. I'll make sure Mum and Uncle Nob get down OK.'

As soon as Frankie left, I touched Elizabeth on her arm, conscious of the flinch that I knew was automatic.

'Look after Frankie,' I said. 'Don't let him out of your sight.'

She nodded, her eyes wide and serious. She'd taken a carving knife from the block behind her, but I didn't let on that I'd noticed.

'Probably a false alarm,' I said.

I hurried upstairs. Mum was in Nob's room, trying to get him out of bed. She turned to me with an exasperated look. Nob was huddled under his blanket, eyes squeezed shut.

'There's no budging him,' she said. It had happened once before. An hour spent pleading with him, while he lay rigid, eyes shut tight, until we'd given up.

'You go down,' I said. 'I'll stay with him.'

Her eyes flicked to the landing.

'Go and look after the children,' I said. 'Probably nothing anyway.'

She put her hand on Nob's hand. His was trembling, but no more than usual. She held it, decided, and hurried downstairs.

'Looks like we're in it together,' I said to Nob. I didn't expect an answer.

I stood at the window, looking out across the moonlit fields.

The air-raid siren sounded again. More short pips. This wasn't a drill. The farmhouse was solidly built. It had survived several centuries of the worst the English weather could throw at it. If a bomb detonated outside, the walls would probably hold, depending on how close the impact. If there was a direct hit, we'd all be gone, whether we were in the cellar or not.

Either way, I was out of ideas for how to get Nob down into the cellar if he didn't want to play along.

A shot echoed across the fields. A rifle. Probably someone's ancient Lee–Enfield, brought back from the first war. One of my distant neighbours, getting over enthusiastic. Perhaps up at The Rocks, the country house between my farm and the town. I pictured a party of men in dinner suits, standing on the terrace, taking potshots at shadows in the sky.

I felt it before I heard it. A vibration. A low buzzing noise, barely audible. I scanned the sky without much hope. Clouds were drifting in front of the moon, and it would be impossible to see the small dark shapes of planes in the dark sky, unless they were flying low.

The Bofors gun fired from its hiding place. Four shots in quick pairs, the percussion hitting the house. Pom pom pom pom. Then silence, the two young women reloading, sighting. The gun fired again, another four shots. They sounded louder, which meant the gun had turned towards us. I hoped they knew what they were doing, it would be a bad joke to get taken out in your own farmhouse by an anti-aircraft gun.

I saw it, above the tree line to the south, heading straight for me. The house shook as it roared overhead. It was low. I hurried out of the bedroom to the landing window where I could see north. A Heinkel. One of their large bombers, flying slowly with no fighter escort. It was already disappearing into the distance, heading up over Ashdown Forest towards London.

It was about to pass out of sight when a glimpse of white flashed in the moonlight. It dropped below the tree line on the horizon, but not so fast I couldn't register its shape.

A parachute.

8

Every instinct told me to run out of the house and drive up to the Forest, where I'd seen the parachute fall below the tree line. I forced myself to slow down.

I pulled out my map and fumbled for a pencil and ruler. I'd watched the bomber come in over the fields. I could plot its route, up the river, across the woods, over my house. I marked those points on the map, using the ruler to continue the line up to the Forest. One minute from clearing the house to releasing the parachute. If it flew at three hundred miles an hour, the drop would be five miles away. I used my pencil to roughly line up the distance on the scale, and translated that to the line of flight. I marked the predicted landing site with a cross, folded the map and stuffed it in my pocket. Of course, any one of my calculations could have been wrong, but better to try for accuracy than to give up on it entirely.

'All clear!' I shouted down to the cellar, standing at the top of the stairs and hoping Frankie didn't have his finger too tightly on the trigger.

*

Every second of the drive dragged for a minute. I pushed the old delivery van to its limits, hurtling along the narrow country lanes, praying there would be no oncoming traffic.

I forced myself to slow down at the worst of the blind corners, opening it up on the straights. Five miles that the bomber covered in a minute took me closer to ten, and felt like fifty.

The road took me past Palehouse Lane, up onto the Forest, the roadside transitioning from trees to heath, and suddenly I was out in the open, touching the sky. At the top, I pulled in at a dog-walkers' layby.

I climbed out of the van and stood, looking out across the expanse, letting my eyes adjust to the dark.

I checked the map. If my rough calculations were correct, the parachute had been dropped to the left of the road, down a long and gradual slope of grass, heather and gorse that stretched away in front of me.

I kept the road squarely behind me, and headed downhill, towards the likely drop site.

My boots crunched on dry heather and scuffed up white sand. It had been a hot, dry spring and the Forest was an arid place at the best of times. The War Ag wanted to put it into useful production, but I didn't see it working in the short term. Sheep would improve the soil eventually with the nutrients from their manure, but it would take years. Perhaps the War Ag were thinking long-term. Perhaps they knew something the rest of us didn't.

The slope started out gently, but got steeper the further I got from the road. When I looked back towards the car, it was out of sight, a big expanse of dark sky, filled with stars.

I should have brought a gun. I'd run from the house without thinking. Still caught in the trap of confusing the comforts of home for the security of being far from the fighting.

I saw the man before I saw the parachute. He was scrabbling around, searching the heather. Above him, the parachute hung lifeless on one of the few tall trees, a skinny birch that had somehow got a foothold in the sandy soil. He was panicking, looking about without much of a method, going over the same spots again and again.

I froze, looking for cover, but there was none. I was exposed, surrounded by heather, glowing white in the moonlight.

He turned towards me. I put my hand in my pocket, where I would have had a gun if I'd had any foresight. I hoped he'd assume I was better prepared than I was.

He would run or he would attack. If he was hoping to maintain secrecy he would be unlikely to shoot me. If I were him I'd use a knife. Rush your opponent and put the blade across his throat. Let him fall and bleed out, get back to the task at hand. I readied myself for the attack. Assuming this was his first combat mission, he'd be inexperienced. His heart would be pounding. He'd overdo it, come at me too fast, overblown gestures. I've fought a lot of men who were in their first fight to the death. And their last.

He didn't run, and he didn't attack. He peered at me, and took a hesitant step closer.

'Who's there?' he called out.

'Who are you?' I shouted.

The moment of truth.

9

The man strode towards me with his hand outstretched, as if we were old chums meeting at his club. He was dressed for dinner: tailored suit, pressed white shirt with starched collar, regimental tie. Only his rubber boots, scuffed white with sand, incongruous against his black trousers, gave any sign that he wasn't strolling into the dining room.

This was not a man who'd just jumped out of an aeroplane.

'Vaughn Matheson,' he said, as we shook hands. I didn't give my own name, and in the excitement he didn't notice.

He gestured behind him, to the parachute hanging in the tree.

'Did you see it?' he asked. He was excited.

'Where's the parachutist?' I asked, stepping past him to the base of the tree. I looked up, on the off-chance there was a Nazi stormtrooper caught up in the tree. Better safe than sorry.

'I had him in my sight,' Vaughn said, 'but I fell. I was looking up at the sky and tripped. Scuffed up my jacket.' He held up his sleeve as evidence, it was smeared with mud, ghostly white in the moonlight.

He returned to his kicking around in the heather.

'Hello, what's this?'

I joined him. Half hidden by the foot-high heather, a smashed wooden crate lay open. I leant down and pulled it apart.

'Some kind of machine,' I said, pulling out handfuls of packing straw, presumably meant to cushion the impact. The machine itself was the size of a suitcase, encased in shining black Bakelite. Like a large portable typewriter. An embossed manufacturer's name – Lorenz.

I pictured the crate being closed up in a Luftwaffe base somewhere across the Channel. It looked like an important delivery. There was no way it would have been sent without a clear plan for its recovery. That meant an agent, operating in my territory, free to move about. It was a big crate, so he presumably had a car or a van. Was the machine light enough to be carried by one person, or would he need help?

There was a carry-handle on the machine. I gripped it and pulled. It was heavy, but not too heavy. Designed to be man-portable. There was a tinkle of broken glass as I lifted, and I put it down as gently as I could. The boys from Military Intelligence would be glad to get their hands on it, and they'd want it to be as operational as possible.

I stood up and looked around. It was quite an exposed spot, with the odd tree here and there. Every ten yards or so there was a gorse bush, head height. Big enough for someone to hide behind if they were waiting for a drop. Perhaps they'd have a light to signal the plane. When the parachute came down, they'd run to it and collect the delivery.

If he'd brought a vehicle, where was it? There hadn't been any other cars up on the road I'd come from. I listened in the silence for the sound of a car starting up, but I didn't hear anything. Presumably once Vaughn stumbled on the drop site, the agent abandoned the recovery. Easier to send another machine on another drop than to replace an agent. He would have gone on foot.

Most likely, he wasn't aiming for a road at all. Dozens of cottages littered the Forest, hidden down farm tracks and quiet lanes, tucked away from the outside world. Places like the Leckies' house.

Of course, there was another explanation for the case of the mysterious disappearing agent. The simplest explanation – in other words the most likely – was that the agent was standing in front of me.

'Have you seen anyone out here?' I asked.

'Just you.'

'Someone was waiting for it,' I said.

He stopped his search and looked around.

'Do you think they're still out there?' he asked.

I didn't reply.

Vaughn put two and two together. He took a step back.

'This is a bit awkward,' he said.

10

A roar came out of nowhere, and we both looked up as a Hurricane momentarily blocked out the stars overhead. Chasing the bomber. I didn't envy him, trying to follow a dark shape in a dark sky when you're both moving at hundreds of miles an hour.

'We'll have to send for help,' I said. 'One of us will have to stay with it.'

I'd given him a way to salvage the operation. He could tell me to go for help, take the machine once I was gone. He'd be a wanted man, but if he was a German spy, he'd have known that was part of the plan. He'd have a contingency.

'I'll go,' he said. 'I've got a phone at my place. I can be there in five minutes.'

'Where are you?' I asked.

He pointed to the northern slope. There was a glimmer of light.

'Shit,' he said. 'Bloody door must have swung open.'

'Go,' I said. 'Call Uckfield police. Charlie Neesham.'

There was a low rumble. Quieter than a plane. We listened. It was a car, making its way up a hill. Difficult to locate the source, but it sounded like it was coming from the opposite slope.

A light winked on, then off. The car rounding a corner, perhaps, or someone with a lantern, signalling to the agent sent to pick up the crate.

The light winked on again.

*

I ran down the slope, to where the valley bottomed out with a wooded section that hid a fast-rushing stream. I recognised it. I'd played there as a boy, making dams in the freezing water until I couldn't feel my feet or hands.

I made my way through the trees, my feet crunching on generations of beech nuts. If there was someone out there hiding they'd hear me coming, but that ship had sailed. I was going for speed, rather than stealth.

An earthy smell told me I was nearing the stream at the bottom of the valley. There was an old railway sleeper forming a makeshift crossing. It was damp, and slippery with moss.

The light showed through the trees again. Either lazy blackout procedure, as Vaughn had claimed for his place, or a deliberate signal. There'd been so much hoo-hah about the blackout it was more likely the second.

I pulled my way through the undergrowth, up a steep slope, slick with rotting chestnut leaves. This was a different landscape to the open slopes of the rest of the Forest – sandy soil, heather and gorse replaced by the rich growth of ancient woodland, part of the original royal hunting ground that gave the area its name.

There'd been a path here, but it had been neglected. Chest-height bracken blocked my way, and woody brambles caught my clothes. It was slow going.

At the top of the slope, chinks of moonlight shone through the trees. There was a clearing. I neared the edge, but lingered far enough back that I wouldn't be seen.

A white house glowed in the moonlight, surrounded by lawns. The house was an art deco monstrosity, like the bridge of an ocean-going liner. Every window was blacked out apart from the one I'd seen from the heath. There was a lingering smell of coal smoke from a damped-down oven, incongruous against the modernity of the building.

There was a car by the front door. Big, black, sleek, like something from a gangster flick.

The car idled. A waste of petrol. This wasn't a driver who was paying for his own fuel, or even worrying about rationing.

I waited and watched. A fox barked. From behind me, the usual rustles of the woods at night, but nothing from the house.

The car door opened, spilling laughter from a conversation in mid flow. Two people climbed out. A woman and a man. They were both well dressed, as if they'd been out for a night on the town.

The woman laughed. There was a muttered response from the man.

'You'll be late,' the driver said. It wasn't the tone you'd expect from a servant.

'Not like they can start without us,' the man said.

They opened the door to the house and stepped inside. The door closed behind them.

The car engine revved quietly and the car sprang forwards in a tight circle, thin beams of yellow light painting the leaves around me before I was left in darkness.

*

The parachute was still there, a reminder that this war was going to be different. Instead of trenches in France and Belgium, this one was going to be decided on our own soil, and in the air above. We'd known it was coming since the armistice. It had only ever been a temporary pause, a chance for both sides to draw breath, raise another generation of men, fodder for the machine-gun and the artillery shell.

Vaughn's house was a distant silhouette on the northern slope. It would have taken him five minutes to get there. If he'd phoned the police straight away, they'd be on their way.

The wireless set was too valuable to leave, so I sat in the heather, a lonely guard duty. I'd wait for the police constables, see it safely in their hands before I let it out of my sight.

The parachute shifted in the breeze, the ghost-like shape billowing. The storm's coming, it seemed to say, and all that you know and love about this country will be destroyed, turned into the mud of the battlefield.

II

I drove down from the Forest, the road swallowed up by a tunnel of trees. I could have had my lights on full and no German airman would have seen me.

The police constables had arrived, breathless with excitement. Young men, who'd grown up with the tales their fathers told, ready to do their bit. They'd approached the parachute the way I'd approach an angry bull, abundant caution mixed with a sense of awe at being in the presence of something with a power beyond the everyday.

As I drove, I let my mind wander. Vaughn Matheson. A name from the past. A name I hadn't expected to hear in the Sussex countryside.

When he'd stepped forwards to shake my hand, I'd been curious to see if he'd recognise me. We'd met before. I had a suspicion he wouldn't remember, and I'd been right. But I remembered.

I remembered very clearly.

It was 1916. I was a new private, my first rotation into the front line. Four weeks of training at Aldershot, drilling on the parade ground, a chaotic few weeks being shuttled around between reserve bases in northern France. All too soon, the orders we'd all been waiting for and dreading. The long, slow train journey in a cattle wagon, the march to the support trenches that had until recently been the enemy's front line, fragments of bodies still embedded in the mud.

The final march as far as the linking trenches would allow, slithering over the top and hugging the ground across an exposed wasteland to get to the front line.

I'd dropped down into the forward trench as an enemy mortar hit our line ten yards to my left. The zigzag of the trench layout protected me from the shockwave, but the cloud of red mist mixed in with the cordite showed me some of my mates hadn't been so lucky. When my sergeant major slid down into the trench beside me and asked for volunteers to carry shells back from the front line to our artillery positions in the rear, my hand went up as if it had a mind of its own.

I was to be part of a small party of mud-covered Tommies, slipping on duck-boards, plunging waist deep into a soup of mud, oil, and human waste, carrying my armful of brass shells. My first initiation into the fact that most of soldiering is moving heavy things from one place to another and back again.

The artillery position was a mile behind the line. A gunner took my shells, one by one, like a well-rehearsed rugby manoeuvre. Each shell passed from man to man, rammed into the rear of the massive gun, steel door slammed shut and locking mechanism rotated into place, the order given, the gun fired. Each shot, the gun bucked, straining free of its shackles, landing with a crash that shook the ground. Each shell traversed the sky, presumably landing beyond the horizon. Out of sight, out of mind. Then the gun breech was opened, with a cloud of smoke, the empty shell removed, and the process repeated.

I found myself alone, ashamed of myself for being so quick to volunteer to leave the line. I was about to slip away when the gunnery sergeant spotted me and pressed me into another mission. A message to take to the higher-ups, further behind the line. All things considered, not the worst thing.

The officers' mess was a ruined church, two miles back from the artillery position. Three miles from the front. As close to the fighting as many of the senior officers liked to get, preferring to learn about conditions on the ground from three-day-old copies of *The Times* that were shipped over from England along with their freshly laundered shirts.

My message was for Captain Vaughn Matheson. He wasn't in the officers' mess, and nobody knew where, or when, he'd turn up. I wrote the whole thing off as a bad job, and left the letter for him, in the care of an aging batman who must have started his military adventure when Victoria was a young woman.

The day was warm, and this far from the front the countryside was pleasant, not so different from the fields and woods I'd been desperate to leave behind in Uckfield. I took my time on the way back, towards the front lines.

I heard an elderly woman shouting, the sound coming from the ruins of a farmhouse a hundred feet up the road. I didn't understand French, but I understood she was angry. None of my business, I thought, as I neared the house. The shouting got louder. There was a pistol shot, muffled, fired in the confines of an enclosed space, the sound dampened by thick stone walls. The shouting stopped. I stopped walking.

Another voice started up, an elderly man, remonstrating. Another shot. Then a third.

I stood in the road, exposed, planning my response if a rogue German came running from the farmhouse. But it wasn't a rogue German. It was an English officer, dapper in his spotless green breeches and puttees, and his ironed white shirt. He strolled out of the farmhouse holding a painting under his arm. He was whistling.

He noticed me, and his smiled slipped, just for a second.

'Don't you know you're meant to salute an officer,' he said.

I looked from him to the farmhouse, and then back to his face. He was watching me closely, putting two and two together. He knew what I'd heard.

I raised my hand and snapped a salute, clicking my heels for good measure. I kept my eyes locked on his, wondering what it would take to wipe away the smirk.

'What's your name, private?' he asked.

'John Cook,' I said. 'Eleventh Battalion, Royal Sussex.'

I paused, counted to three silently. One. Two. Three.

'Sir.'

*

When I came to Maresfield, with the road to Uckfield laid out in front of me, I took a right turn instead, past the watchful sentries at the army camp, through the lanes to Isfield, to Margaret.

Isfield Park was dark. The staff had been reduced to bare bones, and they all lived in the village. How much longer did these old houses have? Relics of a different age that wouldn't be missed by many.

The kitchen door was unlocked. Nothing worth stealing, Margaret had told me when I'd suggested she raise her level of security. She'd said it with such a level of challenge I'd known better than to press the issue.

The house was silent, and I was loath to disturb it. I didn't belong here. The house knew it as well as I did. I passed through room after room, all empty of furniture, stripped of anything of value over the years. One room was lined with empty shelves, and I lingered, imagining the great library that must have once been housed there.

The stairs creaked as I made my way up to the first floor. I was still new enough here that I hadn't worked out which steps to avoid, or where to tread. I waited for Margaret to call out. Perhaps she was asleep.

Margaret's rooms were at the far end of the long corridor. She'd dragged every scrap of furniture she could find into a suite of rooms and made the best of it. The first time she showed me, I asked why she didn't choose rooms nearer the stairs, to minimise the walk. She'd chosen the old nursery, she said, because that was where she'd stayed when she'd visited her aunt as a child.

The bedroom was empty.

I sat in a sagging armchair in a dark corner of the bedroom, my back to the wall, facing the door, listening to the creaks of the empty house as the wind picked up outside. Margaret was probably at the pub. It was after hours but who was counting. Easy enough for the landlord to lock the door and have a quiet drink with a few of his regulars until they ran through their pay packet. The chair was damp. Everything in this house felt damp; the humid summer combined with centuries of cold leaching out of the stone walls.

I must have dozed off. Voices intruded on my half-sleep. Murmuring. Urgent. I was in a dugout, at the Somme. Huddled in a greatcoat passed down from a German lad who wouldn't need it any more, pressed into the damp earth, hoping it would absorb me. Feeling the thump of shells and smelling the soil that would claim me. The soil of the farm I'd turned my back on, only to find again on the other side of the Channel. Earth to earth.

I felt Margaret's hand on mine. Her hair smelt of cigarette smoke.

We undressed quickly, fumbling in the dark, silent in the empty house.

We tunnelled under the covers that felt as damp as everything else in the house. I pulled her to me, my arm around her waist, tracing the curve of her lower back. I met her urgent kiss, her tongue flicking mine, sending a bolt of lightning through every nerve in my body.

She pushed me back, and climbed on top of me, her hair falling down onto my face, a curtain between us even in the darkness. She groaned as I slid into her and she flattened her body against mine. She was a life raft holding me up to the surface of a dark sea, keeping me from dreams of earth and greatcoats and the concussion of shells creeping ever nearer.

'You're a good man, John Cook,' she whispered to me, her head resting on my shoulder. She was lying, of course, and we both knew it, but I was glad she thought enough of me to say the words.

12

I left Margaret at dawn, praying I had enough petrol left to get me home. The personal use ration had shrunk to almost nothing. I'd have to top up at the farm, but that would mean using the dyed petrol that was meant to be reserved for agricultural use. The police were cracking down, rightfully so, but it was a chance I'd have to take.

Bill Taylor, my farm manager, was pacing in the yard.

'Sorry,' I said, as I climbed out of the van. 'Got caught up.'

Bill was worried. Normally he was unflappable. He held up a brown envelope.

'We've got the review. Next Wednesday.'

'I thought we had a month,' I said.

He pulled out the letter and handed it to me, as if seeing it would help me understand. It was from the War Ag, Crowborough branch, Kent and Sussex sector. The War Ag was a layer of bureaucracy between us farmers and the Ministry of Food. It had complete control over every aspect of food production in the region.

I read the letter. We were to be inspected. An exhaustive review. Inputs, outputs, utilisation, waste. The results of the inspection would determine our ability to keep control of our farm.

'They can take it away if they don't like what they see,' Bill said.

'Unlikely,' I said. Thanks to Bill, our farm was a well-oiled machine.

We walked out, across the fields. The wheat fields were nearest the house, on the high ground where the soil was well drained. We'd tried a new variety, Hold Fast, and it was coming on better than I'd expected. We'd be harvesting in a few days if the weather held. Further from the house, the long field along the Isfield road was green with oats sown the previous November – a gamble that had also paid off. All told, a lot of arable. At Bill's urging, we'd bought a tractor three years earlier, when everyone else had been sticking to horse-drawn ploughs. It had been a stretch, financially, but it was paying off, as the number of labourers available was shrinking rapidly, along with the supply of horses.

'I'm worried about Elizabeth,' Bill said. 'I'm going to try to get her more involved. We could use the help, and it might be good for her.'

'Are you sure?' I asked. 'Don't want to put more weight on her shoulders.'

'Worth a try,' he said, 'a wheel to set her shoulder to.'

I'd seen the way she was slipping away, but what I knew about raising children you could put on the back of a postage stamp and still have room to spare.

We pushed our way through a hawthorn hedge, thick with fragrant white blossom. There was meant to be a gap, but it had grown over.

'I'll have this cut back,' Bill said, as we picked our way through, brambles catching at our trousers.

The meadow ran down to the river. We flooded it throughout autumn. The wetter the meadow, the better the grass. The better the grass, the better the hay we could cut. Of course, hay was only useful when you had livestock, and we'd got rid of our cattle months ago, at the direction of the

War Ag. The ground was packed hard now, after the dry spring but that wouldn't last. As soon as the weather changed and the autumn rain came, it would be jelly, good for nothing. The Germans would know that. They'd made the same calculation the previous year when they timed their invasion of Poland – a calendar dictating military manoeuvres in Europe all the way back to Roman times. Hitler's generals were as aware of soil conditions in Southern England as I was. They'd have reports covering soil type, rainfall, drainage, all of that. They'd be wanting to get their tanks rolling across my lower meadow within the month, or they'd miss their window.

'We'll have to bring this into production,' Bill said, looking at the meadow with dismay. 'Everyone I've talked to has heard the same thing. If it's not underwater or sheer rock, it's got to be ploughed up.'

We walked down to the river. The water was low.

'They'll come up the valley,' I said. 'Good flat land all the way from the sea.' We looked down-river. If the blitzkrieg across France was any guide, the attack would be fast-moving divisions of tanks, penetrating the country and encircling our troops. The infantry would follow behind, mopping up.

'What'll you do after the invasion?' I asked Bill. He hadn't fought in the Great War. He'd been a conchy. Refused to serve. I didn't agree with his politics, but since he'd come to work for me I'd got to know him as well as I knew any man. People thought the conchies were cowards. A lot of those people could learn a lot from Bill Taylor.

'Whatever they tell me,' he replied. 'They'll need men who know how to farm.'

I hoped he was right, but I didn't share his optimism. I'd seen what happened when an army overran a civilian population. It didn't end well.

'Maybe use the river,' he said. 'Take the rowing boat. Slip away when it's dark.'

He'd clearly been thinking about it. You could get to the sea, but then what? The Germans had the French ports. You'd have to head further south, past Normandy. Better if there was a fishing boat waiting for you, a mile out, keeping watch.

Bill turned back to the field.

'The man from the War Ag will want to see progress by the time he visits,' he said. 'I've been thinking about making a mole. Weld a torpedo shape to an old plough, pull it along underground, make some drainage lines.'

'Have you got what you need to make it?' I asked.

'Reckon so.'

I liked that about Bill. Always thinking of little improvements, putting in the work to make them happen. In my experience, a lot of people have a lot of ideas, but not many of them turn them into action.

13

Tea was sausages and mash, with fried tomatoes from the kitchen garden. The sausages had been getting worse, more gristle than edible meat. I made a show of eating every bite, aware I was being watched by Elizabeth and Frankie. Important to set the right tone and all that.

'This is the BBC,' the radio newsreader announced. We'd got into the habit of listening to the radio as we ate. Some people thought it common, preferring to keep the receiver in the sitting room, covered with lace, next to a picture of the King. I didn't care what other people thought, and the wireless was one-way communication, meaning the man at the BBC was unaware he was coming to us in our kitchen, while we were eating our tea.

'The French premier Paul Reynaud has announced that there will be no defence of Paris. In the early hours of this morning, German troops marched into the French capital, and met no resistance, following yesterday's declaration by the city's French military governor General Héring that Paris was declared an open city, a move he justified as the best decision for the nation, a tactical move to protect the city's ancient monuments.'

Mum looked at me in disbelief. I shared her shock. Four million of our young men had died defending France, barely twenty years earlier. Now the French had handed over their capital city to the Germans and fled. It was hard to stomach.

The newsreader continued, 'The French government is retreating to the southern city of Bordeaux. It's estimated that up to eight million citizens of Belgium, France and the Netherlands have left their homes in the face of the German army's swift advance, the largest mass migration in the history of Europe.'

I looked at Uncle Nob, in his grimy armchair by the fire, his plate on his lap, struggling to cut his sausages with hands that never stopped shaking. What did he think of the news? Did he hear it? Or was he still hearing the shells pounding the trench where he lay, cowering, waiting for the one with his name on it. Four days of artillery before each big push. Three million shells each time. The silence that could mean only one thing. Climb out of the mud to claw your way through the corpses of your brothers, towards the machine-guns.

'You win every fight you don't have,' I said. It was the sort of thing Blakeney, my old CO, would have said. As with all such aphorisms, it was true sometimes, and useless at others. This time it felt empty. With Paris fallen, London would be next. I knew how I'd feel when the time came. I pictured an armoured division advancing on my farm, parachutists falling out of the sky, Mum and Uncle Nob and the children cowering behind me.

'Churchill's going to have some words about that,' Mum said.

'We'll fight them on the beaches,' Frankie said, parroting Churchill's recent speech. It had been a fine speech, but I'd seen those beaches. A lot of coastline to defend for a country that had been placing all its bets on the fighting being in France.

'Just us, then,' Mum said, with a grim sense of satisfaction. Just us. No French allies to worry about offending.

No false hopes of white knights riding to the rescue. Backs to the wall, that kind of thing.

I didn't share her optimism. We'd been banking on the French tying up the Germans for the summer, digging in around Paris, slowing down the advance. Now there was no advance. No front line. No division of Europe into us and them. It was all them, all the way to the Channel.

'Can I have another sausage please?' It was Frankie. The first time he'd ever asked for more.

Elizabeth pushed a sausage from her plate to Frankie's. Seemed the boy had undergone a sudden change of heart. Until now he'd been at great pains to let us know they made him gag.

'What are you going to eat?' I asked Elizabeth, noting her untouched plate of food.

'Not hungry,' she said. I was worried about her. Since she'd come to live with us, she'd been slipping further and further into a fog.

Frankie's arm caught my eye. He was a fidgety boy at the best of times, but there was something about the way he slipped it under the table.

'Frankie?' I looked at him squarely, searching his face. He glared back at me.

'What are you doing?'

He flushed red, guilt written all over his face.

14

We strode out across the fields, towards the woods, Frankie reluctantly leading, nervously juggling a battered old cricket ball. Me following. Elizabeth dawdling behind.

'I told them I'd keep it a secret,' Frankie said, turning back to me.

'We're going for an evening walk,' I said. 'You haven't said anything to betray your confidence.'

'We should have brought a weapon,' Elizabeth said, quietly.

'I don't need a weapon on my own land,' I said. But I felt foolish. She was right. Things were changing.

Frankie dropped back as we reached the woods. I went first, stepping across the drainage ditch at the edge of the field, and gingerly climbing through the barbed-wire fence. The woods were old, hardwoods, a mix of oak, birch and chestnut, and in the June heat the green canopy was a shield against the evening sky. Centuries of leaf mould made the going springy underfoot.

I looked to Frankie for directions, and he pointed, but stayed behind me, Elizabeth behind him.

I moved quietly, carefully, each footfall on leaves, avoiding any sticks that might snap and announce my presence. A young birch blocked my way, and I gently held back a branch of quivering leaves as I stepped past. I smelt woodsmoke, and heard voices.

Three men had made camp. Two lay on the ground, one sat on a log, tending to a small fire. A tin kettle hung over the fire and the man on the log held an enamelled mug. The mug was filthy and dented, like it had been through a lot. The man looked worse. His eyes were hollows. His hands shook and he watched the flames of the small fire as if he was looking for answers.

'Bad camp security, sergeant,' I snapped. The man glanced up at me, then returned his gaze to the fire. His companions squinted up at me. One of them sat up. None of them seemed concerned by my arrival.

'You should have someone on perimeter,' I said. 'Otherwise any Tom, Dick or Harry could walk in and finish you off.'

'They're welcome to it, mate,' the man who'd sat up said. He looked past me, where Frankie was peering around the birch tree.

'All right lad. Got any grub?'

'Come back to the house,' I said. 'We can give you a proper meal and you can clean up, before you're on your way.'

'Tell them to go away,' the man still lying on the ground groaned, keeping his eyes closed. 'This is the best kip I've had for three months.' His voice had a thick accent. He was wearing an English uniform, but he sounded Polish.

'You can't stay here,' I said.

'Says who?' the Polish soldier asked.

'I do.'

'You and whose army?' said the man by the fire, the sergeant, his eyes not leaving the flames. The way he spoke, he was clearly the leader. There was a menace in his voice. It would have worked, if I'd been a farmer, intimidated by three battle-hardened soldiers, fresh from the front. But it didn't work, because the last time I'd been intimidated by three soldiers, all three of them had been pointing rifles at me, and I was three miles behind their lines, in the mountains overlooking the Khyber Pass. That situation had ended in my favour. So standing over three unarmed men on my own land wasn't going to raise my pulse much, no matter how much menace any of them put into their voices.

'We can fight, or we can eat,' I said. 'I've eaten already, so I'm easy either way. But it looks like you boys could do with a meal.'

The sergeant tore his eyes away from the fire. He stared at me, thinking. I let him look. Looking never hurt anyone. Better than fighting.

'Let's get the fucking food,' the Polish soldier said. 'We kill him after.'

15

We were picking our way back through the undergrowth when we heard the German. Everyone froze, even the children.

The sergeant turned to his two men. He made a hand gesture, forking his fingers, pointing at each man in turn and giving them a direction. They nodded and slipped silently into the trees.

I pulled Frankie and Elizabeth towards me and knelt down, face to face with them. They were pale with fear.

'Probably someone messing around,' I said, keeping my voice low.

Frankie shook his head. I knew what he was thinking. It was what we were all thinking.

'Parachutist,' he said.

Parachutist.

I hadn't told Frankie about what I'd seen last night. I hadn't told anyone. But the word was on everybody's lips, on every front page. Hitler's not-so-secret weapon, responsible for the fall of Belgium and the Netherlands. Elite troops dropped behind enemy lines, tasked with killing and gathering intelligence.

'There aren't any parachutists here,' I said, hoping my confident tone would cut off any further discussion.

I scanned the area, looking for somewhere I could hide the children. I found what I was looking for, an ancient holly bush, dense with green leaves. I pointed to it and whispered.

'Hide in there.'

Elizabeth clutched my arm and shook her head vigorously.

'Don't leave us,' she hissed.

'I can do more if I'm alone,' I said. 'I'll find out what's going on, then I'll come back and get you out.'

Elizabeth was vibrating, her jaw clenched.

'You said you'd look after me.'

'I'll come back,' I said. 'I promise.'

She dropped her eyes, and I felt the last bit of trust she had in me disappear.

I pushed them towards the holly bush. Frankie pulled a branch aside and crawled in. They'd get a nice collection of scratches, but better that than be found by an advance party of Germans.

Elizabeth followed him. I'd have time to apologise to her later, if all went well.

The German voice came and went. One man, talking, as if he was giving a speech. It was difficult to work out the distance. One minute it sounded close, then it seemed to get more distant. At times it disappeared entirely.

The sergeant had gone, following the sound. I followed.

It sounded like the man was at the edge of the woods, or in the field. Either way it was between me and the farmhouse, where Mum and Nob were left unprotected. I picked up my pace.

At the edge of the woods, I caught up with the sergeant, crouched in the drainage ditch on the other side of the barbed-wire fence. The Polish soldier was forty yards to our left, same position, crouched in the ditch. I looked right. The third soldier slid under the fence, down into the ditch. We had a good vantage point across the open field, looking north up towards the house. The field was empty. No German scouting party. No parachutists.

I rolled under the lower strand of barbed wire and slid down into the drainage ditch to confer with the sergeant. As I reached him I heard the voice again. Difficult to locate. It sounded like it was from above us, coming out of the ether. I didn't speak German but he sounded like he was giving a briefing. A confident man, an officer perhaps.

The sergeant looked at me, at a loss. I shook my head. We looked along the ditch. The Polish soldier shrugged.

I stood up, wincing against the anticipated zip of a bullet, followed by the crack from the rifle. I put my hand on the fence, superstitious, like the barbed wire had conjured the voice.

The voice stopped. Rabbits nibbled grass along the edge of the field. They watched me warily. If there had been another man out there, they'd have disappeared back into their burrows.

The three soldiers stood up, looking around, as confused as I was.

16

The soldiers sat at the kitchen table. Mum stood with her back to the sink, torn between a desire to help three young men fighting for King and Country, and a fear of what they represented. Nob, as always, sat in his chair by the fire, shaking hands gripping the wooden arms. I'd sent the children upstairs. It was one thing for Frankie to read about soldiering in his comics, another to have him confront the reality.

'More potatoes?' Mum asked, as they wolfed down their food.

'Yes please,' the Polish soldier said, not looking up from his plate. 'And sausages.'

Mum looked at me and I nodded. It would finish up our meat ration, but I knew a man who could get us more. Potatoes weren't rationed, so as far as I was concerned the soldiers could eat them all night. Mum added the last batch of sausages to the pan with a splatter of grease and set about peeling more potatoes.

'What's your plan?' I asked.

'Get back into the fight. Kill more Germans,' the Polish soldier said. The other two looked at each other.

'What about you two?' I asked.

'We got separated from our company,' the sergeant said. It wasn't an answer, and we both knew it.

'It was chaos,' the other soldier said. 'Hold your ground. Retreat. Hold your ground. Retreat. As soon as they get across the Channel we're fucked.'

'How did they do it?' I asked. 'What's their secret?'

'No secret,' the sergeant said. 'There are more of them, they're better trained, better armed, and they've got a taste for blood. If I were you I'd take those kids and your old people and go north. If you're all here in a few weeks you won't like what happens.'

'We'll fight back,' Mum said, her back to the men.

'No, you won't,' the sergeant said. 'You'll be dead.'

Conversation stopped. The only sound was Mum pushing the potatoes and sausages around in the pan.

The Polish soldier finished the food on his plate and wiped his mouth with his sleeve.

'In Poland, our cavalry was on horseback,' he said. 'We charged their lines with sabres. They didn't slow down.' He brought his hands together with a loud smack, his right hand moving on. 'And the whole time the sky was full of their fighters and bombers. They took out our air force before they even admitted they were invading.'

'It's the speed,' the sergeant said. The others watched him as he chewed his food. 'It's overwhelming. They come at you as fast as their tanks can move. If one part of your line holds them up, they go round. It's like when you're a boy, trying to dam a fast stream with a few rocks.'

'What about parachutists?' I asked, still getting used to the new reality. Until now I'd thought this was just newspapers whipping up fear to sell copies.

The men all shook their heads, looking at each other for confirmation. Like they had a story they didn't want to tell.

'What?' I asked.

'Word went out,' the sergeant said. 'Jerry were dropping people behind our lines dressed as nuns and priests, with their regular uniforms underneath their habits.'

The other two men looked down at their plates.

'We were told to shoot any civilian dressed as a nun, or a priest, or wearing a long coat.'

I thought of a parachutist lying low in my woods, and I realised in my narrow thinking I'd assumed he'd be wearing a German uniform. Of course he wouldn't. He'd be dressed like a farm labourer, or a poacher, someone you'd see out in the fields and the woods and wouldn't think twice about.

The other soldier piped up. 'My captain said we were to shoot farmers if they were ploughing their fields, because they might be laying out instructions for the parachute drops.'

'And did you?' I asked.

The soldier looked down. I turned to the sergeant. He looked me in the eye, defiantly.

'We did what we were told,' he said.

'You can stay in the barn tonight,' I said. I wasn't being completely altruistic. I was thinking about the German voice. If there *was* a man lying low, likely he'd move on before daylight. Perhaps he'd have a *rendezvous* arranged, a safe house where he could meet up with others, get ready for action. But perhaps not. Perhaps his orders were to engage. Instil fear, spread panic. My farmhouse would look like a soft target.

Keeping the deserters around didn't sit well with me, but better to have my home front defended.

17

'The Germans are not the enemy of the working man. We should be making a treaty with Berlin for a peaceful future. If we don't, we'll be trapped in this cycle of endless war until there's nobody left to fight.'

The speaker limped across the makeshift stage, a war wound slowing him down. Not many men our age without some kind of injury. He was dressed in an approximation of a working man's clothes – starched tweed and a cloth cap – but his voice gave him away. This was a man who'd been educated in all the right places. Probably had a collection of ties that got him into various London clubs. And now he was here to tell us little people what to think.

As he stepped into the dim pool of yellow light that passed for a spotlight, I realised who it was. Vaughn Matheson, the man I'd bumped into on the Forest, underneath the freshly arrived parachute, turning up again like a bad penny. I wondered if he could see me, in the dark of the auditorium.

The church hall was packed. Chairs had been set out in rows, theatre style. Margaret and I had arrived with only minutes to spare and were forced to take seats near the front. It was a warm evening, and we'd had to hurry to get there on time.

The council had been putting on debates once a month. I'd seen the posters around town and ignored them until now.

My preferred evening activity was sitting quietly at my local with my old friend Doc, putting the world to rights over a few pints.

Attending the debate was Margaret's idea. Said it would be good for us to open our minds to new ideas. I didn't agree. I liked my own view of the world perfectly well. It had kept me alive through the worst days of the Great War, then through the campaign in India against the Afghan tribesmen. But I liked Margaret, and it was a small price to pay, sitting through an hour of talk before we strolled up to the pub. Could I get away with closing my eyes?

'The war to end all wars,' Vaughn said. 'How many times have we heard that? The ultimate sacrifice, made so our children could grow up in a world without war. That's what they promised us. The French know. That's why they gave up so quickly. They lost even more than we did last time. It was their villages that were reduced to rubble. Their farmland turned to poisoned mud where nothing will grow.'

He knew his audience. Rural men and women. Mothers and fathers. Farmers. People who wanted a quiet life with a good harvest and stable prices.

'Look around,' Vaughn said, and the packed church hall obeyed. Several hundred people turned to look at their surroundings, an unremarkable space, walls and woodwork painted pea green, dusty windows lit orange by the setting sun.

'They had church halls like this in Flanders,' he said. 'And churches beside them. And villages around them. Pubs. Shops. Houses. Schools. Until the bombing started.

'Every shell we fired destroyed everything for a twenty-yard radius and left behind a crater ten feet deep,' he continued. 'By the time we'd worked out what we were doing, we had one gun for every twelve yards of the front.'

He pointed to Margaret.

'Would you mind standing up, madam?'

Margaret looked around, embarrassed, but obeyed the speaker. She stood up.

'Imagine my gun targeted on Mrs . . .'

'Margaret,' she said, resting her hand on my shoulder.

'*Lady* Margaret,' an elderly woman sitting behind us said.

'*Lady* Margaret,' Vaughn said, peering into the darkness. From his point on the stage it would have been difficult for him to see us. But he seemed thrown. Perhaps he'd seen me.

'My apologies, Lady Margaret,' he continued. 'Now. Imagine my gun targeted on Lady Margaret. Set to kill her. But not only her, set to destroy every living thing, everything bigger than a grain of sand, for a radius of twenty feet.'

Margaret looked around, taking it in.

He scanned the crowd and pointed at another woman, at the far end of the row. A farmer's wife I'd seen at the market.

'Would you stand up too? Mrs . . . or is it Lady . . .?'

'Spratt,' she said, standing up, her face flushing a deep red. 'Mrs.'

'Mrs Spratt,' he said. 'The next gun is aimed at Mrs Spratt. Another twenty-foot crater, everything turned to ash and rubble. Now imagine that line of violence extended across Sussex, all seventy miles. A line of complete destruction. Imagine my next shot, twenty feet further north, at the back of the stage here. A walking barrage we called it, moving the destruction forwards so our boys could walk behind and mop up. Imagine what's left behind. Nothing.'

He let that sink in, pausing for effect.

'Nothing's left behind,' he continued. 'Hell on earth.'

Margaret sat down. Mrs Spratt, taking her cue, did the same.

'Raise your hand if you lost someone last time,' he said. 'Brother? Father? Uncle? Friend?'

I raised my hand and kept my eyes facing forwards. I didn't need to look around. There wouldn't be a single person without their hand raised. I felt Margaret raise her own hand. We'd never spoken about her family. The speaker raised his hand in solidarity with us all.

'Did that feel like victory?' he asked. Nobody answered.

'When Churchill says we'll fight to the last man, that's what he means. When he talks of victory, he means being the last person left alive. But what's victory if everything's destroyed? Go and talk to the farmers in Flanders. Ask them what victory looks like.'

'You'd have us lay down our arms and let the Germans invade?' Margaret called out, the steel in her voice serving notice. Vaughn might have been treating this like a philosophical debate, but to most of us on the invasion route it was a matter of life or death.

Heads turned. Someone brave enough to challenge the man on the stage.

'Why would they invade if we weren't fighting them?' a new man stepped forwards on the stage. Whereas Vaughn had tried to dress down to the occasion, this man hadn't bothered. He had a flamboyance that would mark him as an outsider in any village hall or pub in the county.

'We declared war on Hitler, remember? It wasn't the other way round. The Germans don't want to fight us. Hitler looks at the British Empire and he sees a natural brotherhood. All we need to do is give the word, and we'd be left in peace.'

Vaughn held up his hand as if to ward off his opponent.

'Now this is where we need to be careful,' he said. 'My friend here will tell you the Germans and the English are all from the same stock, descended from the same mix of Saxons and Vikings. Our aristocracy are all part of the same family, particularly our royals. We even share a love of beer. And I'm not here to argue that with him, or with you.'

I admired his tactics. Admit that some of what your opponent says is sensible, show you're a reasonable person. Get everyone in the room agreeing with each other. Then, once you've established your reasonableness, take the audience with you to the new ideas you want them to consider.

'But I can't accept that everything the Germans want is right for us. They want to build their own empire, bringing civilisation to the empty spaces of Eastern Europe. We want no part in that. They want to take control of the foreign agitators and international financiers that have been ruining their economy, just as ours was ruined in the last decade when we had all that mess with the gold standard. And even though we may share their sentiments, I don't think we suffer from the problem to the same degree. But where we can't agree, where we can never agree, is on the path forwards for England. I say it has to be rooted in a strong sense of what makes us strong and unique. Our sense of fair play, our love of tradition. In short, the things that have made our country great will be the foundation for our future greatness.'

There was a small ripple of applause. Perhaps the speaker had seeded the audience with sympathisers, or possibly he was getting through to some of them.

The flamboyant one waited for the applause to die down. He looked out at the packed village hall and nodded.

'You've been listening to us for far too long.' He paused for the ripple of polite laughter. 'You've heard that we both agree on the need for peace. We both agree that the Germans aren't our enemy.' He paused again, walking the stage as if deep in thought.

'So why are we fighting?'

He let the question hang in the air.

'Why are we fighting? Who's got an answer for me?'

'Poland,' shouted a brave voice from the back.

'Poland,' the speaker repeated, thoughtfully. 'Who's been to Poland? Raise your hand.'

I looked around, a sea of swivelling heads as everyone did the same. No hands raised.

'Raise your hand if you've got a Polish friend, or a Polish relative,' he said.

Still no hands.

He walked to the front of the stage. I checked my wrist-watch. The debate was due to end at half seven.

'Here's the thing,' he said. He lowered his voice. Whereas before he'd been projecting, performing even, now he sounded like it was a chat between friends. 'War makes money,' he said. 'My colleague told you how many shells his company fired before a big push. Who paid for those shells?' Another pause, for effect. 'We did. The people. Everything we bought, someone was making a profit. Every scrap of bacon, every mouthful of bully beef, every shell, every bullet. Huge fortunes were made in the last war. Ask yourself who made those fortunes. Men with foreign-sounding names like Rothschild. Men who don't claim allegiance to this country, or to any other. Men who control your lives without you even knowing they exist.'

'This is what the Soviet revolution was about,' he said, raising his voice steadily. He paced back and forth. 'Taking the capital back from these international financiers and giv-ing it to the people. Creating a country where the people who do the work end up with the money, and the class of people who exist solely to profit from your work are cut out of the system. That's the future for England.'

'What about the royal family?' Mrs Spratt called out.

'What work do they do?' the flamboyant man asked. 'Why should they lord it over us, when we're the ones producing the food and working in the factories?'

'Go back to Russia and leave us alone,' shouted someone, I couldn't see who it was.

He'd over-egged it. He'd had the sympathy of the audience until he'd turned on the royal family. Not surprising in my experience – a lot of fanatics are good at drawing you in with their logical arguments, but their fanaticism keeps pushing them, the gleam in their eyes gives them away. They don't want to make small changes, they want to burn it all down.

18

We stood in the late-evening sun outside the church hall as the good people of Uckfield filed out, many of them muttering to each other. Had either of the debaters won over any new members to their respective causes? Vaughn had seemed slightly more persuasive, but I could imagine his opponent's bit about financiers ruining the economy had hit a few marks. A lot of people had lost their farms in the thirties. There'd been headlines about the gold standard and dark stories told about international finance. When the opponent emerged, a couple of young men rushed up to him, recent converts perhaps. He hurried off, talking excitedly to his new disciples.

Vaughn was the last out. He saw me, and strolled over, unhurried. I noticed his limp had vanished, presumably an act aimed at generating sympathy from the crowd.

He held out his hand and we shook.

'Vaughn Matheson,' he said. 'I believe we've met.'

He turned to look at Margaret with an intense gaze that bordered on insolent.

'Mags,' he said, 'you look ravishing as always.'

He hugged her, then held her at arm's length for a further inspection.

'Vaughn,' she said, 'this is John Cook. John, this is Vaughn. Old friend of the family.'

I gave Margaret a look. I had the feeling I'd been duped somehow.

'Did Cook tell you about our adventure last night?' he asked.

Margaret was confused.

'Quite the team,' Vaughn said. 'Defending Sussex against the invasion.'

'The parachutist I told you about,' I said to Margaret. 'Vaughn was there.'

'Cook was rather convinced I was the recipient,' Vaughn said.

'Were you?' I asked.

'That would be telling,' he said, and winked at me.

'How do you two know each other?' I asked Margaret.

'Mags and I knocked about in India,' Vaughn said to me. He turned to Margaret and grinned. 'Are you two . . .' He looked back and forth, an amused expression on his face.

'Yes, we are, Vaughn, and don't be such a pig about it,' Margaret said. I hadn't seen her like this. She was pleased to be with him, but she was alive with a nervous energy.

'I'm parched,' Vaughn said. 'What are we drinking?'

Perhaps my kind of man after all.

★

Vaughn drove, his scarlet MG rocketing along the lane to Isfield like a fighter plane yearning to leave the runway.

Margaret had jumped in next to Vaughn, which left me in the dickey seat behind them, a space designed for a child at best, more a place to throw your jacket. The windscreen, barely a foot high, may have provided some kind of protection for driver and passenger, but I was squarely in the slipstream. Vaughn and Margaret had a lot of catching up to do, judging by the way they had their heads together. I gave up trying to listen. Easier to sit back and close my eyes.

As we descended the long hill into Isfield, Margaret leant over to Vaughn, her mouth practically touching his ear. He down-shifted, gunned the engine and messed about with the clutch more than necessary, the engine roaring as he used it to slow the car. With a deft flick of the wheel he took the sharp turn, under the arched gatehouse echoing the roar of the engine back to us, through to the long avenue of ancient oaks that led to Margaret's ancestral home.

19

We sat on a picnic blanket in the walled garden that was now mostly unkempt lawns. The crumbling old brick walls radiated the heat from that day's sun. Margaret's cook had left a plate of sandwiches, which we supplemented with a few bottles of wine, dug out from the furthest corner of the cellar. Since I'd got to know Margaret, I'd come to learn that her hospitality invariably left a lot to be desired. Despite inheriting one of the largest houses in Sussex, she was broke. If any one of her creditors knew the full picture there'd be 'for sale' signs up in an instant.

'So how do you know Mags?' Vaughn asked me.

'I was going to ask you the same thing.'

'Well, that,' he said, leaning over and putting a hand on Margaret's thigh, 'is a long and complicated story, which I'll tell you once we've become better friends.'

'What's the headline version?' I asked, with a calm I was surprised I was able to muster.

'How about . . . Bombay Nights . . . an epic tale of intrigue, love and lust in the declining days of the Raj.'

Margaret took Vaughn's hand off her thigh.

'Vaughn knew my father in Bombay,' she said.

Vaughn clasped his hands over his heart.

'Such ruthless brevity,' he gasped. 'Somebody top up her wine glass, maybe she'll find her tongue again. Or maybe somebody else has already found it.' He winked at me.

I did my best to smile.

Vaughn clicked his fingers as he remembered something. He pointed at Margaret.

'I say, Miriam's down for a few days. We'll have to have you over. She'd love to see you.'

'What's she up to nowadays?' Margaret asked. 'The last time I saw her she was a child. I can't imagine her out in the world.'

'We'll have a party,' Vaughn said, ignoring Margaret's question. 'Push the boat out. You're both invited, and I won't take no for an answer.'

'That would be lovely,' Margaret said.

'So, Cook,' Vaughn said to me. 'What did you make of our show at the church hall?'

He was right to call it a show. It would have been scripted on each side. Carefully crafted and performed, designed to elicit an emotional reaction in an audience.

'You both present the same point of view about the need for peace,' I said. 'You pretend to debate the finer points. It creates the impression that peace with Germany's a natural conclusion. You have the young chap go off the rails about the royals, which gives the crowd something to feel scandalised about. Meanwhile, you hope that one or two of them start to ask their friends about Poland, or about the Rothschilds.'

'You think we're being too obvious?' he asked.

'I'm the wrong person to ask about the finer points of propaganda,' I said. 'Plus, I don't agree with you.'

'What's *your* solution to the Jewish problem?' Vaughn asked.

'You're doing it again,' I said. 'You're stating an opinion as a fact, inviting me to debate you on the finer points.'

'You don't think it's a problem that the great families of Europe are in debt to people who don't claim allegiance, or owe any duty, to any country?'

'I don't know anyone in high finance,' I said. 'The only banker I know's George Crafts, who holds the loan on my land. Hard to imagine anyone getting particularly worked up over that arrangement.'

I had more to say about Vaughn's theories, but I was interrupted by a roar overhead. A flight of Spitfires, returning from the continent. Seventeen planes, two formations of six, and one of five. One man lost.

'All right,' Vaughn said, as the roar of the Merlin engines receded. 'What do *you* believe in?'

Margaret put her hand on my arm.

'I believe in England,' I said. 'This countryside. Those people who came out to the church hall to educate themselves, to better themselves. I believe it's worth fighting for, and I believe I'll die fighting for it, likely sooner rather than later.'

Vaughn leant towards me and refilled my wine glass.

'*I* believe,' he said, 'that we all need to get hammered.'

He raised his glass in a toast.

'To the delectable Lady Margaret –' he took a deep draught – 'and her gentleman farmer, Mr Cook, who's going to die fighting for us all, sooner rather than later.'

20

It was dark by the time we got rid of Vaughn, his car roaring off down the drive. He'd polished off most of the wine, and he drove recklessly. I gave him a fifty per cent chance of navigating the drive home without incident. I had my own feeling as to which side of that fifty per cent I'd prefer.

'You didn't mention you'd had a fling with him,' I said, as I picked up the glasses.

'I didn't, because I didn't,' Margaret said, with a certain amount of amusement evident in her voice. 'He's too old for me now, and he was certainly too old for me when I was in India. Plus, he's a bore. He was a bore then, and now he's a double-bore.'

'So that was all a story?'

'It's Vaughn being Vaughn,' she said. 'He'll say anything to get a reaction. You've listened to him talk for the last few hours.'

'Unfortunately.'

The house was big, and dark, and empty. It smelt of old stone, like a church, damp even in the middle of the longest, hottest summer on record. I took the stairs two at a time, forcing Margaret to hurry to keep up, a childish way of punishing her.

'Cook!' she called out, as I reached the bedroom door. I stopped. She was twenty yards behind me, still only half-way along the corridor.

I let her catch up. Told myself I was being ridiculous. She passed me as I held the door open. I followed her into the bedroom and closed the door behind me. We were alone in the house, no soul within a mile radius, but closing the door changed things. A private space.

She took out her earrings and put them on top of the chest of drawers. She had an old saucer she kept her things in.

'Do you want to argue about Vaughn, or do you want to make love?'

She took her necklace off.

'I can see the merits of both,' I said.

She pushed the straps of her dress off her shoulders, letting it fall to the floor. Her slip followed.

'You don't want to help me with this?' she asked. She reached behind her back to unhook the straps of her bra. I closed the distance between us, and took over, always the gentleman. With the clasps undone I slipped my hands underneath the cups, caressing her breasts.

'You're quite an infuriating woman, you know.'

'I think you like infuriating women,' she said, as she turned to undo my belt.

'You've been misinformed.'

She kissed me, lightly at first.

'Let's put this conversation on ice until tomorrow,' she said. 'That wine's got me feeling quite racy. See if you can keep up.'

21

Mrs Leckie was on her knees in her front garden, a large sunhat her only concession to the heatwave. There was a breeze up on the hilltop, and she had the hat tied under her chin with a scarf. I'd never seen her without a heavy cardigan and this morning was no exception. She had a punnet full of strawberries, and was busy pulling out runners, tutting at each one, as if it were a naughty schoolchild.

'You turn your back on these for one minute,' she said, pulling up a long chain of plants, linked by thin tendrils. She shook the soil off and dropped the offending plants in a trug by her side.

'Had any more trouble from your landlord?' I asked, standing politely on the other side of the garden wall.

'No, I don't think they'll be back, do you? You were very effective,' she said. 'Glad you found your métier. Certainly wasn't schoolwork.'

'I was a late bloomer.'

'That's all right,' she said. 'We're not all cut out to be poets. Someone's got to do the dirty work.'

She looked across the road.

'Where's your van?' she asked. 'Don't want to leave it on the road. Those lorries don't slow down for love nor money.'

'I walked. Wanted to stretch my legs.'

'I'm surprised they let you through,' she said. 'They're meant to be on the lookout for suspicious-looking men.'

'Had to go the long way round. Came around past Underhill.'

The shortest route would have taken me through Maresfield, but what was normally a sleepy hamlet was fast turning into a no-go area, fenced off and guarded by clipboard-wielding sentries. A large contingent of Canadian troops had been barracked there, and rumours in town said an additional camp was being built for prisoners of war.

'I was worried about you,' I said. 'I heard rumours of a parachutist.'

'You don't strike me as the kind of man who listens to fishwives' gossip,' she said, giving me a piercing stare.

'You haven't seen anyone suspicious?' I asked. 'Heard any German voices coming out of the ether?'

'If Hitler wants to send someone to spy on me, that's his lookout,' she said. 'Can't imagine it'll do him much good.'

'What about those lorries?' I asked.

She shuffled along on the grass to the next section of the combined flower and vegetable bed, grabbed the trug and pulled it closer, and set to work again.

'Some kind of works,' she said, 'all very hush hush.'

'What do they do there?' I asked.

She shook her head.

'I've got better things to do than go playing detective. Leave all that to the youngsters.' She looked at me meaningfully. Based on my performance at school she probably thought I was a bit dull, had to drill the point home.

'Go out through the gate at the end of the back garden,' she said. 'You don't want to walk up to them on the road. They'll shoot first, ask questions later.'

It was a glorious morning, out on the open heath, under the vast sky. The gorse was popping in the heat, giving off waves of vanilla. I kept Palehouse Lane as a reference, off to my left, a hundred yards away through head-height gorse and thickets of birch. Close enough to keep my bearings, far enough that I wouldn't be seen by anyone on the road. I was doing a recce of what sounded like a military installation. That could be taken the wrong way. People had been taken away and not seen again. The War Powers Act gave the security services unlimited power.

To my right I had a grand view of the upper slopes of the Forest, mostly clear heath, with clumps of towering pine trees at some of the highest points. I wouldn't have liked to live here. The views were magnificent, but it was too exposed. No defensible perimeter. One of the things we'd learnt quickly on the Afghan frontier – wherever you set up camp, you want a perimeter of defences. The only way to sleep easy.

I looked back towards the Leckies' house but the slope of the hill had hidden it beyond the horizon. I was completely alone, with no signs of civilisation in any direction. With the brown of the sun-parched grass and heather, and the sound of the insects, I could have been on the savannah. Only the criss-crossing vapour trails above me, fighters out to intercept the Luftwaffe over the Channel, indicated any sign of life.

The slope led me gently down to the bottom of a valley, the vegetation closing in, more birch and pine, and the peaty smell of water as I came to a slow-moving stream. Without noticing, I'd got closer to the road. The distant roar of a heavy engine signalled another lorry.

I slipped back into the cover of the undergrowth as the lorry swept around a corner. It had come from behind me, from the Leckies' house. It was loaded down, khaki canvas covering odd shapes on the flatbed. Delivering supplies, pre-sumably. As it rounded the corner, the clutch crunched and the lorry jolted as the driver put it into a low gear. It started

its slow grind up the next hill, working its way back up
through the gears.

I let it get a good distance from me, waiting until the quiet
returned. No point trying to sneak up on a secret installation
if I couldn't hear what was going on around me. When it
was completely quiet, I retraced my steps back into the
woods, then headed onwards, uphill again. I kept the road a
hundred yards to my left.

As I climbed the slope, the undergrowth thinned out again,
a subtle change minute by minute, but half a mile of it put
me back onto the top of the next dome, back in the sky with
the Forest laid out at my feet. Behind me, the Leckies' house
was now a feature on the horizon, commanding its own
hilltop.

'Hello!'

I spun around, shocked that I'd let another man come up
on me without me hearing.

'Over here,' he said. He was sitting in the shade of a gorse
bush. That explained why I hadn't heard him, he hadn't
been moving. I'd been the one blundering through the
heather, giving my position away.

It was the young man from the debate. Vaughn's opponent, who'd wanted to do away with the royal family.

I put a genial smile on my face, the way men do when
they've gone for a walk to get away from humanity but bump
into another person. The mutual pretence of civility. As I
approached, I sized him up. Mid-twenties. Expensively
dressed in an urban man's approximation of the country life
– plus fours, tweed, a jaunty cap.

'Morning,' I said.

'Going to be another scorcher by the look of it,' he said.

He was sitting on a small stool, a clever device that looked
like it was designed to fold up, all steel tubes and webbing.

In front of him, he had a canvas propped up on an easel. He held a palette in his left hand and a knife in his right.

His painting was a work in progress, but he'd already captured the sweep of the skyline. I recognised the Leckies' cottage – a dab of white amidst the slopes of purple heather.

'Such a peaceful spot,' he said, 'apart from those blasted lorries.'

'I gather there's a works up the way,' I said.

He looked over his shoulder, following my nod, but he didn't seem overly interested.

'You should be careful,' I said, 'I hear it's hush hush, you might get in trouble if they see you out here painting pictures.'

'Oh, I don't think I'm much of a threat,' he said, returning to his work. He smeared a generous dollop of black across the white canvas, above the purple slopes. I looked up at the sky, a pure deep blue.

'Enjoy the day,' I said to him, setting off. I'd have to change my route, couldn't let on to him where I was heading.

'It's more to the left,' he said. I stopped, my foot crunching on a dried clump of heather.

'The secret installation,' he said. He winked at me. 'Not that you're going there, of course.'

22

Mrs Leckie had called it the works. I'd pictured a factory of some sort. Maybe a workshop. Brick or concrete. Corrugated-iron roof. Rusting detritus.

There was a fence, with a gate, guarded by a sentry.

Beyond the fence, there was a brand-new building. Brickwork, with decorative detailing. Twice the height of a house and wider than my biggest barn. It had tall windows flanking a large loading door, designed to fit a lorry.

I sat in the trees and watched. Based on my experience so far, and what Mrs Leckie had said, I didn't expect to have to wait long. I wasn't disappointed.

After ten minutes, the large door opened inward. It was too dark to see anything inside, compared to the brightness outside. A lorry nosed out, through the door, which closed behind it. The gate was opened, and the lorry headed off. The gate closed, and all was quiet.

Five minutes later, the sequence was reversed. A lorry roared up the hill, pulled up by the sentry at the gate. Papers were checked, jokes exchanged, the gate opened. The lorry pulled in, waited on the concrete forecourt in front of the looming building, the large doors opened inward, and the lorry drove in.

For the sake of completing the cycle, I sat for another twenty minutes until the doors opened again, and the lorry emerged.

The building must have been spacious inside. The lorry had gone in forwards, and came out forwards. That meant there was space inside for it to turn. If a lorry had tried to turn inside my barn, it could conceivably do it, but only if the whole place was empty.

I decided to follow the fence around the back, to see what else I could find out.

The fence was new, and endless. Concrete uprights every ten feet, angled out at the top. Taut barbed wire, threaded through the concrete posts, every six inches. The wire was new. Give it a few months and it would take on a dull patina. A year and it would start to rust.

I pushed my way through the undergrowth, alternately in leafy shade and blazing sun, thinking about who would want the Leckies out of their house. Mrs Leckie thought her house was owned by Kate's family, but Kate had refuted that. She was an administrator. A property manager. So who was paying Kate's wages and issuing the orders? Was it connected to the works? Perhaps someone wanted her out to create a security cordon. Mrs Leckie said the works were hush hush, which meant the War Office. But the Ministry wouldn't mess about with hiring hoodlums as middlemen, it would send a grey-faced civil servant with official paperwork. If it needed to evict someone, that person would be evicted. No arguments. No shotguns on either side.

If it wasn't the government that wanted the Leckies' house, who did? Was it someone who might be interested in knowing more about the works? Someone who might like to count the number of delivery lorries being driven past the cottage, or even to sabotage whatever was happening inside that large brick building?

Perhaps the answer was the simple one – money. People were anxious to move out of the big cities, as the fear of bombing or invasion grew every day. Presumably there was a big demand for quiet cottages tucked away in the country.

The first thing I learnt from my walk along the fence was that I wasn't the first to do so. Grass had been trodden down, more damage than a deer would make. Halfway around, I found the clincher, two cigarette butts. Someone had stood here and looked through the fence. Blakeney, my former CO, always said that successful reconnaissance was fifty per cent showing up, fifty per cent paying attention, and fifty per cent not smoking. Harder than you'd think for the average soldier.

Since my predecessor had chosen this spot as the one in which he lingered, I did the same. He'd chosen well. I had a good line of sight through the fence to the apparently idyllic and undisturbed Forest, while behind me was dense under-growth. I was unlikely to be surprised from my flank or rear.

The land inside the fence was a significant size. I'd long since left behind the brick warehouse. The fence hadn't felt like it curved, and I'd walked a mile along it so far. I looked along it to my right, and I couldn't see a point at which it changed course inwards. It could easily run for another couple of miles before it reached the woods in the distance. Likewise, if I looked straight ahead, I couldn't see any sign of fence. No glints of sunlight from the shining barbed wire. No freshly cut trees, removed to keep the fence line straight. Call it four miles wide, and another four miles across. Sixteen square miles would make it the largest piece of enclosed land in Sussex.

At the centre of it all, one feature stood out, silhouetted against the sky. A clump of towering Scots pine. More than a mile distant from me, but it still looked tall. From close up those trees would look like giants, a couple of hundred feet tall. They might have even been redwoods, brought back from America hundreds of years ago. Such clumps were a regular feature of the Forest. Wherever you went, they followed you, always there on the horizon.

'*Gustav Siegfried Eins. Hier ist Gustav Siegfried Eins.*'

I dropped to the ground. Not much cover in the low heather, a foot if that, but better than standing like an idiot in the open. Whoever it was, I'd almost let him creep up on me.

The voice repeated again. The same sentence.

'*Gustav Siegfried Eins. Hier ist Gustav Siegfried Eins.*'

Then silence.

No footsteps. No responses from any other voices. It sounded like someone was making a transmission.

The parachutist.

I raised my head above the level of the heather and looked around. Next time he spoke I'd be able to get more of a sense of where the voice was coming from.

'*Gustav Siegfried Eins.*'

The voice seemed to come from in front of me, but looking through the fence all I could see was an expanse of heathland, rising gently to the clump of trees in the far distance. A few birch trees. He could be hiding in the shadow of one of those. Perhaps he had a transmitter rigged up in a tree, or maybe even between trees.

I stood up. I'd been standing before, so my position was already blown. He hadn't shown any inclination to shoot me. It would have given away his own position.

I needed to get inside the enclosure. Whether I'd been spotted or not, I needed to get closer to the trees. If he shot at me, at least he'd prove his existence. I'd take my chances on his accuracy.

'*Gustav Siegfried Eins. Hier ist—*'

I put my hand on a strand of barbed wire, testing the tension. I put my boot on the bottom strand. It took my weight. As long as I didn't put my hands on the barbs, I could climb it. The top would get a bit hairy – I'd have to climb outwards. But nothing ventured, nothing gained.

But then I stopped, as I realised what had happened. The voice had stopped abruptly.

I took my hand away from the wire. The voice returned.

'—*Siegfried Eins.*'

I waited for the next transmission. As soon as it started, I put my hand on the wire, and the sound stopped. I took it off, and the sound returned.

★

Two shots echoed across the Forest, in quick succession. I winced, and listened for any sign of the bullet hitting near me. But there was nothing, just the echoing retort of the shot.

Something was wrong. The gun was wrong.

A double-barrelled shotgun, twin triggers, designed to let the sportsman get off two shots while tracking a flying bird.

Nobody sends an advance scout with a shotgun. They'd give him a rifle for this kind of thing. A pistol or a revolver for close-up work.

I thought of the Leckies' house. Stan, sitting in his chair, shotgun by his side, ready to defend his home. Mrs Leckie, on her knees in the grass, keeping an eye on the road.

23

I ran. Chest-height gorse tore at my arms, thick, inch-long spines shredding my shirtsleeves and drawing blood. Clumps of heather threatened to trip me at every step.

Another shot. Closer this time. No second shot. None needed, presumably. The silence in its place as worrying as the gunshot.

I left the trees behind and came out onto the open heath where I'd seen the artist, the Leckies' house a distant shape on the horizon, right at the top of the hill. The artist was gone.

I ran, even though running wasn't going to make a difference.

I hurdled the back gate, into the Leckies' back garden. Rows of vegetable beds. Raspberry canes in a netted enclosure. Curls of metal made from cut-up tin cans dangled from the trees – rudimentary bird scarers. Unnecessary at that moment. The birds had all been scared off by the shots.

Around the front, the house was as picturesque as the first time I'd seen it, a rural idyll, here at the top of the hill, an island in a sea of heathland, under the huge sky.

The front door was open. A rectangle of darkness.

The smell inside told the story. Cordite, blood, and the other smells you get when a human body is ripped apart by gunfire.

The door to the kitchen was ajar. I used my boot to nudge it open. Mrs Leckie was on the floor. The first shot had hit her in the sternum. It had taken her down, but hadn't finished her. She had a knife in her right hand. Fighting to the end. The second shot had finished her off.

Stan was in the snug. He'd died in his chair.

24

Two miles to Kate's house. Thirty-five minutes at a fast walk.

Last time I'd visited, full of righteous anger at the way her sons were mistreating the Leckies, Kate had handled me expertly. Sat me down. Offered me tea. Took the momentum away from me. Let the old study with its shelves of dusty books and slowly ticking clock lull me into a place where civilised discussion was seemingly the only option.

Not this time.

Assuming one of her sons had fired the gun, their hands would smell of gunpowder. They'd be flushed with the excitement of the mission, the exhilaration that comes from breaking that biggest taboo – thou shalt not kill. Men react differently to breaking that law. They'd either be sick with worry, or giddy with power. Either way, the story would be written on their faces.

I pounded on the front door, liking the sound it made. Here I am, it said, defender of the innocent, righter of wrongs. Give up your murderers and let them face the light.

No answer. No Kate. No timid maid. No young man, face flushed with victory. Crows squawked above nearby fields, and in the distance a tractor rumbled, old Beecham, getting an early start on the harvest. His fields all sloped southwards, putting him a few days ahead of the rest of us.

I looked up at the house and breathed deeply, willing the rushing blood to subside. Time for thought, not for action.

I walked around to the back, where her sons had parked their car last time I'd been here. An old farmyard, ancient barns succumbing to rot. No animals. No cars. The house was locked up, and every room was dark.

My conversation with Kate and her sons would have to wait, but not for long. The Leckies' deaths would not go unanswered.

25

I took a detour on the way home, to Newick. I owed Eric a visit, and I had a feeling he'd be the man to talk to about strange voices in the woods.

Eric was in his nan's back garden, shirtsleeves rolled up, jacket hung over the edge of his wheelbarrow, a pack of cigarettes bulging from the breast pocket of his waistcoat. A hot morning to be weeding, but it needed doing. I thought of Mrs Leckie, whose days of pulling up strawberry runners were over.

Eric saw me coming, but kept at his work. He had a bed of lettuce coming along nicely. Enough to feed a battalion, if you could get the battalion to eat salad.

Eric was a young man. If I had to guess I'd have put his age at nineteen or twenty, but he'd already developed a reputation as being a man you could turn to if you wanted something found. If you needed another chicken for your coop, Eric could find you one. If your wife needed a few yards of material for a new dress, Eric could find it. And if you noticed that your barn was missing something you thought you'd put there for safe keeping, it was likely Eric had found it on behalf of someone else. He had a good heart, and he helped more than he hindered, so he was generally a welcome sight. And I knew something about Eric that nobody else did. He'd agreed to be part of my Auxiliary Unit, opting to put himself in harm's way the day the invasion started. Practically begged me to let him join, even though he knew the predicted life expectancy was going to be counted in weeks, once the Nazis rolled through.

He straightened up as I approached. We'd established that since our unit was outside the regular military there would be no saluting, no nonsense about rank. But he came to attention nonetheless.

'I've got an interesting question,' I said, keeping my voice low. We were at least a couple of hundred yards from the nearest neighbour, but better safe than sorry.

'Go on,' Eric said.

'You haven't heard any German voices, have you? When you're out on your travels?'

As well as being a procurer of rationed goods, Eric was a poacher. He spent a lot of time in the woods, on both sides of other people's fences, and I assumed he knew of other people who were in the same line of work.

He shook his head.

'What's going on?' he asked. One thing I'd learnt about Eric, despite the illegalities of the way he made a living, he had a strong sense of duty. Wanted to do his bit. He'd been the first in line to sign up the day we declared war, but they'd kept him out because of an old injury. Working with me, preparing for the invasion, had whetted his appetite to get stuck in.

'There's a Nazi spy hiding out nearby. I think he's trying to send radio signals back home.'

'Nothing on our wireless,' Eric said, looking back up towards the house where his nan would be sitting by the receiver all day, hopping between the BBC and illegal stations coming from Europe. A BBC-only diet was a bit much for most people. Only so many brass band performances a person can listen to. The foreign stations got the latest music from America. You had to listen to a bit of propaganda between the performances but I doubted Eric's nan was going to be convinced Hitler was doing the right thing by a smooth-talking radio announcer.

'Not just on the wireless,' I said. 'You might hear them coming out of nowhere when you're out in the woods or the fields. Long fences seem to bring them in.'

'Voices, or Morse code?' Eric asked.

'Voices. In German,' I said. 'Probably encoded.'

Eric looked around at his own fences. He had quite a collection. Lots of things to keep in, and people to keep out. Eric was clearly a believer in the saying that good fences make good neighbours.

'Do you think it's him?' he asked, after a while.

'Cyril's gone,' I said. 'And the voice I heard didn't sound like him.'

The previous month, another member of our unit had disappeared under suspicious circumstances. Took most of our weapons. Cyril was an expert on radio signals. I hadn't thought he had any love for the Germans, but I'd misjudged him. He'd been through every day of the Great War, from signing-up to armistice. Probably saw enough war for a lifetime.

'I saw a parachute come down on the Forest,' I said. 'There was a broken radio. Maybe the parachutist's met up with someone with another set.'

'I'll check Cyril's place again,' Eric said. 'Then I'll ask around. See if anyone's been hearing anything.'

'Good man.'

Eric blushed. A good lad, trying to do his bit. I was glad to have him in my corner.

'When are we going to meet up again?' he asked. 'You know. . .'

'Let's get this thing with the parachutist squared away,' I said. 'No point in us training for the invasion if it's already started.'

26

The Polish soldier was sitting on the wall, in front of my house. Bees buzzed lazily amongst the lavender. A picture of English country life, apart from the white lines drawn on the blue sky by our boys flying non-stop sorties over the Channel.

'What are you doing here?' I asked. I had a bowl of strawberries from Eric, and I set them down on the wall, feeling the warmth radiating from the sandstone.

'Waiting for you,' he said. 'Your mum said you were out. Said I could have dinner.'

He looked over his shoulder. Elizabeth was at the window, watching us, face blank.

'What's up with the girl?' he asked. 'All through dinner, looked like she was deciding whether to run away or stick me with a knife.'

'Why were you looking for me?' I asked.

'You're not so friendly,' he said. 'What have you got to be so miserable about? Nice farm. Nice family. No Germans.'

'I'm sure they're on their way.'

'We thought you were coming,' he said. 'After your Prime Minister made the treaty with us. Promising to come to our aid if Germans invaded. Day one, they crossed our borders, everyone said, "the English will come". Even when their Luftwaffe destroyed our cities, and their soldiers raped our wives and daughters, people were saying "the English will come". But the English didn't come.'

He finished his cigarette and ground it into the mud.

'You'll get us a black mark with the War Ag,' I said. 'They don't like litter. Corrupts the food chain.'

He lit a new cigarette and took a long drag.

'I think you English like your rules more than you like fighting.'

'I think you like talking,' I said.

He shrugged.

'You heard the news?' he asked. 'Italy declared war. Now it's you lot against all of Europe.'

'They'll be wanting to claim a piece of France,' I said. 'Like neighbours when a farm goes under. All wanting their own corner.'

'I came to talk to you,' he said. 'Been waiting all fucking day it feels like. So you want to hear what I got to say?'

'What is it?'

'I was at the pub in town last night. Looking for any more Poles. No Poles, but I heard something interesting. A man was drunk. Big deal, everyone's drunk. But he was too drunk. Sloppy. Too much talk. Talking about some people who needed killing.'

'People are allowed to talk in a pub,' I said.

'He said your name. Something about sticking your nose in.'

'Was he a Tommy?'

'Not Tommy,' he said. 'Civvy. With other civvies. Not a farmer. Looked like he worked in a . . . what's the word . . . shop where you sell furniture.'

'Was his arm in a cast?' I asked.

'You're not so dumb, for a farmer,' he said.

'Which pub?'

'I don't know the name, by the station.'

'The Fireman's Arms?'

'If you say.'

It wasn't a pub I usually frequented.

'I'll drop in this evening,' I said. 'Buy you a pint if you and your mates are there.'

'Bob's gone,' the Pole said. 'I think military police got him last night. Got a whole bunch of the English boys. Rounded them up and sent them on their way, like sheep.'

'But you got away?'

'English MPs aren't interested in me,' he said. 'Besides, I'm not sheep.'

27

The Fireman's Arms was in prime position, at the bottom of the high street, next to the station. It had changed hands since I'd last visited. The new landlord had spruced things up, to the extent that putting a few pots of geraniums on the window sills could be considered spruced up. A blackboard by the front door promised sandwiches. Another innovation.

I had to push my way through a crowd of soldiers outside, and when I made it inside, I was surprised at how busy it was. I'd been expecting the usual quiet evening – working men quietly drinking away their lives – but the place was full, and there was an electric energy in the air. A fug of smoke hung down from the yellow ceiling, and men were shoulder to shoulder, drinking and talking. Most were soldiers who looked like they'd slipped away from the trains shuttling men from the coast to barracks inland.

For every soldier, there was a girl. I recognised a few faces. Others looked like they'd arrived from out of town for professional purposes – their dresses more revealing, their make-up more expertly applied.

Watching over all of this, two military police officers stood at the bar, their red berets folded and stowed under their shoulder lapels, a warning to everyone. They had a practised nonchalance that I knew, from experience, could switch to action in a second. I'd had my fair share of brushes with MPs, and had learnt to give them a wide berth when I'd been in uniform. Now, though, I was invisible to them. Another old man in for a few beers after his day on the farm.

I pushed my way through the crowd. A commotion in a group of gunners rippled out and one of them staggered into me, spilling his beer. I put my hand on his back, keeping him away from me, and at the same time another man bumped into me from behind.

'Steady on!' he said. I turned, ready to apologise.

'Hello!' the man said. We recognised each other at the same time. He was the artist I'd seen that morning, near the Leckies' house.

'They didn't catch you,' he said, with a smirk.

'What do you mean?' I asked, leaning in to hear him over the noise of the crowd.

'I watched you,' he said, 'doing a recce.'

'Just out for a walk,' I said.

'That's all right,' he said, and he winked at me. 'Our little secret.' It was unsettling. His wink was intimate, like we were old friends, in on a private joke. Before I could come back with a retort he slapped me on the shoulder and left. I watched him push his way through the crowd, on his way to the gents.

I made it to the bar and ordered a pint of best, still thinking about the artist.

'Kate Davidson's lads been in tonight?' I asked.

The barman shook his head. It could have meant no, or it could have meant he wasn't going to tell me.

'Someone was in here last night talking about people needing to be killed,' I said. 'Hear anything like that?'

'Look around,' the barman said. 'Take your pick.'

The Polish soldier joined me at the bar.

'You heard the latest rumour?' he asked. 'Local priest caught with wireless set in his belfry.'

'That one's been going around since last year,' I said. 'Your source is out of date.'

I bought the Polish soldier a drink, keeping an eye out for the Davidson boys.

'You hear any more German voices out in the fields?' I asked.

'It's the fence,' he said. When I looked surprised, he smiled, pleased with himself.

'I figured it out,' he continued. 'Last night. I heard the voice, hid in a bush, but got fed up hiding, so went looking for a German to kill. It's your fence.'

I nodded.

'Makes me wonder,' he said. 'You haven't signed up to fight, and your fence talks German.'

I drank my beer, looking around at the busy pub.

'If I was on their side, I wouldn't be using my fence to take orders,' I said. 'I'd have a nice little receiver tucked away in the attic, like that priest you heard about.'

He finished his beer and waved to the barman for another round.

'Still,' he said. 'Germans on the radio. People getting killed. Doesn't sound like quiet English countryside.'

'How long are you sticking around?' I asked.

'A while,' he said. 'They've set up a, what's the word . . . cordon . . . on the roads out. No one in or out without the right papers. Protecting the rest of the country from people like me.'

'Or trying to filter out the spies and saboteurs who came over on the boats,' I said. 'If I were a German commander I'd have rounded up everyone I could lay my hands on with passable English, shoved them into a Tommy's uniform, and told them to get themselves onto a boat.'

'How do you know I'm not one of those,' he said.

'I don't.'

'You should get me drunk,' he said. 'See if I give up my secrets.'

'Let's start with your name.'

'Milosz,' he said, holding out his hand. We shook.

We spent the evening drinking, and I kept an eye out for Kate's sons, but they didn't show up, presumably lying low until the dust settled.

I left Milosz buying a round, and took myself off to the toilets. I kept my eye out for the artist, as I pushed through the crowd. He'd been close to the Leckies' house when the attack happened, and now he was here.

The urinal was full, four men standing shoulder to shoulder. In the stall behind us, a rhythmic thumping told me one of the professionals had found a client.

A man buttoned up and pushed past me. He avoided my eyes, and I reciprocated. It was only as I unbuttoned my flies that I looked forwards, at the wall above the urinal. There was a row of leaflets, all the same, all roughly printed. Large text. A simple message.

SAY NO TO A JEWS' WAR

It wasn't the first of its kind I'd seen. For the last five years, as the threat of war built, there'd been an undercurrent of debate, which often turned violent. Germany had its Nazis, and so did we. But the tide had slowly turned since the outbreak of war. The British Union of Fascists had been outlawed in May, and Oswald Mosley, our homegrown Hitler, had been arrested.

This leaflet was different. It stood out. The apostrophe showed the poster had been created by someone with a high level of education, and a finicky sense of detail. Most people, even if they'd realised they needed an apostrophe, would have guessed wrong and put it after the W. Or they'd have left it off, not wanting to get it wrong.

Regardless of grammar, the paper in front of me wasn't destined for a long life. As I stood there, it unpeeled itself from the wall and slid into the urinal to join the mess of yellow piss and cigarette butts. The next leaflet along was on its way there too. It looked like they'd all been kept rolled up in someone's pocket, and the paper wanted to revert to the rolled shape. They'd been hastily pasted onto the wall, but the wall itself was covered with glossy paint that was damp with condensation. Not the ideal surface for a quick smear of wallpaper paste.

As I returned to the bar I scanned the drinkers to see if anyone was watching me. Someone had posted up propaganda posters for their cause. Perhaps they'd decided to stick around to see if anyone looked stirred up by their slogan. Maybe there'd be some kind of effort at recruitment. Maybe a secret society, dedicated to posting up more notices. But nobody tried to catch my eye or start up a conversation about the merits of the war. No loud comments about Jews, testing my thoughts on the subject.

One man did catch my eye, though. He was sitting at a table in the corner, flicking his eyes around the pub, scanning faces. He had his back to the wall, and from where he sat he had a view of both the bar and the entrance.

When I got back to my place at the bar, I used the mirror behind the landlord to study the man in the corner in more detail. He was my age, forty-ish, with close-cropped hair. He had a red scar across his cheek. He was dressed in worn tweed, his jacket slightly large, allowing freedom of movement in a fight, and useful to conceal a weapon.

Two other drinkers sat at his table, either side, talking across him. They must have known him, otherwise they wouldn't be sitting with him, but they were ignoring him, like he was a servant, or a relative. A boring uncle perhaps. The other two were younger, a man and a woman. They were flushed from drink, laughing, caught up in each other. I let myself watch the woman. She was glamorous, dressed up for a night out, sure of herself.

I realised where I'd seen them before. The night of the parachutist. Getting out of a luxury car.

'Don't be too obvious about it, but have a look at the three people in the corner,' I murmured to Milosz. 'Young man and woman, older man in the middle. Have you seen them before?'

Milosz watched for a minute before turning back to the bar.

'The older man had rushed field dressing,' he said. 'Bullet wound. Not deep, but messy. Probably sewn up at front lines, got infected. Lots of old men like that in Poland from last war.'

'Was he in yesterday?'

'Don't think so,' he said.

As I watched, the young woman held her glass up and said something to her companion. He got up from the table and made his way towards our position at the packed bar.

I stood back, giving him a path to the bar. He nodded his thanks and caught the landlord's attention.

'Another pint and a G&T please, heavy on the G,' he said.

Curious, buying two drinks, when you'd come from a table with three people. It added to my impression that the older man was a third wheel.

'Let me buy you a drink if you've come over from Dunkirk,' I said. He turned to face me and I got a good look at him. He was older than I'd thought. Older than the woman. Mid-thirties at least. He had a tanned face, with deep lines by the corner of his eyes, like he'd spent too much time in the sun. He'd shaved before he'd come out, and had a fresh nick on his neck, with the faintest trace of toilet paper attached.

'I'm not with that lot,' he said, gesturing to the soldiers. 'You?'

'Just a farmer.'

'No *just* about it. Equally as heroic. Keeping the nation in feed,' he said. I couldn't tell if he was mocking me or not.

'Where are you from?' I asked.

'One and four,' the landlord said, pushing the two drinks across the bar. It gave the man a second to think.

He reached into his pocket for the right change.

'Sorry,' he said, 'not allowed to say. Loose lips and all that.' He said it in a friendly enough way, but there was a firmness underlying it.

He put his coins on the bar, confirming the amount with a quick flick of his eyes.

'I saw your poster in the toilets,' I said.

'Not me, I'm afraid,' he said. 'Although . . .' he smiled, 'if you're looking for the culprit . . . I'd say someone older than you or me. Well educated. Someone who knows their grammar and believes the printed word has power.'

The scar-faced man in the corner was watching our exchange. He stood up and muttered to the woman. She complained but he cut her off. He was clearly in charge. She finished her drink hurriedly and grabbed her handbag.

'Nice talking with you,' the man said, unaware that his companions were making plans for a hurried departure.

I felt a strong compulsion to keep him talking. Something was wrong, and some part of my subconscious had registered it but was declining to pass on the information. The longer I kept him talking, the more chance I gave myself to get to the bottom of my sense of unease.

But then the evening changed.

28

'Cook, you cunt!' a drunken voice broke through the hub-bub. I felt a hand on my left shoulder. It grabbed me, jerking me back.

I went with it, letting the hand pull me around. When somebody grabs you like that, they want you to turn into their punch. Spin you around, take a wide swing at your jaw, or a looping fist to your nose. Standard pub brawl. So I turned, but I leant my head back. As expected, by the time I was facing my assailant, his fist was whistling past my nose. It was Kate's younger son.

Things were looking up. The pub had looked like being a bust, but the man I'd come looking for had shown up and volunteered to be taken down. I let his swing pass me by, threw a short underarm jab into his large stomach. My fist disappeared into his solar plexus, and I drove upwards. A woof of stale air was forced out of his lungs, and he doubled over. I grabbed the back of his head, pushing it down to meet my rising knee, which crunched into his nose.

He staggered backwards, blood spurting from his broken nose, crashing into a table, sending glasses and ashtrays flying.

His older brother, Victor, arm in a plaster cast, took his place. There was a glint of light on the blade in his hand. I backed away. Regardless of whether my opponent had a broken arm, a knife fight was at the bottom of my list of preferred evening activities.

A buzz of anticipation rippled through the crowd. The ancient thrill of a fight.

'Outside!' the landlord shouted. 'Both of you!'

Outside or inside, either was fine with me. Kate's sons had hidden behind their mother's skirts the last time our paths had crossed, but now we were going to have words.

*

The crowd in the car park organised itself into a circle, surrounding an empty patch of tarmac the size of a boxing ring, with me and my opponents in the middle. The younger brother pulled off his blood-soaked shirt.

'I'm going to teach you a lesson,' he said, throwing his shirt to a supporter in the crowd. 'You don't mess with the Davidsons.' Probably a mantra he'd had running through his head all the way to the pub.

I let him talk. He didn't know it yet, but he was already beaten. He'd lost the fight the second he'd put his hand on my shoulder. That's not how you take out a threat. If you walk up behind a man you want on the ground, you put him on the ground, before he knows you're there. Anything else is play fighting. And if he wanted to play, I'd be happy to oblige, although I predicted that each round would diminish his enthusiasm considerably. When he was finished, I could hand him over to the police and let the law take care of the rest.

Victor concerned me more. He'd already shown he was happy to use the knife, and since then he'd had time to stew on the injustice of being beaten by me the first time. Add to that, I was worried about the feeling he would have got from killing the Leckies. It hits every man differently, but for some, it's like opening the floodgates.

There was a ripple in the crowd behind me. I risked a glance back. The three strangers were threading their way through. The man with the scar, the young woman, and the man I'd talked to at the bar.

My assailant swung his fist at me while I was distracted. A long swing, theatrical, designed to impress everyone in the car park that he meant business. It had failed him the first time. Trying the same thing again told me everything I needed to know – he wasn't a threat, and he was stuck in a loop without assessing how it was working for him. If he was a normal drunk, and this was a normal day, I'd have put him down quickly and left him to tend his wounds. But he wasn't a normal drunk. He was a killer. He and his brother had beaten the Leckies, then when they hadn't acted the way he'd predicted, they'd gone back and finished the job.

I stepped forwards, into the arc of his swinging arm. I got his arm across my ear for my troubles, but his fist was now behind my head, useless. He crooked his arm, pulling my head towards his chest, where he could bring his left fist up into my face. But I kept my forward momentum, and head-butted him. His nose was already broken, and this time it disintegrated. He screamed and put his hands to his face, all thoughts of attack gone. I pushed him backwards, and he stumbled into his brother.

Victor pushed him aside. No love lost between the brothers, it seemed. If anything, Victor looked disgusted. Didn't want the failure rubbing off on him.

With his unbroken arm, he reached into his back pocket and pulled out a second knife. Now he had one in each hand. It was very theatrical. Like some kind of assassin from a Fu Manchu story. I didn't put much stock in his ability to co-ordinate both knives, but I've learnt to be cautious when it comes to knives. Better safe than sorry.

I turned to one of the MPs, standing behind me in the crowd. He was watching the unfolding fight with the air of a connoisseur, like a first-class batsman watching a sleepy village match.

'Captain,' I snapped, in my best sergeantmajor voice – quick, efficient, trained to bring my superiors solutions, not problems.

'These men are deserters,' I said. 'Found them stripping off their uniforms in my barn. This one said the King could fuck off. Said he'd like to get the young princesses alone for the night and give them what-for.'

A prostitute in the crowd gasped. She'd been ready to see two men beat each other to a pulp, but hearing a profanity about the royal family was a step too far. A sense of moral outrage that demanded action.

The MP had brought his pint out with him, and he took a long draught. I wasn't sure he would take the bait. But once he'd had his drink he tugged on a lanyard around his neck, pulled out his whistle, and blew a piercing blast. The ACME police whistle, designed to be heard up to a mile away in a crowded city. My pulse quickened at the sound. A Pavlovian response. The same whistle had been issued to every officer on the Western Front. Every time I'd heard that sound had been one of the worst moments of my life.

The effect was instant, and massive.

'Move, move, move!' from the back of the crowd. Before people had a chance to move, four MP sergeants rushed forwards, pushing people aside with no regard for civilian versus soldier, male versus female. If you were between them and the man who'd blown the whistle, you were out of luck. Glasses smashed on the tarmac. Women screamed as they were pushed aside, and the MPs arrived in the circle, ready to subdue a riot. They'd been selected for size and aggression, trained to run towards a soldier who looked like he was thinking about disobeying an order. The MP with the whistle pointed at Victor, who stood in the middle of the circle, his knives out. The MP nodded, and the four sergeants piled on.

Victor swung with his knife and nicked the first MP to reach him, drawing blood. Not a wise move. He'd been in for a rough time of it as it was. Now he'd bought himself the strong possibility of life-altering injuries.

'Both of them?' the MP asked, as the brother tried to crawl away from the melee, blood gushing from his twice-broken nose.

'Both of them,' I said.

Behind the crowd, a large black car pushed its way through the periphery. The scar-faced man was at the wheel, and he caught my eye. He gave me an ironic salute, and I had the same feeling I'd had when I first noticed him. He was a man like me. Someone who'd get the job done, whatever the job was, whatever it took.

29

First thing in the morning, the high street was quiet. A brisk walk from my farm, into town, to the police station, ready to report my findings.

Two police constables pushed past me. The phone was ringing, unanswered, and shouts came from the depths of the station. The constable at the desk held up his hand for me to wait.

'Is Neesham in?' I asked.

Detective Sergeant Neesham was an old acquaintance from school. A good man, give or take. We'd butted horns over a recent murder. I'd cleared my name but left a trail of collateral damage – men who'd deserved to die.

A door slammed and Neesham appeared from his office, grabbing his overcoat from a rack. He didn't slow down as he opened the hatch on the counter and made for the front door.

'I saw a parachutist,' I said. 'The one Vaughn Matheson reported. He's making radio transmissions.'

'Not now, Cook,' he said.

I followed him out to his car.

'I also found the Leckies' killers,' I said, as Neesham pushed past me.

Neesham hesitated.

'Get in,' he said.

He pulled out of the station car park, onto the high street, and flicked a switch on the dashboard. His siren wailed into life.

We hurtled down the hill towards the railway crossing, past the Fireman's Arms. Neesham took the crossing without slowing down, testing the suspension on the car. He sped up the high street, towards the cinema. He gunned the powerful engine and shoppers crossing the road had to step lively as we sped past.

'The War Ag's taking Streatfield's farm,' he said. 'He's got himself holed up in the house with a shotgun, threatening to kill anyone who cares to get close.'

Arthur Streatfield had a failing farm on the Newick road, between me and Eric. He'd been letting it go to the dogs since his sons were killed in the Great War. Three sons on the same day. A suicidal attack the day before the Somme. Turned out later it was designed solely as a diversion. Went down in regimental history as 'the day that Sussex died'.

'I thought that was the War Ag, not you lot,' I said.

'How's your place?' Neesham asked. 'Ready for the inspection?'

I didn't answer.

He took the s-bend carved through sandstone outcrops, under the footbridge that let the owners of The Rocks estate cross the road to their pleasure gardens without having to interact with the rest of us.

'I had an irate call last night from the barracks at Maresfield,' he said. 'Someone encouraged their MPs to snatch a couple of civvies.'

'Kate Davidson's boys,' I said. 'They killed the Leckies. They wanted them out of the cottage. They'd already tried violence, but they weren't getting things their way.'

'So you thought you'd step in and play detective.'

'They'd still be at large if it wasn't for me.'

We shot down the straight, heading out of town, hemmed in by mossy stone walls. I looked left as we passed the turn-off to my farm.

'It wasn't them,' he said.

'How do you know?'

'They've got an alibi,' he said. 'We know where they were when the killings took place.'

'And you believe them?'

'I believe my own eyes,' he said. 'They were at the station. First day of training for the local defence volunteers, along with every other man in Uckfield. Apart from you, I might add.'

Churchill had put out a call for able-bodied men to sign up at their local police station. No planning. No infrastructure. No weapons. Give the masses something to do.

'Doesn't sound like their cup of tea,' I said.

'They were first in line.'

Neesham killed the siren as we bumped along the rutted track to Streatfield's farm. Three police cars circled the abandoned well in the middle of the yard. Each car had a police constable sheltering behind it. Each constable had a shotgun. Like a Bogart film. One of the constables had a bloody handkerchief pressed to his face.

'This is going to be a mess,' Neesham said. 'Stay in the car.' He got out and hurried around the back of the car, keeping low.

A shotgun barrel protruded from an upstairs window of the farmhouse. Streatfield, presumably. He'd be drunk, which meant his aim would be useless.

I got out of the car, slamming the door behind me. I wanted Streatfield's attention, wanted him to see it was me, not a police constable.

'Streatfield?' I shouted. 'I'm coming in. If you shoot me, we're going to have words.'

'Cook!' Neesham shouted. 'Get back in that car!' I ignored him and strode across the overgrown yard. The last time I'd been here had been to borrow a harrow, when I'd got back from the North-West Frontier, and I'd been putting everything I had into keeping my farm afloat. Streatfield had been the only one willing to lend me his kit. One of the problems with farming. Everyone needs the same machines at the same time, so it's hard to share them. Streatfield had given up, so his tools were always available.

I made it to the shelter of his barn, attached to the side of the house. The barn was dark, and smelt of rotting straw. Rats scurried in the dark. They didn't sound like they were running away, more like they were trying to get a good look at the unexpected visitor. Or planning a co-ordinated attack.

There was a side door from the barn into the house. I hoped it was unlocked. Kicking a man's door down wasn't the best way to get him on your side.

The kitchen was as rank as the barn, possibly worse. Fewer rats, but only just. Or maybe the rats in the house were quieter.

'Are you going to come down and sort this out, or am I going to have to come up?' I shouted.

'They're not taking my farm,' Streatfield shouted down.

'Nobody's taking anyone's farm,' I said. 'But if you keep pointing a gun at all those lads out there one of them's going to get upset and decide to shoot you first.'

'Tell them to go away,' he said.

'I think it's a bit late for that.'

There was silence for a while.

'Bit of a problem,' he said.

'I'm coming up,' I said.

Streatfield was sitting on a wooden chair to the side of the window, his ancient shotgun resting on the sill. He was dressed in his underpants and a filthy vest. The room was dank with mould and it smelt worse than it looked.

'They want to take the farm,' he said, as if I didn't know. As if I'd dropped round for a social visit.

'Maybe not such a bad thing,' I said. 'Let a young man have a go with it. The country needs feeding.'

He looked at me with watery eyes. Tracks on his grimy face showed he'd been crying.

'Meant to be *my* boys.'

'That's all in the past,' I said. 'We all lost people. Got to get on with it.'

He looked around the room.

'Did I hurt anyone?' he asked.

'You winged one of them. Probably given him a few weeks off sick.'

'They're going to put me in jail.'

'They want the farm,' I said. 'Come down and we'll talk with Neesham. He's all right.'

'Charlie Necsham?' he said, his face lifting.

'Let's go,' I said. 'Sort it out over a pint.'

He looked up at me with hope, a vision of a way out.

'Stay away from the window,' I said, as Streatfield got up from the chair.

'Right,' he said, leaning across the window to grab his gun.

A volley of gunfire erupted from outside. Like a pheasant shoot; a frenzy of gunfire until everyone had emptied their chambers. I got a mouthful of dust and blood before I could back out into the upstairs hall.

The shooting stopped.

'You in there, Cook?'

It was Neesham. A bit late.

'He was coming out,' I shouted.

No answer. An honest mistake, Neesham would be thinking. Paperwork, but nothing worse.

I looked back into the filthy room. Streatfield was on his back, what was left of him.

I walked out through the barn, into the yard. Police cars were already backing out, places to be, things to do, lives to ruin.

Neesham shook his head.

'You all right?' he asked.

I stared at him, hoping to convey all the contempt I felt for everyone who'd ever sent a man over the top. For the generals who'd murdered Streatfield's sons as surely as the constables had murdered their father.

'I'm all right,' I said, walking past him, walking home.

I'd got the Leckies killed, and I'd made a mistake about the Davidson boys. But the answer wasn't to put my faith in Neesham and his constables. Nothing good would come of Streatfield's last stand, but something useful perhaps. A reminder of my guiding principle. One that had got lost in the mess of the last few days. One that I'd learnt the hard way.

If you want something done, do it yourself.

30

Kate's front door was open. I was still thirty yards from the house, walking loudly on the deep gravel. I wasn't going for the element of surprise, happy to announce my presence.

Kate and I were going to have words. She'd sent her sons to get the Leckies out, but that hadn't worked out. Perhaps the second time she'd got someone else in. Perhaps she'd told her boys to get themselves an alibi for the day.

There was a crash, like someone had pulled a drawer out past the stops and let it clatter to a stone floor.

I reassessed the situation. People don't walk into their own house and leave the front door open. They don't pull drawers out and let the contents clatter over the floor.

Someone else was in there.

The parachutist?

I took cover behind an overgrown rhododendron.

I had two choices, stay and get involved, or leave and live to fight another day. Rule number one, you win every fight you don't have. But walking away wouldn't give me any answers about what had happened to the Leckies, just more questions. So I stayed. Not inertia. A conscious decision. Get involved.

Treading softly on the grass, I closed the distance to the house, until the only thing between me and the front door was gravel. No way to cross it quietly. I ran, aiming at a spot three feet to the side of the front door. No point in giving the intruder a silhouette to aim at through the open door.

I pressed myself against the wall beside the front door and listened. Another clatter. Someone was ransacking the place. Lucky for me, the noise they were making had covered the noise of my approach. Which told me something. I wasn't dealing with any great military or criminal genius.

I crouched down and looked in through the open front door. If anyone had been watching, their first shot was likely to come at waist height, where a man would comfortably hold his gun. I kept lower than that, raising the odds of me surviving that first shot.

But there was no shot, and the clatter from the back of the house continued.

Inside the house, I saw a slipper, discarded on the flag-stone floor. Next to it, a foot, protruding from the drawing room. Someone was down.

I hurried in, staying low. Ducked into the drawing room.

It was Kate.

At first glance I assumed she was dead. She lay on her back. Her chest was a mess of blood. Two shots, close up. She'd probably answered the door and been hit straight away. Stumbled back as her heart stopped pumping, col-lapsed into the study as her muscles failed without the hydraulic support from the heart.

I felt her neck, making sure, and her eyes flickered open.

She looked at me, pleading. I touched her face.

She'd told me her boss would be disappointed, the last time we'd been in this room.

Her lips moved soundlessly. I leant in close, but I still couldn't hear.

It wasn't like in the movies, where the dying man gives a monologue, then gently closes his eyes. It doesn't work like that. The body has shut down. The lungs have expelled their last breath. No air to make the words.

I watched her lips. She brought her bottom lip to her teeth. It looked like an 'f', then her mouth went slack.

'Fault,' she said.

Another crash from the kitchen. I was crouching on the floor in the drawing room, my back to the door. Every fibre in my body screamed at me to turn, to face the threat.

I stayed with Kate for her last seconds, my hand on her cheek, my eyes locked on hers. I owed her that much.

People talk about the dying finding peace in their final seconds. It's a comforting thought. It's coming to us all, so we tell ourselves fairy tales about the experience. Kate wasn't at peace. Her eyes widened in panic, her brain pleading with her lungs to breathe, refusing to believe the truth. I held her gaze. Even blinking would have been cowardice, allowing myself a respite. I kept my eyes locked on hers until the hundreds of muscles in her face slackened in death.

The back door slammed, and the house was quiet. I listened carefully. Nothing. No creaks of someone shifting because they'd had to hide. No quiet steps of somebody determined to deal with an unwelcome visitor. Just the distant call of wood pigeons in the trees.

'Your fault,' she'd said. She was right.

*

The kitchen was a mess. The younger son, his nose black from our fight, sat in his armchair by the fire. A cup of tea and half a slice of toast on the table next to him. A few minutes ago he'd been eating his breakfast, back from his overnight stay with the MPs. Now he was dead.

A slight breeze on my neck was the only warning I got. Displaced air, pushed in front of a fast-moving object. A fraction of a second that made the difference between victim and participant, from dead to still fighting. Something was swinging towards the back of my neck. A killing blow.

Instinct kicked in. I launched myself forwards, away from the threat, buying myself more time to assess the situation and plan my counter-attack. I hit the ground and rolled across the tiled floor, my boots clattering against the enamelled stove as I ran out of room. My assailant was already following. He had a knife in his hand, a short, double blade. A soldier's knife.

I'd been expecting a German uniform, like the parachutists in the comic books Frankie read. But he was dressed in a Tommy's uniform. Salt stains at chest level, from where he'd waded out into the sea, from the beach at Dunkirk.

It took me a second to recognise him. One of the deserters I'd found in my woods and given dinner. The sergeant. The back door was open behind him. He'd come back.

He paused. He had me cornered, he could allow himself a breather. A mistake, which told me I was dealing with someone who hadn't yet become habituated to killing. Here was a man for whom the rules of society still held some sway. A fact I could use against him.

'I don't care what you did here,' I said.

Not true, of course, I rather did care, but he had a knife and I didn't.

In his hyper-alert state, his logical mind had to fight for resources. The expression on his face telegraphed the turmoil. Hard to think straight when your blood's up and adrenaline has shut down everything apart from your fight-or-flight reflex.

The decision was telegraphed on his face. His jaw set, his eyes focused.

Above me, a rack of pans hung above the stove. Heavy, black, cast iron. I made a show of looking past him, to the back door, and feinted that way. He took the bait and shifted to his left, blocking my escape. But I wasn't interested in escape. I'd given him a chance to run, and he'd made his choice. It was a decision that was going to work out badly for him if I had anything to do with it.

I reached up and grabbed a frying pan eighteen inches across. Its grey oak handle fitted my grip perfectly. I could have spent hours trying to design the perfect weapon to bring to a knife fight and not improved on this. Three feet from the tip of the handle to the end of the pan. A large mass, impervious to the knife and certain to do damage to any part of the human body it struck, if swung with force.

He made the same calculation. He backed away, pushing aside a chair with a screech of wood on stone.

He transferred the knife to his left hand, freeing up his right. My heart sank. I could only think of one good reason for that, and he proved me right. He reached behind his waist and came up with a Webley revolver, standard army issue.

I raised my hands. It was what you were meant to do in that situation, if you were to believe the movies. Your assailant would be duty-bound to treat you with grudging respect, take you prisoner, or leave you to fight again another day. Not massively realistic based on what I'd seen in Flanders, or the North-West Frontier. If it was you and another man, and one of you had a gun, there was only one way that encounter was going to end.

But my assailant was a young man. He hadn't been at Flanders, or in the dusty mountains of Afghanistan. He thought he was dealing with a man of honour.

He was wrong.

Putting my hands up had increased the frying pan's potential energy. A large mass, held up high. I let the weight of it drag my hand down, and I pulled it, through an arc, like swinging a cricket bat towards a ball arriving at waist height, giving it everything and going for the boundary. I let go of the pan, on a trajectory towards the man's head. He had a fraction of a second to react, and he wasted it, raising the gun towards the pan as if he were shooting at a target. The pan knocked the gun from his hand without slowing down. It took him in the neck, its momentum unaltered until it was embedded in the full depth of his soft tissue.

The pan thumped to the ground with a clang, and the man went down, clutching at his throat. I kicked his gun away. Better safe than sorry.

I pulled up a kitchen chair and sat, waiting for him to die. Asphyxiation takes a long time. I didn't feel any sympathy. He'd killed Kate and her son in cold blood. Odds were he'd done the same to the Leckies the day before.

But why? I could think of a few reasons that would fit if this were a murder novel, one of those paperbacks that were all the rage. He was looking for somewhere to lie low while his unit was transported out of the area, back to their base. He was a long-lost son, back for revenge over some long-harboured slight. Or perhaps he'd heard a story from a mate about a buried treasure kept in the garden. All unlikely, but basically feasible.

The crunch of stones from the driveway warned me I wasn't going to be alone for long. It was an effective alarm. A car. Idling, then silent. Then the sound of doors opening.

I slipped out the back door and waited to the side, in the shade of an ancient pear tree. I was invisible to anyone in the house, but if I got the chance I'd be able to peer in. I wanted to know who it was. Perhaps the killer had accomplices, coming to retrieve something, or to make sure the job was finished to their satisfaction.

Voices filtered back from the front of the house. They'd found Kate. From the tone of the voices, it didn't sound like they were affiliated with the killer. They sounded surprised. One of the voices was clearly in charge. He was giving orders. Calm, measured.

I recognised the voice.

Neesham.

Stay or go. Leaving quietly seemed sensible. I was an innocent bystander. The police might not see it that way.

A rustle of leaves warned me I wasn't alone. Someone pushing through the beech hedge at the side of the house.

I turned quickly, assessing the threat. A police constable, truncheon raised, ready to take me down.

The truncheon was a fearsome weapon. Thirty inches of solid lignum, the densest and heaviest wood in the world. Designed to subdue the angriest and most intractable criminal. It didn't leave me with many options. Either get hit hard, or take out the man wielding it. Me or him.

I hesitated. I'll do whatever it takes to survive, even if it means killing the man in front of me. But this man wasn't my enemy. He was a young lad, barely out of school, who'd signed up with the police to do his bit. An honourable choice. Not his fault that doing his bit and smacking me on the head with a truncheon were one and the same thing.

My hesitation made all the difference. Inaction instead of action. Always a poor choice. More footsteps behind me. Leather soles. Another threat. I turned, my attention divided. My head exploded in a bright light, and the next thing I felt was the ground digging into my cheek.

31

'Tell me,' Neesham said, 'from the beginning.'

I was laid out on the couch in the drawing room. I tried to raise my hand to my head, but handcuffs cut off my movement. I pulled myself up to a sitting position, intending to stand, but the room spun alarmingly.

Neesham sat on the opposite couch, where Kate had sat the last time I'd been here. He looked tired.

'How did you get here so quickly?' I asked.

'What do you mean?'

'The murders took place about five minutes before I got here. You got here five minutes after me. You were on your way already.'

'I don't have to explain my methods to you, Cook.'

My head was pounding. I closed my eyes.

'You're not the law, John,' Neesham said. 'Let the rest of us have a chance. Some of us might surprise you.'

I didn't respond to Neesham, but I could feel his satisfaction in the silence. Since our days together at school, he'd always been in my shadow. Since I'd come back from the war we hadn't crossed paths much, but I knew how he thought of me. Cook, the man who'd lost his mind and stayed in the army after the war. Seen so much killing he couldn't come home. Damaged goods.

'Tell me again,' he said.

I told him about taking Mrs Leckie home from the station. About her and Stan being bruised, threatened and evicted. I told him about coming to see Kate, and her promise to leave the Leckies alone.

'I was back there yesterday and I heard shots. I was too far away to be useful.'

I didn't tell Neesham about Kate's last words. *Your fault.* That was between her and me.

'What were you hoping to achieve coming here?' Neesham asked.

'I wasn't thinking that far ahead.'

'You wanted revenge.'

He was right, of course, but it wasn't just revenge.

'She killed the Leckies,' I said. 'Even if it wasn't either of her sons pulling the trigger, she was behind it. I wanted to put it to her. See what she said.'

Neesham wrote on his pad. He looked at me, thinking carefully about his next question.

'I assume the soldier was dead when you arrived.'

I didn't answer. It hadn't sounded like a question.

'What's his connection to the Leckies?' he asked.

'He was a deserter,' I said. 'I found him lying low in my woods with a couple of others.'

'He's not from Dunkirk,' Neesham said.

'How can you tell?'

'Orders from the top. The absolute top. We're not going to find any of our returning heroes committing any crimes, least of all deserting. These are all gallant young men who can't wait to get back into the fray and give Jerry what-for.'

'So they get a free pass on anything they decide to get up to?'

'If we catch anyone in the act, we hand them over to the military police. Let them worry about it. But if it's a report of a crime, we file it at the bottom of the in-tray. Leave it there for a year until this is all over.'

The last thing the country needed was stories of Tommies misbehaving. One of the advantages of conducting wars overseas was that the public could be kept unaware of the various realities of forcing young men to put themselves in harm's way.

Neesham looked up as another car pulled up in front of the house. We listened to the door opening and closing, footsteps.

Doc Graham carried his medical bag. He looked at the two of us, on our opposite couches. Me in handcuffs, Neesham with his notebook. He didn't comment. He knelt by Kate's body.

'Nasty,' he said.

'That's your medical opinion?' I asked. Doc and I were old friends. The three of us, Neesham included, had gone to school together. Small-town stuff.

'In medical parlance, she's deceased.'

It wasn't like Doc to be so flippant. He was a precise man, in words and in action. Something was wrong. More wrong than walking in on a dead body and two of his old school-mates at loggerheads, one of them in handcuffs.

'There's a couple more in the kitchen,' Neesham said.

*

Doc went through his checks on the soldier while Neesham paced. I sat on a kitchen chair, next to the son, or what remained of him. Neesham had let me out of the handcuffs, grudgingly.

'Well?' Neesham asked. Doc was crouched on the floor, he looked up at Neesham and shook his head. He'd been feeling the man's ankles. Rolled his trouser legs back down. He shuffled along, repositioning, and unbuttoned the shirt. The soldier's neck was destroyed, the frying pan had done its job. Doc examined the man's chest, and looked under the arms. Once again, he looked up at Neesham and shook his head.

'One less thing,' Neesham said.

'What are you looking for?' I asked.

'You were saying something earlier about a parachutist,' Neesham said.

'I saw one come down on the Forest,' I replied. 'Vaughn Matheson said he'd call it in. I told him to ask for you.'

Neesham shook his head. Apparently the message hadn't got through.

Doc felt inside the man's jacket, and produced a crumpled wad of paper. He unfolded it. Two twenty-pound notes, blood leaching into the paper, and a map. He unfolded the map and looked at it. When he looked up, he didn't look at Neesham, but at me.

'What?' I asked.

Doc spread the map out on the kitchen table. Uckfield and Ashdown Forest. Standard Ordnance Survey, one to twenty-five thousand. Sheet TQ 42. You'd find a copy in every house in the district, scuffed at the corners, coming apart at the folds.

A cross, crudely made with thick pencil, showed our current position.

'Someone gave him this and the money,' Neesham said. 'Gave him his marching orders.'

'This is the Leckies,' I said, pointing at another cross, at the end of Palehouse Lane, stuck out like an island in the middle of the open space of the Forest.

I'd been wrong about Kate. She hadn't hired this man. Why would you hire a killer and put yourself on his list?

'Cook,' Doc said. His earlier flippancy was gone. Doc was my oldest friend. My only friend. He wasn't a man who wore his emotions on his sleeve, but in that one word, there was fear, and urgency.

Doc pointed to another point on the map. A third cross, crudely drawn with thick pencil. A job to be done. Forty pounds up front. A year's pay. Probably more to come on completion.

My vision blurred and I couldn't focus on the map. I didn't need to. I knew every lane, every hedgerow, every contour. I knew what was hidden beneath the thick cross. A farm-house. Outbuildings. Barns. Sitting alone and vulnerable at the end of a half-mile-long country lane, a mile west of Uckfield.

My farm.

32

Neesham's car slid to a halt in the farmyard. I had the door open before it stopped. My heart was pounding from the adrenaline, and my mouth was parched. The yard was quiet, baking in the afternoon sun.

I was too late.

The kitchen door was ajar.

I pushed through the door, blind in the darkness after the bright sun, no attempt at stealth. Everything I'd ever learnt cast by the wayside. Training and craft were for the battlefield. This was my home.

The kitchen was still. Dark shapes loomed.

A lifeless shape was slumped in Uncle Nob's chair.

I looked for rage to comfort me, that old friend that got me through the worst, time after time, but instead I felt a complete emptiness, as if every part of my soul had been scooped out and discarded. I walked slowly to Nob's chair, tears filling my eyes.

It took me a second to realise what I was seeing.

Nob's black coat, thrown over the chair. Impossible to mistake. A coat, in the dark.

The shot was distant. A single explosion, echoing back from the woods, followed by a cacophony of crows as they took off, cawing and complaining.

Neesham followed as I sprinted from the house, through the farmyard to the fields beyond. My boots pounded on the concrete track that led from the yard to the gate. Neesham's leather shoes slapped the ground, keeping pace with me.

Crows wheeled above the far meadow, the low-lying field we didn't farm, too water-logged for crops. There was a shout of anger and another shot. A cry. A young woman. Unmistakable. It was Elizabeth. I'd rescued her from a hell no girl should ever know, and promised to keep her safe.

But I'd failed her.

I ran, giving it everything I had. I'd been too slow to save the Leckies. This time I'd be faster. I'd get there in time.

An engine roared. A plume of black smoke rose above the distant hedge – the only barrier between me and the far meadow. Between me and that hedge, a field of young spring wheat, its green shoots eighteen inches tall. A fine crop. I was on the edge of the field and the track followed that edge in a big loop. Following it would take me on a detour, out to my right and then back again. I didn't have time.

I struck out across the field, my boots sinking into the soft, tilled earth, leaving a trail of crushed wheat. Every step I took, my boots picked up another layer of mud. It was heavy going, and my heart was already racing. I was slick with sweat.

All the complexities of the world reduced to me, the mud weighing down my boots, the heat, and the distant hedge, now seemingly on the other side of the world and receding over the horizon even as I raced towards it.

Neesham stuck to the path, taking the long way. Even so, he was ahead of me – easier to run on the grassy verge at the edge of the field. He reached the gap in the hedge and his shoulders slumped as he looked into the far meadow. There was another shot, and Neesham winced. He turned to me and shook his head.

★

'Next time, bring a gun,' the Polish soldier said, scanning the woods at the edge of the meadow. 'You thought we were under attack. So what was your plan?'

The Fordson tractor backfired, the sound ringing out like a shot across the field, the retort echoing back from the line of trees at the far end of the field.

Elizabeth was up in the driving seat of the tractor. The plough lines behind her told the story of the day, wobbly for the first few rows, but increasingly straight. Behind her, Frankie and Bill Taylor laughed as they rode a makeshift plough, standing on it like acrobats riding horses in a circus ring.

Frankie fell off the plough, and yelled at Elizabeth to stop. She looked around and saw me watching her. As she let in the clutch, the tractor backfired again. I flinched, and noticed Neesham did the same.

'I skipped the planning stage,' I said. 'My old CO always said I had a bias for action.'

'Like our cavalry charging those Panzers,' he said. 'Bias for action will get you killed nine times out of ten. Ten out of ten for those boys.'

'I want you gone,' I said.

'I'm not with those others,' he said. 'I met them on the boat, but that's all.'

'Too much going on,' I said.

'I could help on the farm,' he said. 'Keep my eyes open. I'm a useful person to have around.'

It wasn't a terrible idea. Bill Taylor needed the help, and we had the harvest coming up.

'A few more days,' I said. 'Keep watch. Any more deserters, let me know.'

33

The Cross was quiet. I nodded to familiar faces as I carried two pints to my usual table in the corner.

Doc drank half of his pint in one gulp, his face grim.

'You've got something to tell me,' I said. Not a question.

He knew me better than to pretend he didn't know what I was talking about. We'd sat at this table most evenings for the better part of twenty years.

He pulled a pamphlet from his inside pocket and laid it on the table. It was well thumbed. Slips of paper marked favourite pages.

It was a flimsy publication. Cheap paper. Government issued.

'Joining Up?'
A Handy Guide For Every Recruit
All you want to know!
6d

There was a picture below the text. A drum, with a Union Jack, an anchor, and a pair of RAF wings. Designed to appeal to a young man like Eric. But Doc wasn't a young man. He had responsibilities. A wife. Children.

I couldn't look at him, so I flicked through the pamphlet. It was mostly advertisements. Ovaltine (Ask for Ovaltine at your canteen. Best for health – for sleep – for nerves). Gillette (On all fronts, men of self respect use Gillette).

Julysia Hair Tonic (Handy flasks! Ask for Julysia at your NAAFI canteen).

'You've decided,' I said. An observation, rather than a question.

I put the pamphlet on the table. It sat amidst our empties and curled beer-mats like a grenade with its pin removed. The air felt heavier.

'I have.'

'What does Jane think?'

He drank more, looking at the blackened fireplace. Avoiding my eyes.

'She understands,' he said. He was bad at lying. He didn't believe it himself.

'When do you go?'

'I don't know. They'll call me when they're ready. It'll be Aldershot.'

I remembered my own journey to the barracks at Aldershot, a lifetime ago.

'No point me telling you we need you here,' I said.

'No.'

'Well,' I said, 'you've built a backlog of rounds you owe me. Better drink up and get buying.'

'I thought we were even.'

'Last Christmas,' I said. 'You were getting them in, and Jim got festive behind the bar, gave you a free round. The summer before that, you said you were going to be late. You didn't show up, I had to drink yours.'

'What about all the times we've gone back to mine for a whisky after?' he said.

'Doesn't count,' I said.

He finished his pint.

'All right,' he said. 'Can't leave you complaining I'm a cheapskate.'

He got up and went to the bar. Easier that way, not having to look at each other.

★

We didn't talk more about his joining up. He was a grown man and he'd made his decision. Instead, we spent the rest of the evening on the usual subjects. Doc was always good for a few stories about his patients, suitably anonymised of course.

'I've been thinking about the Leckies,' he said, later in the evening. 'They're not the only ones who've been encouraged to leave.'

'What do you mean?'

'Former patient of mine. Lived up on the Forest. Top of the hill somewhere. Gooch. Left suddenly a few months ago.'

'Where did he go?' I asked.

'I'll dig out his forwarding address,' he said. 'Let you know.'

34

The train was full. All eight seats were taken in our compartment, the luggage racks were bulging, and several cases filled the space between the two rows where ordinarily our legs would have fitted. I kept my legs pressed awkwardly against the window, the metal sill digging into my knees as I watched the countryside rush by. Margaret sat across from me, with her own view out the window.

We'd taken the train up from Uckfield to Victoria, made our way on foot to Waterloo to catch the train for the west country. London was eerily quiet. As we'd hurried across Southwark Bridge, we'd stopped and listened.

'I wonder what it's like in Paris this morning,' Margaret said. Only two hundred miles away, Nazi tanks were rolling along ancient boulevards. German officers were sitting at tables outside coffee shops, toasting their victory. Did it feel real to them? Or were they, too, marvelling at the oddity of being in an ancient foe's capital city, emptied of most of its residents, taken with barely a shot fired.

It took the train forever to get clear of London, with its interminable suburban stops, but now we were making good time, rushing west, out of harm's way. The atmosphere in the compartment had been tense in the city, always the fear of what was to come. Now, everyone relaxed. Newspapers were rustled, sandwiches unwrapped, legs recrossed.

We were going to pay a visit to Doc's old patient, who'd left the Forest in a hurry a few months ago. Mr Gooch had sat as a magistrate for a long and distinguished career. I wanted to hear why he'd left. A last-gasp effort to put some kind of logic to the mess I'd put in motion when I inserted myself into whatever had been going on. I owed the Leckies that much, at least. I also wanted to ask him which of his former neighbours on the Forest would be most likely to harbour a German parachutist. A man like Gooch would have made it his business to know the people around him. What kind of people they were.

There was a discarded copy of yesterday's *Evening Standard* wedged between the seat and the armrest. I picked it out and flicked through it. I read a shrill opinion piece, telling us to watch out for fifth columnists – people who sympathised with the Germans and were planning to defeat us from within. The phrase was the current darling of the press. It had come from the war in Spain. General Vidal had encircled Madrid with four columns of infantry and artillery. He referred to his supporters inside the city as his fifth column. Civilian agitators who could make a nuisance of themselves and undermine the loyalist government.

I didn't set too much stock in what the papers wrote. They were trying to increase their circulation numbers. But the idea held a certain logic. Not everyone in the country wanted war. Some people actually supported Hitler's politics, especially when he talked about the Jews and Communists. I thought about the poster in the urinal.

Say no to a Jews' war.

★

The train deposited us at Greenway, and we took the chain ferry across the river to Dittisham, then walked up a steep hill that left both Margaret and me pretending not to be out of breath.

'How well do you know these people?' Margaret asked.

'I don't,' I said.

I looked further up the road. We still had a good stretch of hill to climb. I stopped and took in the view. Dittisham lay below us, the river Dart snaking into the distance, to where the sea glittered in a haze of misty afternoon light.

'Doc said Gooch was a good man. Not likely to be scared off by the prospect of a few bombs, or even the invasion. No nonsense. He said he thought it was curious when he said he was leaving.'

'So we walk up to his door and ask him to explain himself?'

She looked at me carefully.

'Do you want to sit down?'

'Wanted to take in the view.'

'Might want to cut down on the sausages,' she said, with a glint in her eye.

35

'I was a magistrate for more than thirty years, so I saw a lot of the worst side of humanity,' Mr Gooch said. 'Kate Davidson wasn't the worst, but she was far from the best. As a landlord she left me alone, as her father had. But she sold the property a few years back, and from that point, I knew it was only a matter of time.'

Gooch was an elderly man, in his late seventies. He sat stiffly in the shade of a rose arbour, a rifle leaning against the trellis, within reach. Ready for parachutists, no doubt. From his spot up here, on the hilltop, he would have prime shooting rights.

He poured tea, and passed a cup to his companion, a woman of a similar age.

'I'd been meaning to come down this way to be with Dotty. Her husband died at Ypres, and she's been by herself since then. Kept asking me to come and visit. In the end, I did.'

He held out his hand, took Dotty's and squeezed affectionately.

'You said Kate sold your property?' I asked.

'She had to notify me,' he said. 'As a tenant I was within my rights to stay on, so I did, until the threats started.'

'Threats?'

'Kate's sons. The eldest in particular. Always in and out of trouble. A bit of burglary, minor theft, that kind of thing.

Neither of them struck me as natural enforcers. There must have been some kind of financial incentive. Get the tenants out and there's a bonus in it for you, you can imagine the kind of arrangement. Used to see quite a lot of it when I was on the bench.'

'You think the Leckies were killed because they wouldn't leave?' I asked.

'Victor, the eldest one, spent six months in Lewes for GBH. Not a criminal genius by any means, but I could see him moving up to murder if the money was right.'

'The police tell me he had a cast-iron alibi.'

'Did you know most crimes of violence take place within the family? Something about seeing the same face over the dinner table night after night. I can't tell you how many men have been sent to the gallows because their wife said the wrong thing, night after night. And it's not just husbands either. Wives too.'

'Who bought the property from Kate?' I asked.

Gooch shook his head.

'They were under no obligation to divulge that, and they didn't. I could have enquired at the land registry if I'd been interested, but I was already planning to leave.'

He turned to Dotty. 'I told you I should have done more.'

'You've done enough, Harold,' Dotty said.

Gooch handed Margaret a cup of tea.

'And what's your interest in the matter?' he asked.

'I gave the Leckies the impression I'd take care of their problem with Kate and her sons. Now they're all dead and I'm left with the feeling it's my fault.'

'You can't be responsible for everything that crosses your path,' Mr Gooch said, giving me a piercing stare. I could imagine him in his days as a magistrate, getting to the heart of the matter with a reluctant witness. 'You learn that soon enough on the bench.'

I didn't answer. I've found that's the best response when you don't agree. Cuts down on unpleasantness.

There was a distant droning sound and we all looked up at the sky. Three dots, coming out of the south-east.

Dotty pulled a pair of binoculars from a well-used leather case. She trained them on the sky.

'Spitfires,' she said. 'Mark twos.'

'Coming back from France?' I asked.

'No,' she said, 'it's a delivery run, from the Supermarine factory over in Southampton.'

'How can you tell?' I asked.

'The formation's tighter than a combat mission,' she said. 'A few yards apart. No need to risk that level of precision if you're on your way back from the front.'

She handed me the binoculars.

'Women pilots,' she said. 'They ferry the planes around the country. Frees up the boys for the fighting. The girls have got more to prove, so they train harder and fly closer.'

I looked through the binoculars as the flight of Spitfires roared towards us, brand new Rolls Royce Merlin engines purring. Dotty was right, they were flying only feet from each other, their wingtips practically touching.

'Some of my girls are in that unit,' Dotty said. She waved as the Spitfires buzzed the house, only clearing the roof by a few yards.

'Dotty's a schoolteacher,' Harold said. 'Brought her out of retirement to help with the evacuees.'

'More tea?' Dotty asked.

I handed her my cup for a refill.

'Have you talked to any of the others?' Gooch asked.

'What others?' Margaret and I said at the same time.

36

Margaret took my hand as we walked back down the steep hill into Dittisham. It was late afternoon and the sky was deep blue.

Gooch had given us a list of names and addresses. People he knew who'd left the Forest in the same time frame as him.

With my free hand I loosened my tie. It was as hot as any day I remembered on the North-West Frontier, albeit the company was more pleasant.

There was a whistle in the distance, echoing along the valley.

'We'll miss the train,' Margaret said. She fumbled in her purse and came up with something. It was a ring.

'I think Mr and Mrs Cook deserve a honeymoon,' Margaret said. 'Don't you think?' She grinned as she slipped the plain gold band onto her ring finger.

'Who gave you that?' I asked, trying to sound nonchalant. I'd only known Margaret for a month, and I realised I hardly knew anything about her past.

'It was Mummy's,' she said.

Booking into a small bed and breakfast, or getting a room at a pub, would be a lot less complicated with that bit of metal on her finger. The country may have been in its last week of freedom before annihilation, but certain social codes weren't ready to be broken.

'Mr and Mrs Cook,' she said. 'How does it sound?' She took my hand. I felt the ring on her finger.

'Sounds like it would take a bit of getting used to,' I said.

★

There was an inn by the river. We took a room, no eyebrows raised by our checking in as man and wife. The landlady was glad of the business, especially when I asked if she could arrange a couple of rounds of sandwiches.

The room was stuffy, but when I opened the window fresh air flooded in, cooled by the river, directly below us. On the far bank, azaleas swept down to the water's edge, and higher up I could see glimpses of a grand house.

Margaret joined me at the window.

'That's Greenway,' she said, looking across the river to the roofline of the imposing white house. 'Agatha Christie lives there. I went to a house party once.'

'I didn't know you moved in that set,' I said.

'There's a lot you don't know about me,' Margaret said.

'Evidently.'

'I wonder if she gets any of her story ideas from spying on this window,' Margaret said.

'Let's hope not.'

'Maybe we should give her something to put in one of her books,' she said, as she undid my tie and set to work unbuttoning my shirt.

'I didn't know she wrote *those* kind of books.'

★

It was dark when we made our way down to the quiet bar. Our entrance caused a couple of glances, but nothing more. People had their own things to worry about without getting too concerned about a couple of day trippers.

'I've been thinking,' Margaret said as I brought two pints from the bar. She'd found a quiet table in the corner where we could talk without being overheard.

'Somebody's been encouraging tenants around the Forest to leave their homes,' she said. 'That must mean they've got another purpose for those homes, assuming they don't want them empty.'

'The Forest's in the middle of the invasion zone,' I said. 'A good place to land your parachutists. Send them south, hitting the rear of our defences. Cut supply lines between the coast and the rest of the country.'

'Agreed,' she said. 'But you don't need to buy up properties and threaten people into leaving for that. When the invasion starts, they'll drop their people where they want to drop them. Whether Mr Gooch or the Leckies are sitting in their air-raid shelters or not isn't going to change Goering's plans for his parachute regiments.'

'Maybe you want to bring together a group of like-minded people,' I said. 'Somewhere convenient for London, but remote enough to be private.'

I sipped my pint and kept quiet as the barmaid brought over a plate of cheese sandwiches. The perfect meal. A few pints, a few sandwiches, me and Margaret, somewhere nobody knew us. Maybe we should stay. Make friends with the writer across the river. Go to dinner parties.

'Multiple houses suggests multiple people,' she said.

'Could be. Like that Bloomsbury lot, buying up properties around Lewes. Some kind of artists' colony.'

The sandwiches were terrible. The bread was stale and the cheese thinly sliced. Margarine instead of butter.

'Maybe you're right about wanting them empty. Somebody's buying privacy.'

'It would have to be someone rich,' she said. 'That's a lot of income you're choosing to forego if you leave houses empty. How many names on Gooch's list?'

I pulled the paper from my shirt pocket.

'Six, plus Gooch.'

'Let's say they're being rented out at a pound a month,' she said. 'That's twelve pounds a year per house. Multiply that by seven, that's over eighty pounds a year. Make it a hundred, because there must be one or two more that Gooch doesn't know about. A hundred a year, that's a small fortune.'

'We need to find out who's been buying up the properties,' I said.

I finished my pint. The beer wasn't much better than the sandwiches. It was cloudy, from the bottom of the barrel, and overpriced.

'What are you thinking?' she asked.

'I'm thinking we should go back upstairs.'

She took her pint glass, three-quarters full, and downed it, holding my eye.

'I think you're right,' she said.

37

We took the coast route back. Better to avoid London, and I wanted to stop at Lewes. The county town was the site of the records office. If there had been sales of properties on the Forest, there'd be paperwork.

'I feel like a farmer's wife going to town for a big adventure,' Margaret said, as we stepped out of Lewes station, with the town laid before us.

'I'm not sure how many adventures Lewes has to offer,' I said.

'Nonsense,' she said, 'I hear the women at the WI talking about it all the time. Apparently the slices of cherry cake at Schofield's are quite the thing.'

'Sounds like you've got the morning planned out,' I said.

*

Lewes was full of troops, spilling from the pavements onto the narrow streets. Most shops had their windows boarded up against potential bomb blasts, and those that weren't boarded up were covered in tape, criss-crossed to hold the glass together against potential shock waves. There was a buzz in the air. If the Germans invaded, Lewes would be in their way, a strategic gap in the otherwise impassable barrier of the South Downs. The Norman castle on the hill was a constant reminder that this was a strategic position between the coast and the rest of the country.

'Excuse me, sir.' A policeman stood, watchful. 'Can I see your identity papers?' he asked, polite, but alert.

'We're allowed to be here,' Margaret said.

I pulled my identity card from my inside pocket, glad I'd brought it with me. Margaret made a show of digging through her handbag. The policeman took mine and studied it. He was doing his job, I reminded myself, doing his bit to keep the country safe.

'What brings you here?' he asked, addressing me as if Margaret didn't exist.

'Cherry cake, apparently,' I said, raising my eyebrows and nodding to Margaret.

The policeman didn't smile.

'This is a quarantined area,' he said.

'We're exercising our right to travel in our own country,' Margaret said, 'before the Germans get here and put an end to it all.'

She found her card and handed it to the policeman.

'Is there a problem?'

He read her card and I waited for the change.

'Lady Margaret,' he said, his face colouring.

'I asked if there was a problem.' She put some edge into her voice. She knew what she was doing, using her status as a weapon. A side of her I hadn't seen before.

'No ma'am,' he said, studying every detail on the card as if the security of the whole country depended on it.

'As Mr Cook said, I was hoping to get a slice of cake. Could you direct me to Schofield's?'

He gave us our papers back.

'Past the town hall, ma'am,' he said. 'Can't miss it.'

'Thank you,' Margaret said.

'Keep your hand on your wallet when you're in the street,' he said, now our protector. 'Whole place is under siege from pickpockets, down from London to help relieve the Tommies of their pay.'

'A bit hard on the man, weren't you?' I said, as we walked away.

Margaret snorted. 'That's rich,' she said. 'He didn't look at me once, just the little lady, and your way of getting him on your side was to ridicule me.'

Margaret had a way of putting things that made sense. I'd been a fool.

'And when I bare my claws the tiniest bit I get a rebuke from you.'

I didn't answer. Probably best.

38

The county records office was in the town hall, near the top of the high street. It faced the gatehouse to the ancient castle, the heart of the town.

I explained I was thinking of buying some property on the Forest, wanted to check some chains of ownership, and we were shown to a reading room. After a couple of minutes' wait, an elderly man brought in an ancient map, hand-drawn on heavy cloth and lacquered with some kind of protective layer that turned the whole thing yellow. He laid it out on the table for us and handed me a clipboard with a slip of paper and a pencil.

'Write down the number of the property you want the information for, and we'll retrieve it from the archives,' he said, with difficulty. He wheezed as he talked.

'Gas?' I asked.

He shook his head. Didn't want a fuss.

'Where do we find you?' I asked.

'I'm always here,' he said, as he closed the door.

We pored over the map. I traced Palehouse Lane from the main road. *Ford* was written in blue in elegant italics where the stream crossed the road. At the end of the lane, more italics, this time in capitals – *WORKS*. An inch back along the road, surrounded on all sides by pink contours, was the Leckies' house. There was a short column of handwritten numbers next to the house, and I copied them down. I assumed they referred to historical transactions.

Margaret had the list from Gooch. She read out each address in turn. I found it on the map, and she copied the numbers onto the clipboard.

'We need pins,' I said, 'so we can see the pattern.'

'This'll do,' Margaret said, rummaging in her bag and producing an old train ticket. She ripped it into pieces and put a piece of the coloured card on the location of each of the houses.

We looked at the map. The pieces of card covered a random selection of properties on the Forest. There didn't seem to be a pattern.

At the front desk, I gave the clipboard to the wheezing man. He looked dubiously at the list of numbers.

'How long do you think it'll take?' I asked.

He looked at his watch.

'Two hours.'

★

'You're not eating your meat roll?' Margaret asked, as she finished her own meal.

'You can have it,' I said.

'Sure?'

I swapped plates and she set to work. She was welcome to it. The meat was mostly fat, and the first mouthful had been enough for me.

We were sitting in a dusty church hall, newly repurposed as a 'British Restaurant' – Churchill's name for a communal kitchen – designed to give people a chance to supplement their rations. They were all the rage, and we'd had to queue for twenty minutes to get a table. The food wasn't worth the wait. A grey concoction designed to make a few pounds of low-quality meat go a long way. I'd eaten enough mutton in the North-West Frontier for any man, so I sat and watched Margaret as she tucked in.

'How's your cook doing with your rations?' I asked, as she put away my portion.

'I'm going to have to let her go. Can't afford to pay her.'

'So what's the plan?' I asked. I didn't see Margaret doing very well, rattling around what I presumed was a massive kitchen in her stately home. 'Do you know how to cook?'

'How hard can it be?' she said. 'If I can learn to field-strip a Bren gun, I think I can learn how to cook a pork chop.'

'How much trouble are you in, financially speaking?'

Margaret glared at me.

'I can take care of myself,' she said. 'Don't worry about me.'

I returned to reading the paper. The early edition of the *Argus* had a photograph on the front page. A German officer in handcuffs, being escorted onto a train. The photographer had got a good shot of him. He looked familiar, something about the scar on his face.

'They found the parachutist,' I said.

I read the short article below the photo.

'Bailed out of his plane over the Forest. Wreckage found north of Hartfield.'

I turned the page.

'Presumably there's a distinction,' Margaret said. 'A parachutist would be someone sent to deliberately jump out of a plane. An invader. A pilot bailing out's a different kettle of fish. More of a win for us.'

I read the article closely. Understandably, information was sparse.

'Does it specify whether he was a pilot bailing out or a parachutist?' Margaret asked.

'No,' I said.

'Maybe it's your man, maybe not,' she said.

She took the paper from me.

'Handsome-looking chap,' she said. 'Looks a bit like you in the right light.'

'What's for pudding?' I asked, peering up at the menu board.

The pudding was more of a success. Spotted dick. Hard to mess that up, although they'd clearly done their best.

*

The wheezing man was waiting for us. He'd found something. Could barely contain his excitement. Probably as good as it got in his line of work.

He pushed a sheet of paper across the reception desk. The form from the clipboard – one code number per property. He'd researched each property and filled in the salient information from the files. He'd completed each line in immaculate handwriting. Each line was the same.

'No information on file.'

'What does that mean?' Margaret asked.

'It means there's no information for those properties,' he said.

'That's impossible,' Margaret said.

He shook his head.

'Records get lost. Or they get returned to the wrong file. Once that happens it's impossible to track them down. They show up when they show up.'

'But you don't think this is a coincidence,' I said.

'Seven properties, all connected,' he said. 'Unlikely.'

'What's the connection?' Margaret asked, looking at the old man for the answer.

'We're the connection,' I said. 'Or rather, the criteria that put each property on the list. On the Forest. Recently vacated by the tenants. And now we've got proof that something's going on. Someone's been here and messed about with the records to make it hard to find who owns them.'

We hurried back to the map room. The yellowing map sat on the table, with its pieces of colourful card seemingly placed at random.

'Is there another way we can find out who owns these properties?' I asked.

'You could find out who did the conveyancing,' the old man said. 'But I doubt they'd tell you.'

The answer was in front of us, I was sure. I walked around the table to look from another angle. A trick I'd learnt from Blakeney, my old CO. But all I could see was an upside-down view of Sussex.

Then I saw it.

39

'Look at the contour lines,' I said. 'The Forest is a number of peaks, each one with a clump of trees.' I pointed to five high spots on the map, each surrounded by close-set red contour lines.

I used my pencil as a pointer, moving away from one of the high points, pointing to a succession of fainter red lines.

'These lines show we're going downhill from the peaks, but quite soon the ground levels out again. We end up with a plateau, lower than the peaks but higher than the surrounding countryside. It's like a tabletop, and the peaks are additional bumps on the table. The rest of Sussex is somewhere down below.'

I found the contour line I was looking for and traced it with the pencil. The wheezing man kept a close watch, making sure I didn't mark his map. The contour line made a large shape, encompassing a fair portion of the Forest, with seemingly random inlets and extrusions.

'This is the edge of the tabletop,' I said. Anyone inside that edge has a pretty good view across the whole area. Anyone outside that edge can't see up onto the top. They'd see sky.'

I squatted down, my eyeline level with the table.

'Look,' I said. 'When I'm above the level, I can see across the table.'

I lowered myself, so my eyes were below the table.

'But now, I can't see the top at all.'

I stood back, letting it sink in. Margaret crouched down and looked for herself. The wheezing man tried it, then stood back and looked at me as if I'd discovered the secret of the ages.

Whereas before there had been a random collection of houses with crosses and others without, now there was a clear explanation for why some had been emptied, and others had been left in peace. Every house with a marker was inside the contour line.

'Hang on,' Margaret said. 'There's one we don't have a marker for.'

She pointed at a large house, big enough to merit a blocky black shape on the map, showing a large main building with two wings, and a collection of outbuildings. Hatched shading showed a collection of glasshouses. The estate sat on the northern edge of the Forest. It had an uninterrupted view of the area within the contour line.

'Perhaps Gooch didn't know about it,' I said. 'We should check.'

'No need to check,' the wheezing man said. 'Everyone knows who lives there. Been in the same family for generations.'

I looked at him expectantly. He was enjoying being the centre of attention.

'I thought he was out in India,' he said.

I had a sinking feeling. I looked at Margaret.

'Vaughn Matheson?' Margaret asked.

'Lord Matheson to the likes of you and me,' the wheezing man said. 'Met him once at a village fête, a long time ago. Lovely chap.'

40

Vaughn's place was the grandest house on Ashdown Forest, sitting in several hundred acres of private woodland surrounded by thousands more of heathland, all preserved for the exclusive use of one family. It was built in the same style as the Houses of Parliament – gothic, black stone dripping with damp even in summer.

Margaret parked her wreck of a car, an Alvis F series that seemed to burn a pint of oil for every gallon of petrol, in a glade of redwoods in front of the house. Each tree was larger at its base than her car, and I felt the bark of the nearest one as Margaret messed about with the car, topping up the oil, anticipating a quick departure. The redwood was soft and fibrous, unlike any native tree I'd ever felt. I looked up into its canopy, several hundred feet above.

The front door was open. There was a delivery van outside and large displays of fresh-cut flowers were being carried in. It looked like the place was being prepared for a function.

We were intercepted by a butler dressed in formal wear. He looked familiar. My age. I tried to place him and got an image of him running at me, red-faced, aiming to do me an injury. He bowled every now and then for Fairwarp cricket club. Deadly on occasion with a well-placed yorker. If I remembered right, I'd hit him for a couple of sixes the last time we'd met, before he'd got my middle wicket. William

Washington, distantly related to the American President, or so everyone always said.

'We want a word with Vaughn,' Margaret said. Washington didn't blink, presumably it was part of his job not to look surprised.

'I'll let Lord Matheson know you're here,' Washington said, turning to leave.

'No,' I said.

Washington froze.

'It's a surprise,' Margaret said. 'Where is he?'

Washington glanced through a set of double doors. In the distance we could see patio doors leading out to sunlight, thin curtains fluttering in the slight breeze.

We found Vaughn on the tennis court, alone, hitting a ball against a wooden wall painted green with a white line at net height. He was in his whites. The way he was hitting the ball made me wonder what was on his mind. It looked like he was trying to destroy the wall, or the ball, or both.

He saw us out of the corner of his eye, but kept at it. Perhaps he was on track for a personal best. But he was off his rhythm, knowing he was being watched, trying too hard. He wound up for a backhand that would have sent the ball to France if he'd connected, but he missed, with a whiff of air through the strings.

He smiled. A good approximation of a man happy to see his friends.

'Mags!' he said.

'What happened with the Leckies?' I asked him. Better to be upfront than beat about the bush.

He didn't answer. He pulled his shirt off, over his head like a child, picking up a towel from a chair.

'You had some tenants on Palehouse Lane,' I said. 'They were killed.'

He didn't seem self-conscious, drying off the sweat from his torso in front of a lady and a relative stranger.

'What's this all about, Cook?'

'You've been playing Monopoly all over the Forest,' I said. 'The Leckies were killed so you could repossess their property. Gives you the full set, every house with a view over the high ground.'

'Look, it's no secret I've been buying up a few places—'

'Actually, it is,' I said.

'What do you mean?'

'All the records have been removed,' I said. 'Someone's trying to hide something.'

Vaughn looked to Margaret as if she were the referee. She kept her face blank.

'No,' he said. 'This is backwards. I'm the one being threatened. The Leckies were a warning to me. And then my land agent.'

'You don't deny you've been buying the properties?' I asked.

'Why should I? Last time I checked, the law allowed a man to buy a house or two.'

He looked at Margaret, then me. Back and forth. He realised we weren't there to be fobbed off with a few pleasantries.

'If anyone treated any of my tenants badly, I can assure you it wasn't on my instructions.'

'Why are you emptying your properties?'

We both knew the answer. There was only one reason to move out the only people who had a view over the massive expanse of the Forest, right in the middle of the invasion zone, halfway between the coast and London. I expected him to be evasive, but he wasn't. His face lit up, as if he'd been dying for me to ask.

'I'll show you!' he said. 'Come on!'

41

We walked, leaving his ornamental gardens behind, crossing a stream, out across the open expanse of heath, following a ribbon of white sand where the thin layer of soil had been worn away by years of footsteps.

A small downslope appeared gradually in front of us, the way it can on the Forest – an expanse that looks featureless from a distance resolving into hidden details as you close in, like the countryside between the Leckies and the works. We found ourselves amidst birch and pine. I smelt woodsmoke, and heard laughter.

Vaughn grinned, like a conjuror showing us a new trick.

We emerged from the trees, into a clearing of short-cropped grass and a small, thatched cottage, like a fairy tale.

Two elderly women sat on kitchen chairs that had been brought outside onto the lawn. Both of them had easels in front of them, with half-finished paintings. One of the women was dressed in a pastiche of the country life, a big floral dress and a floppy sunhat. The other was dressed in trousers and a shirt. Both were barefoot, and both were smoking.

An axe smacked into a log, splitting it with a satisfying thunk. It was the artist, down by the side of the cottage, hidden in the shade. The young man squinted at us, then returned to his task, picking up another log and dropping it onto the chopping block. His trousers were rolled up to his knees, his shirtsleeves past his elbows, black braces holding his trousers up. Like the women, he was barefoot. He was sweating from the exertion.

'Hello!' Vaughn said cheerily, 'mind if I pop in?'

'Of course not, darling,' the woman in the floppy hat said. 'Always glad of an excuse to stop work on this abomination.' She waved her cigarette at her painting.

'Speak for yourself, dear,' the other woman said, delicately dabbing a touch of colour to her own canvas.

'I'm giving Mr Cook the guided tour,' Vaughn said, as I followed him out of the woods, onto the lawn. The artist swung his axe and the blade glanced off the log, burying itself in the grass near his feet.

'You don't want to be doing that barefoot,' I said. 'Easy way to lose a few toes.'

'See, Freddie? I told you, didn't I?' the woman in the hat said.

Freddie scowled and set up for another swing. He inched his feet back. This time he got the log square-on and the blade sunk in without splitting it. He rocked the axe back and forth but it was firmly stuck.

I joined him.

'Got any steel-capped boots?' I asked.

'Must have left them in London,' he said.

It was a miracle he hadn't taken his foot off. I took the axe from him and pulled it out of the log. He had a respectable pile of split wood to one side.

'You did all that?' I asked.

'I was doing fine,' he said.

'That's the thing with equipment like this,' I said. 'When it works, you can get a lot done. But you've got to be ready for the time it doesn't work.' I placed my foot next to his and showed him a split in the leather on the side.

'I was doing the same thing once,' I said. 'Wasn't concentrating and the axe bounced off. Went through my boot like butter.'

'Did it hurt?'

'No, but I felt pretty stupid when I had to go in and tell Mum.'

I handed him the axe.

'What size are you?'

'Eleven.'

'I've got an old pair of boots that would do the trick,' I said. 'Drop by sometime and you can pick them up. Home Farm, on the way to Uckfield.'

The blousy woman, Constance, poured tea. She'd brought out a plate of bread and jam, with apologies for not having biscuits or cakes.

'How long have you been here?' Margaret asked.

'A few weeks,' Constance said. 'Right, Kay?'

Kay, the other artist, shook her head.

'Four weeks tomorrow.'

'We're so grateful to Vaughn. It's amazing what he's doing. Everyone thinks so.'

I must have looked quizzical. Constance answered.

'The artists' colony. Such a perfect idea, especially now.'

'Where were you before?' I asked.

'We have a small house in Bloomsbury,' Kay said.

'It's getting unbearable in town,' Freddie said. 'Blackouts, air-raid sirens. You can't hear yourself think.'

'Freddie's sensitive,' Kay said. 'He needs peace and quiet for his work.'

'What do you do?' I asked.

'He's a poet,' Constance said, slapping Freddie's hand as he reached for a second piece of bread. 'Leave some for our guests, darling.'

'Mr Cook was a bit suspicious of me, moving out some of my old tenants,' Vaughn said. 'I think he thought I was clearing the way for a Nazi invasion.'

'How diligent of you,' Kay said. 'Can't be too careful.'

'You're not worried?' I asked. 'You've moved right into the invasion zone. This could be a battlefield in a few weeks.'

'I don't think so,' Constance said. 'It won't be as bad as that. More of an administrative change-over, like after a general election. I don't think it will need to bother people like us.'

42

The terrace was buzzing. Vaughn was throwing a party and he'd pressed Margaret to agree to stay. Said his sister would have something she could wear. I'd turned down his offer of a dinner suit, and in solidarity with me he'd stayed in his shirtsleeves from the afternoon. Everyone else was dressed formally.

I took a glass of champagne from a footman bearing a silver tray. I looked around for the butler, Washington. I wanted to talk to him, get some intelligence about Vaughn, but I hadn't seen him since we'd returned from the artists' cottage.

The champagne was chilled. Important to get the little things right. There must have been an ice-house somewhere on the property, stocked with large blocks of ice cut from wintery lochs in Scotland and rushed south on an express train, packed in straw and newspaper. A working man's annual wages spent so we could stand on the terrace sipping wine that was chilled a few degrees colder than it would have been without the effort.

There was a murmur from the crowd as Margaret appeared at the patio doors. She looked stunning. Every inch the heiress. Beside her stood a young woman with a cane. They'd dressed almost identically, and done their hair in the same style. They looked almost like twins.

'Don't you brush up well, Mags,' Vaughn said as he appeared from the crowd and slipped his arm around Margaret's waist. I was getting tired of the Mags and Vaughn act.

Vaughn made a sweeping motion with his arm, introducing me to his sister.

'Cook, this is Miriam. Miriam, Cook's Mags' latest chap. Quite the surly brute.' He winked at me.

'Oh my!' Miriam said, taking me in. I felt like an exhibit at an agricultural show. Miriam held out her free hand and I took it, unsure what to do with it. I was still taken aback at the effect of her standing next to Margaret.

'Pleased to meet you,' I said.

'My dear Miriam,' the woman from the cottage said as she pushed past me. 'You're limping. Don't say you're hurt.'

I stepped back, glad to be out of the limelight. I caught Margaret's eye and she smiled.

'Tennis,' Miriam said, to Constance. 'I travel from one end of the country to the other without incident, then this oaf pushes me out of the way so he can get in a smash.'

'How was the journey?' Constance asked. 'Was it awful?'

'Hell,' Miriam replied. 'I had to wait at Victoria for an absolute age, and of course you can't get a porter for love nor money.'

'You were lucky to get a train, with all the troop movements,' Constance said.

*

The evening dragged. Margaret was in her element. These were her people and I didn't begrudge her the chance to spend some time with them. From what she'd told me, she'd grown up with events like this, albeit most of them out in India, at the height of the glories of the Raj. Quite a fall, from all of that to traipsing around in the woods with a farmer.

I got caught up in a discussion about the wisdom of investing in war bonds versus silver. The consensus seemed to be to sell the bonds, since they'd be worthless when Hitler invaded and the government fell. I left the conversation before I said something I'd regret.

I took refuge on the edge of the terrace. We were behind the house, looking south, with a view out to where Vaughn had taken us earlier. The gardens were a riot of colour, lit by the late-afternoon sun. Beyond them, the Forest was dull and brown. I had a perfect view of where the parachute had come down. No wonder Vaughn got there so quickly. If he'd been standing here, he'd have been able to rush through the gardens, into the trees, and up to the Forest in a matter of minutes.

And if a plane had been coming out of the south, looking for a marker, Vaughn's house would have been an obvious reference point, especially if he'd left a light on.

'I'll have to show you round.' It was Miriam, Vaughn's sister, leaning on her cane and looking up at me with a tilted head. She looked over the gardens.

'Capability Brown,' she said. 'One of his greatest works, so they say. I've never been much for plants myself but some people get positively worked up. I'd be happy to give you the tour. Show you the hidden gems and all that.'

'You grew up here?' I asked.

'They let us come for holidays, then packed us off to god-awful boarding schools. Vaughn got it worse, of course. When Daddy got posted to India he dragged us both over there. All highly irregular, but what Daddy wanted, Daddy got.'

Margaret's laugh carried over the general hubbub, and I looked for her across a sea of heads.

'She's with Vaughn,' Miriam said, '*quelle surprise.*'

'You knew Margaret in India?' I asked.

'Vaguely,' Miriam said. 'Mostly it was those two, thick as thieves. I was bundled off to Switzerland, and when I did make it home they made it clear I wasn't welcome.'

She studied me openly, with no guile. It made me like her.

'Vaughn said you're up at Cambridge,' I said.

'They let a few of us girls in every now and then,' Miriam said, 'keeps the agitators off their backs.'

'What do you study?'

'I teach,' she said. 'Waves and all that.'

I nodded sagely, as if I knew what she was talking about. The closest I'd got to university was hearing about Doc's exploits, and most of those had involved drinking.

'The sea?' I asked, imagining experiments with floats. There'd be charts involved, and speeches delivered in oak-panelled lecture theatres.

'Radio,' she said. 'Very hush hush.'

Once again, Margaret's laugh carried over the noise.

'You should be careful,' Miriam said, 'if you're intending to keep her. Vaughn's had a lifetime of getting what he wants.'

'Does he want Margaret?' I asked.

'Of course,' she said. 'We all do.'

43

Dinner was everything I'd expected. A long table, silver can-delabra, enough food to feed a small town. Vaughn had been saving his ration coupons for a rainy day.

The room was designed to intimidate. A huge stone fire-place dominated the side wall. Above it, an ugly portrait of one of Vaughn's ancestors.

They'd placed me between the two women we'd met on the Forest. Constance, in a flowery dress the size of a mess tent, on my left, and Kay, in a tailored dinner suit, on my right.

'What do you think about the Jewish problem?' Constance asked, raising her reading glasses in readiness to properly assess my response.

'Is there a problem?' I answered.

'Namely that they live in our countries without consider-ing themselves citizens,' Kay answered, from my right.

'Countries?' I asked, spearing a piece of limp asparagus.

'England, France, Germany . . .' Constance said.

'. . . all the great European nations,' Kay added.

I ate my asparagus. It was a first. Our greengrocer didn't sell it, and I'd never grown it. Too much fiddling around with banking up the soil. It was gelatinous, and whatever taste it had was overpowered by the margarine. Even Vaughn was having trouble getting butter. He should have asked, and I could have put him in touch with Eric.

I didn't respond to the women. I've found it's the best way to draw people out, make them tell you more about themselves than you reveal about yourself. A matter of habit, compounded by my bad mood at being coerced into staying for the party, solidified by the sinking feeling that told me exactly where this conversation was going.

'Hitler's merely doing what everyone's been thinking about,' came from across the table. A vicar with a florid face that spoke of a life well lived.

'He's a brute, of course,' from my right, 'but one can't argue with his underlying philosophy.'

I looked along the table for respite. Margaret was next to Vaughn, at the far end. I couldn't hear what they were saying, but she was flushed, and he was smiling. Her dress was a revealing cut, designed to show off her curves, and Vaughn was having a hard time keeping his eyes on her face.

'We seem to have it backwards,' from my left. 'We're sending good people, from good families, to internment on the Isle of Man, because they have family in Germany, while we're letting the Jews go free. And now we're hell-bent on war, to protect them.'

'I don't know anyone who wants war with Germany,' Kay said, on my right.

'You would, if you listened more than you talked,' I said.

That quietened them down.

I was rescued from further comment by the tinkling of a glass and the scraping of a chair on the stone floor, as Vaughn rose for a toast.

'I'd like to thank you all for coming,' he said, carefully looking around at all of his guests. 'It's heartening to be with so many friends who all believe as I do, that it's not too late for peace.'

This was met with a round of 'hear hear' and even a thumping on the table.

'As most of you know,' he said, 'I've been lucky enough to be involved in an organisation that's been leading the charge on matters of peace. Since the early days, we've been a beacon of hope for fellow Christians across Europe. Good people, regardless of nationality and language, united by our common beliefs. A tribe of peace-lovers, we've been called in the press, as if that's some kind of slur. Well, I accept that slur. I'm a Christian, and a pacifist, and if that means my beliefs run counter to the war-mongers in Downing Street and Fleet Street, I'll shoulder that burden.'

He paused for the round of applause that followed.

I turned to my dinner companions to see how they were receiving the message. They were besotted.

'I know many of you have been anxious to hear reports about our approaches to the King,' Vaughn said. If people had been following closely before, this sealed the deal. The room was silenced. Not a fork on a plate or a chink of a glass.

'What I have to tell you now must stay between us. I say this with absolute seriousness. There will be a time when the good news will be shared, but until I let you know that time has come, what I'm about to tell you must stay in this room.'

Vaughn looked me in the eye. Where did I fit in with his assessment that he was surrounded by friends and confidantes?

Margaret put her hand on Vaughn's. A nice touch. Vouching for me.

'I have it on first-hand authority that we have a supporter at the highest level in society,' Vaughn said. 'The *very* highest level.'

On my left, Constance gasped. She wasn't the only one.

'I can't yet reveal the name of our supporter, but I have his guarantee that when the time comes, he'll be ready to step forwards.'

Vaughn surveyed his party. He had them hanging on his every word.

'Until that day, we're all to carry on doing our bit. Our supporter will be watching us closely, and when the time is right, he's promised to join us here. Based on plans that I've become privy to, I predict we'll be welcoming a guest of honour in a matter of weeks. In fact, depending on sailing conditions in the English Channel, we may be welcoming a whole succession of important guests here.'

This got a ripple of laughter, some of it genuine and some of it uncomfortable.

'I trust you'll join me in a toast.'

Vaughn picked up his glass, generating a rush of activity as the rest of the guests did the same.

'To peace!' Vaughn said.

'To peace!' everyone murmured.

44

The women withdrew, a procedure I'd read about in Edward Forster's books, but hadn't believed happened. When they were gone, Vaughn rose and suggested the men join him in the study for a snifter. In practice that meant an old duffer wearing his Boer war medals, the red-nosed vicar from across the table, sweating in his dog-collar, Freddie, Vaughn and me. Five men at an event with twice as many women. We'd learnt to live with it since the Great War. And now we were sending the next generation of young men into the same slaughterhouse. Perhaps Vaughn, with his desire for peace, had a point.

In the study, we were treated to a minute-by-minute re-telling of the old duffer's experience in South Africa. Freddie suffered through the story with the lack of grace of a schoolboy being kept after class. He was a curious sort. The type who had clearly never been taught to modify his behaviour to suit his surroundings.

The old duffer was interrupted as the door to the study opened. It was Miriam. She was excited.

'It's happening,' she said.

★

Vaughn hurried us all through the house, shouting as we went.

'Ladies and gentlemen,' he said, 'if you'll be so good as to gather your drinks, we've got an adventure in the gardens for you.'

'The gardens?' an old matron sitting in a cosy spot by the fire complained.

'Bring your outdoor shoes, and you might want an over-coat if you feel the chill,' Vaughn said.

It was getting dark outside. Servants bustled about, pro-viding burning torches, lending the affair a medieval, pagan feeling. There was a ripple of excitement in the air, at the prospect of being handed a flame.

'When does the blackout come in?' Constance asked, shoving her feet into a pair of muddy boots.

Washington, the butler, emerged from the shadows. He consulted the day's paper. *The Times*, of course. The black-out times, start and end, were on the masthead.

'Fifty-seven minutes' time,' he said, as if pronouncing a complicated legal opinion.

'Plenty of time,' Vaughn said. 'Come on!'

We trooped solemnly down the steps at the edge of the terrace, into the ornamental gardens, filled with towering rhododendrons in full bloom. The grassy paths were already damp with dew. The air was heady with jasmine, and bats flew above us in the dark.

Washington brought up the rear, and I dropped back to walk with him.

'Didn't have you down as a blackshirt, Cook,' he said, keeping his voice low.

'I'm looking for a parachutist,' I said. 'Any ideas?'

We slowed our pace, letting the party get ahead of us, until we were alone in the darkness.

'Not here,' he said, under his breath.

'You know what's going on?' I asked.

'Not here,' he repeated.

I stopped in his path.

A twig cracked in the trees, a few yards into the undergrowth. A deer perhaps. Or perhaps someone was keeping an eye on us.

'I believe it's a surprise,' he said, projecting his voice into the darkness. 'Lord Matheson's quite excited to show you all. We should hurry.'

We moved on. The path took us onto an ornamental bridge across a waterfall, linking two lakes. The rushing water gave us cover to talk.

'The Green Man,' he said. 'I get off early tomorrow night.'

Footsteps from behind us heralded the arrival of a latecomer. It was Freddie.

'Come on, Cook, don't want to miss this,' he said.

*

We caught up with the party at the far end of the lake. A haze of mist rose from the water. If Excalibur had appeared from the mist, held aloft by a ghostly arm, it wouldn't have looked out of place.

Margaret found me and slipped her arm into mine.

'Has it been dreadful?' she asked.

'Nothing I can't handle.'

A grassy meadow led to the tree line, and we walked through the long grass to an old wire fence, presumably the edge of Vaughn's property.

'They put you between those dreadful women. It looked like they were trying to sell you a magazine subscription,' Margaret said.

'Gather round!' Vaughn yelled, and we formed a loose semi-circle around him, with the fence behind him. With our burning torches, it looked like we were about to conduct some kind of sacrifice, or storm the Bastille.

Vaughn looked at his wristwatch.

'A moment of silence, please!' he shouted.

The last few murmurers quieted themselves. All eyes were on Vaughn. He looked expectant. He checked his wristwatch again.

There was a nervous titter of laughter.

'Could have brought some bloody whisky, Vaughn, if we're traipsing around the country.' This from Constance.

'Bear with me,' Vaughn said.

We waited in the dark, the flaming torches making the only noise as they were gently teased by the wind.

'*Hier ist Soldatensender Calais*,' a voice said, unmistakably German. It came from nowhere.

I looked around for the source and saw it: a long, barbed-wire fence behind Vaughn.

Everyone else looked mystified. People muttered to each other: What kind of play was Vaughn putting on? Did he have an actor lurking in the trees? Presumably some kind of hilarious joke. Good old Vaughn. Always game for something.

The voice continued. I didn't understand the words, but it sounded like an announcement.

'This is Gustav Siegfried One,' Kay, my dinner companion, said, taking the role of interpreter. 'This is the Chief, resuming transmission from Forward Operating Base Delta in Calais, in the territory of the Reich formerly known as France.'

While she spoke, the German voice emerged from the air, seeming to come from all around us. Freddie touched the barbed wire, and the voice disappeared.

'It's the fence,' I said to Miriam, standing next to me. I felt foolish as soon as I said it. She'd told me she was an expert in radio waves and here I was trying to impress her with my rudimentary understanding of the subject.

Freddie took his hand away and the German voice continued, with Kay translating.

'As we mass on the beaches and the mustering points, ready for the invasion of our weakest neighbour, we know that the Jew-loving Churchill will be quaking in his boots, and our glorious leader is only days from his triumphant master-stroke.'

'Exactly,' Miriam said to me. 'The correct combination of wire length and corrosion. We found it yesterday evening and Vaughn wanted to show it off.'

'This will be a triumph of the foot-soldier. The tank commander. The U-boat crew member. But as we march down Piccadilly Avenue, we must keep an eye on our rear-guard, on Berlin, where the profiteers and party . . .' Kay seemed lost, her translation faltered.

'Apparatchiks,' Margaret interjected.

'Yes, thank you,' Kay agreed. 'Where the profiteers and party apparatchiks operate, those . . . leeches who are already syphoning off by all accounts fifty per cent of all funding meant for widows of soldiers, while normal people go hungry in their homes.'

It was good to know that the Germans were having their own problems. The way things were presented in the newsreels, they were unstoppable. This was the first I'd heard about internal issues.

'Thus, as we lie down to sleep on what might be the eve of our invasion, we ask for your blessing, people of the fatherland, and give you in return our warning – watch your backs, and keep the glorious Leader safe from those around him who look to subvert this historic moment. Signing off for this evening, Gustav Siegfried Eins. I repeat. Gustav Siegfried Eins.'

45

'I've heard that voice before,' I said.

Miriam and Vaughn looked at each other. They tried to hide it, but they were excited.

We were back in the library. Vaughn and I had our brandy and the ladies were sipping sherry. Freddie was pacing around the room, bouncing a tennis ball on the parquet floor. He glugged wine from a bottle. The rest of the party had gone, and the servants had withdrawn.

'Where were you?' Miriam asked.

'Southern edge of my land, give or take.'

'What was the alignment of the fence?'

'East to west.'

She rushed to a writing desk, under the window. She pulled down the writing surface and rummaged around in the exposed drawers.

'Vaughn, where do you keep your pens?' she snapped.

'Top right drawer,' he said. 'Ink in the inkwell.'

She brought a notepad back with her, and noted down my answers.

'How long's the fence?' she asked.

The field was two hectares. Roughly five acres. A rectangle, the shorter side butting up against the woods. The drainage ditch keeping the livestock from escaping, with the barbed-wire fence as an extra precaution.

'Hundred and fifty yards, I'd say.'

She drew a rectangle, and annotated it with the numbers.

'When did you hear it?'

'Around the same time, give or take,' I said. 'Around dusk.'

'You're south of us?' she asked.

'About five miles.'

'How loud was the signal?'

'Similar,' I said, 'perhaps weaker.'

'Show me,' she said.

46

Margaret drove. We rocketed downhill, losing altitude as we left the Forest behind us. Through the tight bends of Duddleswell, opening up for the long straight down past Fairwarp, past Palehouse Lane.

'I don't understand,' Margaret shouted over the din from the engine and rushing wind. 'Why are only certain places picking up the transmission? Why not every bit of barbed wire in the country?'

Margaret was a careless driver at the best of times, and as she looked back to Miriam in the back seat, jammed in next to me, the car swerved.

'Drive,' I said. 'Questions later.'

The car sped past Fairwarp church, Margaret peering into the darkness, driving faster than she could see. She'd masked out her headlights according to regulations, only a tiny slit of light allowed, and it turned what was already a hair-raising experience into a pure gamble.

Miriam leant in to me, her mouth to my ear. We were like sardines in a tin, so she didn't have to lean far.

'If we can gather as much information as we can about the receivers,' she shouted, 'in this case your fence and Vaughn's fence, we can make some assumptions about the distance and direction to the source of the radio transmission.'

I turned to her. She was still facing me and now we were inches apart. I leant past her face to shout into her ear, our cheeks brushing.

'Seems like a lot of trouble. The chap on the transmission said he was on the French coast. What's the value in pinpointing it further?'

She grabbed onto me as Margaret swerved suddenly.

'Bloody deer!' Margaret shouted. 'Think they own the road!'

'He's not in France,' Miriam shouted into my ear. 'He's here, in Sussex.'

Suddenly it was clear why she was so interested. A waveform expert from Cambridge arriving in Sussex on the eve of the invasion, putting herself in harm's way. Dragging us out to listen to enemy propaganda in the middle of a dinner party. This wasn't a party trick.

'He's somewhere nearby. And if he's louder for us than for you, that means he's either north of us both, between us and London, or he's somewhere between us.

We rocketed past the turning to Palehouse Lane, where only a few days ago I'd been driving Mrs Leckie home from the station.

'We think he's hiding out on the Forest somewhere,' Miriam shouted.

47

We hurried across the moonlit fields, through the newly widened gap in the hawthorn hedge. The far meadow was half ploughed, and our ancient Fordson tractor was labouring across the mud. It stalled, and a distinct shout carried across the field.

'Fucking hell!'

It was Bill Taylor. Bill and the Fordson had a hate-hate relationship. Bill, precise and thoughtful in all walks of life, didn't get on with the vagaries of the machine. He'd been on at me to replace it, but it would have taken a loan so expensive it would put the whole operation at risk and I'd held off.

We picked our way across the ploughed section of the field.

'Having fun?' I asked.

'No, I'm bloody well not,' Bill Taylor replied.

'I was talking to the Fordson,' I said.

The Pole joined us. He'd been walking along behind the plough, monitoring its progress.

'No good,' Milosz said. 'Plough bit keeps riding up. It needs eighteen inches down to make the drainage channels, but it rides up, first chance it gets.'

'Tried weighting it down?' I asked.

'Then it bogs down.'

'How about a man riding it? Like you did with the children?'

'Could work,' Milosz said. 'Let's try.'

'We'll try again in the morning,' Bill said, 'but we're going to have to have a serious chat about getting that tracked machine we talked about. It'll do much better in the mud.'

'Let's not waste time discussing it any more,' I said. 'Call Allthorp first thing. Put in the order, if they'll let us have it.'

Bill cut the engine and climbed down from the tractor. The way he held his back, it was clear he'd been at it for a long time. I'd been letting him take the lion's share of the work, but I'd been taking advantage of him. Bill wasn't the kind of man to tell you he needed help. I'd forgotten that my role as his employer was to step in when he was doing too much.

'Call it a day,' I said. 'The field'll be here tomorrow. We can do it together.'

I left Bill checking the tractor before he finished for the night. Milosz followed me, as I'd hoped he would.

'Anything to worry about?' I asked, keeping my voice low.

'Nothing,' Milosz said. 'No visitors. I walked perimeter during lunch. No signs of anyone.'

★

'A hundred and sixty-two yards,' Miriam shouted. She'd paced the length of the fence as best she could, helped by her cane, and now she hobbled back to us, stopping to write her findings in a pocket notebook. When she reached us she showed us her work – she'd sketched the construction of the fence, carefully noting the number of strands, the method of attachment to the rotting wooden posts, and the amount of rust on the wire.

'It's what I thought,' she said. 'Perfectly set up to receive eight hundred to nine hundred kilohertz. Your fence should actually be a more sensitive receiver than ours. It's longer, with more strands of wire, and the perfect amount of corrosion. We'd expect you to get a louder signal. But you said it was quieter, coming and going, that means the transmitter's closer to our fence than yours. I'd say that puts the transmitter within two or three miles of our fence.'

'Is there any way to triangulate?' Margaret asked.

'We'd need at least two more locations,' Miriam said. 'But we can't very well put an ad in the paper asking to talk to people who've been hearing German radio transmissions. It would cause panic.'

'We could set up shop at likely places,' Margaret said. 'If you're saying we want a three-row barbed wire fence of more than a hundred yards, that helps us narrow it down. It's a matter of doing the legwork.'

'That could take weeks,' Miriam said, shaking her head. 'I don't think we've got that long. I think we've got days, if that.'

We all looked south, towards the coast.

48

I was up early and took the shotgun and a pocket full of cartridges. Frankie had been keeping it clean after I'd shown him how to look after it. Give him a few months and I'd show him how to shoot, turn him into a country boy.

I walked out to the field of spring wheat, wincing as I saw my boot marks crossing it on the diagonal. If the man from the War Ag saw those, we'd get marked down.

I took up my position with my back to an old oak that cast a deep shadow over the edge of the field. To anyone out in the sun, I'd be invisible in my dark clothing, as long as I kept still. I sat, and waited, and thought.

Miriam had been sent to investigate the radio signals, that much was clear. But Vaughn was openly pro-German. He'd say he was pro-peace, but that was splitting hairs. It was a cover, and a short hop from that to wearing swastikas, as a number of other 'peace' organisations had shown. As it was, Vaughn was treading a fine line, and he'd have to be careful not to end up behind bars with Oswald Mosley. If I had to bet on whether Vaughn would help an arriving parachutist or turn him in, my money would be on him helping him. And if I felt that way about Vaughn, logic dictated Miriam should be treated with the same level of caution.

All of this was a circular argument which brought me back to my initial preference. My founding principle.

If you want something done right, do it yourself.

If there was a parachutist hiding out in my patch, I backed myself to track him down. If he put up a fight, I'd do whatever was required. If he survived that, I'd hand him over to Neesham. The good thing about Neesham – I didn't need to know his politics. He wasn't that complicated. He was an honest copper, who'd do the right thing.

I saw movement in the hedgerow, and raised the shotgun to my shoulder.

I watched, and waited, slowing my breathing, my world reduced to the field of fire laid out in front of me.

I fired, twice, and cracked the gun, but I didn't need to reload. I'd got what I came for. Two rabbits. Two less pests to eat my crops. Two meals for Eric, and his nan.

★

Eric was in his garden, same as last time. He was nailing up an enclosure around a dirty pond. Inside the enclosure he had a coop, and as I approached a pair of ducks waddled into it, hiding from the threatening newcomer.

'Thought you might be able to find a use for these,' I said, handing over the rabbits.

'Thanks, Mr Cook,' he said. 'Stick around, I'll get you a couple of these duck's eggs. Lovely with a bit of bread.'

I let him root around in the coop and took the two eggs he handed me, still warm.

'Any luck with those German voices?' I asked, not expecting much. It had only been a couple of days, and Eric was a busy man.

'I was going to come over,' Eric said, feeling in his inside pocket. He pulled out a page from a notebook – rough paper, flecks of brown pulp still visible. He handed it to me and I unfolded it.

'I can find more if you give me more time,' he said.

I scanned the page. He had at least ten readings. Each one had location, time and date, and a note.

'That's how loud,' he said. 'I asked each person the same question – if the person was standing next to you in a busy pub, would you think they were talking normal, too quiet, or too loud.'

'Good thinking,' I said, and I meant it. It was a clever way of getting people to use their judgment without overthinking. Everyone could relate to being in a busy pub, and everyone would have a similar calibration.

'This is impressive,' I said. Eric shrugged.

'Like I said, I'll get more if you give me longer.'

'This'll be good to be getting on with,' I said.

49

The Green Man had a low ceiling, made lower still by thick oak beams painted black and covered with tarnished horse brasses. I had to stoop as I made my way to the bar, and it reminded me why I didn't drink there more often.

William Washington was propping up the bar. He was in his shirtsleeves, his butler's tails presumably left hanging in his room. The wireless was on. The RAF had bombed Italy. Precision bombing. Military targets.

I bought a pint of porter for myself, and a pint of mild for Washington.

'Not here,' he said, under his breath.

I left the right change on the bar and followed Washington to a quiet table in the back corner, where we could sit without being overheard.

'Well?' I asked, as Washington flicked his eyes around the pub. He was acting like we were planning a bank heist.

'What do you know about Aspidistra?' he asked.

It was an odd question. He saw my confusion.

'Houseplant?' I answered. 'Non-native, I suspect. Asian?'

He shook his head, tired of waiting for me to fumble around.

'Who are you working for?' he pressed.

'I don't work for anyone,' I said. 'I'm a farmer.'

Washington glared at me. I sipped my beer, waited for him to get to the point. He'd told me to meet him here, so I knew he had something he wanted to tell me.

'Lots of organisations are interested in Lord Matheson,' he said. 'On both sides of the Channel. You're not the first stray he's picked up.'

'Who's interested in him on this side?' I asked.

'Organisations that don't get discussed in pubs.'

'Why Vaughn?' I asked. 'His politics are too far right for my tastes, but he seems pretty inoffensive. He's no Mosley.'

'Mosley's taught everyone a lesson,' Washington said. 'They should never have arrested him. Now everyone with a swastika armband hidden in their sock drawer has learnt to keep quiet about it. But you're right. Lord Matheson's no Mosley. Mosley wanted to run the country. Matheson's not that ambitious. He wants the south-east. Sussex would do. Lord Matheson, protector of the county.'

'Where do you sit on this debate?' I asked.

'I'm the butler,' he said. 'I don't have opinions.'

'What happened with the Leckies?'

'Forget the Leckies,' Washington said. 'Casualties of war.'

'What if I can't forget them?'

'You're going to get more people hurt,' he said.

'You think I'm responsible for them?' I asked.

He shrugged and drank more.

'Like I said, I'm just the butler.'

I wanted to tell him the deaths weren't my fault. I'd come to the pub expecting to learn more about Vaughn and I found myself on the back foot. I watched an elderly woman at the bar. She took her half and sipped it, closing her eyes in relief. That first drink, after a day on your feet. She put her coins on the bar and shuffled back to her own dark corner.

The way she'd put the coins on the counter was entirely unremarkable. No need to check the amount. Second nature. It recalled a memory, something I'd been trying to get at, without knowing why.

The man at the Fireman's Arms had given his coins a nervous look. A glance. I'd seen it, but I hadn't noticed because the evening had taken a different turn.

He'd been checking to see he'd put the right coins down. Something only a foreigner would do.

50

I crouched in the undergrowth, watching the art deco house. Ten past eight. Fences across Sussex would be vibrating with radio waves, filling the air with German voices.

I circled round the house to the back, where a lawn ran down from the house to the woods. An ornamental monkey-puzzle tree loomed in the dusk. Beyond it, lawn chairs and croquet hoops spoke of a pleasant afternoon. A teak table overflowed with empty bottles. It looked like there was quite a house party going on.

The wise move would have been to sit and watch all night, but it was time to make something happen, wise move or not.

I ran across the lawn, making sure to avoid the croquet hoops. Coloured balls were spread across the grass, abandoned mid game.

I tried the back door.

I heard it straight away. The voice from the ether, pulled down from the airwaves by my fence. But this time I wasn't hearing it from a fence. I could hear the man himself, Gustav Siegfried, making his nightly report.

I was in a kitchen. It was small and ultra-modern, with formica counters and an enamelled stove. There was a humming from the corner. A purpose-built refrigerator, a compressor on top whirring away. By the stainless-steel sink, a generous collection of dirty wine glasses.

The voice was coming from deeper in the house. I heard other voices, kept deliberately low.

I stepped carefully over a bundle of wires that lay across the kitchen floor. I followed, like Jack following a strand of the beanstalk.

In the hallway, the German voice was louder, and I could see an open door ten feet away. The wires ran down the side of a shining parquet floor, across the corridor to lead through the open door. Where they crossed the floor, someone had put a rug over them. The rug was bunched up from people repeatedly scuffing it.

I'd found German spies, broadcasting openly back to the motherland, helping Hitler prepare for the upcoming invasion. I could back out of the house, retrace my steps, all the way to Uckfield where I could tell Neesham. But there was another option. Deal with it myself.

Blakeney, my old CO, would have had a pithy saying, but I didn't need his advice. I'd go with the principle that had got me through life, through tricky situations in the trenches, in Afghanistan, and on the streets of Hong Kong. It hadn't failed me yet.

Find your enemy. Kill your enemy.

A woman laughed and the German voice stopped. I heard the flutter of papers followed by conversation. The woman was talking in German, but it didn't sound like it was for broadcast. She sounded relaxed, joking around with her friend or husband while they sat by the fire at the end of the day. Bad enough enemy agents were lying low in Sussex. Worse still, they were playing house in the lap of luxury.

As I approached the open door, the German broadcaster restarted, but this time in a heavily accented English:

'It's come to my attention that there are a great many English listeners tuning into my evening reports. To you all I say a hearty welcome, pip pip and all that.'

Again, the woman laughed.

'I invite you all to lay down your arms as soon as your German brethren arrive on your shores. It will go easier that way. Well, easier for us, that's for sure. But seriously, you know that most of our soldiers are young men, most of them just out of school with not much military training. We've grown our army so quickly, you see, that we couldn't waste too much time with the niceties of training. I just spoke to a brave young soldier, Leutnant Sami Werner. He says he hopes he doesn't come across too many Tommies, because he's only been given three bullets. Seems the fat cats in Berlin have been keeping a lot of the so-called investment our glorious Führer has made in our armed forces for themselves.'

I'd heard enough.

Find your enemy. Kill your enemy.

51

I stepped into a spacious drawing room, a glossy grand piano in the far corner. The man I'd talked to at the pub sat on a couch, a notepad in his hand. The woman from the pub sat next to him, making notes in her own pad.

At the side of the room, two young men sat on dining chairs set against the wall. One of them was writing and the other consulting a sheaf of papers. They looked up at me in alarm.

I fired a shot into the ceiling. The man and woman from the pub turned to look at me. They gave each other a knowing look, and the woman raised her hands, rather impishly, like it was a game.

'That's enough,' I said.

I pointed my gun at the young man.

'Stop the broadcast,' I ordered.

He smirked. 'Do you see any microphones?' he asked.

'How's your English?' I asked him.

'We *are* English,' he said. He sounded exasperated. He looked at the woman as if it were her job to solve this little problem for him. Get things back on track.

I assumed the woman was in charge. Probably had a plan for this. Did they have poison capsules in their teeth, like they did in the flicks? I gave them a second. If they wanted to take the honourable way out, that would give me fewer people to kill. A win all round.

The woman looked up at the ceiling, where hurried footsteps echoed, in reaction to my gunshot. I'd have company soon. She looked at me as if to say 'now look what you've done'.

I stood with my back against the wall. I could cover the people in the room and keep my eye on the door, but if someone was out in the corridor they wouldn't see me until they entered the room.

'Anyone in here says a word I'll shoot them first,' I said, in my command voice.

'Bunny!' the woman shouted.

Keeping my eyes on the door, I pointed my gun at the woman. I'd given the ultimatum and she'd broken it deliberately. Like a test. You let one person do that and you've lost control. Only one response possible.

It took a moment to sink in, above the pounding blood in my ears. My finger was on the trigger.

'Bunny!' she shouted again. Her voice wobbled. She was scared. She knew she was hanging by a thread.

Bunny.

Heavy footsteps on the stairs – we were about to have company. Along the corridor, following the bundle of wires, past the kitchen door, over the bunched-up rug.

The door opened. A man hurried in. He was in his sixties, wearing a rumpled suit that looked like he'd slept in it. He beamed when he saw me.

'Cook!' he said, holding out his hand to shake. I moved the gun from the woman to him. He didn't seem to notice.

'You took your bloody time,' he said. 'I told these chaps you'd be here days ago.'

52

I'd met Bunny in London a month earlier, when the Germans had invaded France. I'd travelled to London to sign up, join the army and give my life to the fight against the oncoming Blitzkrieg.

Bunny had told me the army had different plans for me. He'd given me my marching orders and sent me on my way. He'd told me I'd never see him again. Our conversation hadn't taken place. All that kind of thing. Standard military intelligence rubbish, as if we were all playing a big game.

A lot had happened since then.

Now, Bunny looked from me to the couple on the couch, and back again. He beamed.

'John Cook, meet Helmut and Frieda. Helmut, Frieda, meet John Cook. Good chap. Got a farm down in . . .' He looked to me for help.

'Uckfield,' I said.

'Uckfield! Slap bang on the invasion route, as far as we can tell.'

I lowered the gun.

'We've met,' I said.

More footsteps from the corridor heralded another arrival. It was going to get crowded.

'Ah!' Bunny said. 'Cook, this is Adams.'

Adams nodded. I recognised him. The scar-faced man from the pub.

'Adams is one of your lot, Cook. Commando, just back from Norway. You might have crossed paths in India perhaps?'

We shook hands, firmly, a contest. A regimental thing. I was in good shape. Twenty years of baling hay and pulling cows out of the mud. Adams gave as good as he got. I counted to three then we both let go, hands bruised and honour served.

'I saw your picture in the paper,' I said. 'You were dressed as a Luftwaffe pilot.'

'Don't believe everything you see in the newspapers,' Bunny said.

*

We left the young men conferring over their notes. Bunny shepherded the rest of us to a windowless room. All four walls were covered with maps of southern England and Europe, each wall with a desk and chair. The German couple took a chair each and swivelled them round to face the room. Adams followed suit. I left the last one for Bunny but he perched on a desk, so I sat down. No point standing in the middle of the room like the piggy in the middle.

A white-coated butler followed Bunny into the room with a tray of glasses, a bottle of whisky, and one of soda.

Bunny poured five drinks, all the same. Generous amounts of whisky with a squirt of soda. It seemed none of us got a choice in the matter. He handed them around and took a deep gulp of his own.

'Some people have been killed,' I said. 'Friends of mine. Wasn't anything to do with you lot, was it?' I tried to sound casual, but I watched everyone carefully as I asked the question.

'Who wants to take that?' Bunny asked, like a schoolmaster moderating a debate.

'Wasn't us,' Adams said. 'We've got better things to do than go around killing the locals.'

'Good heavens, Cook!' Bunny said. 'We do not, I repeat do not, take out members of our own citizenry.'

'How about the parachutist?' I asked. 'Nothing to do with all this?'

'Everything to do with all this,' Bunny said. 'We've known for some time Berlin's aware of what we're doing. We've been expecting someone to turn up and take a shufti. Counting on it, in fact.'

'And here you are,' Adams said. I kept a close eye on his right hand. He had a pistol in a holster on his right hip. The leather restraining strap was unfastened. A professional's weapon, the hammer filed off, a bullet in the chamber, trigger guard removed, ready to kill a fraction of a second after he had the thought.

I moved my own hand closer to my hip.

'No one's accusing you of being a fifth columnist,' Bunny said.

'So, what's going on?' I asked.

They all looked at each other.

'What do *you* think's going on?' Bunny asked.

I drank my whisky.

'You're putting out a radio show, pretending to be a German paratrooper ahead of the lines, lying low on the Forest,' I said. 'You've got a genuine German as the voice.' I nodded to the man who'd been talking into the microphone, 'but I assume the wording's been carefully vetted. If the audience is German soldiers across the Channel you're trying to feed them some kind of misinformation. Sowing the seeds of confusion. How am I doing?'

The German radio host nodded.

'He's smarter than you said he'd be,' he said to Bunny.

'You've been sloppy,' I said. 'Poor security. You've been going to the pub, being obvious about being a foreigner. All that guff with the coins. And the other night you left a light on that could be seen across half the Forest.'

Bunny watched me, nodding encouragingly. I could see him as a professor, lecturing the next generation of the aristocracy in some dusty classroom.

'What do you make of that?' he asked.

'You're either stupid, or you've been trying to attract attention,' I said. 'Let's be kind and assume you're not stupid.'

'We're not stupid,' the woman said.

'OK,' I said, 'you wanted to be found out. You know about Vaughn. You probably know about all the raving Nazi sympathisers in the country, yet you set up shop here, right under his nose.'

Bunny nodded encouragingly. He seemed pleased.

'You're trying to draw them out,' I said. 'Pushing them into making a move. So you can hold him up as an example of what happens to silly boys who get caught playing for the wrong side. How close am I?'

One of the young men poked his head in the door.

'Five minutes,' he said, before disappearing.

The woman got up. She hadn't touched her whisky.

'Come and watch the show,' she said.

53

I followed them along the hall, towards the stairs. Presumably they had the transmitter in a bedroom, or even the attic. Probably the best place to send a clear signal.

The woman paused before we got to the stairs. She looked back at me, and at Bunny, who nodded approvingly. She pressed one of the panels on the side of the staircase, and a door opened.

'Keep up,' she said. 'We're late.'

★

I followed them through the door under the stairs. There was another staircase, this one leading downwards, as if to a cellar. But it went deeper than a cellar. Before I even started down the stairs, I could hear the woman's footsteps far below, still descending.

I counted the steps. Twelve steps in my house from the ground floor to the cellar. Here we took forty down, more than three storeys. At the bottom, we found ourselves in a narrow passageway, like a miniature version of the London Underground. It had curved walls, painted white, with electric lights on the ceiling. Everything smelt new.

The woman was already thirty yards ahead, her partner hurrying to keep up.

We hurried along for five minutes. Quarter of a mile, give or take. The tunnel was perfectly circular, like the Tube, apart from one point where we passed what looked like an escape hatch above us. All the while, we were on a slight slope upwards. I tried to calculate our heading based on the alignment of the house, and the direction we'd taken, but it was impossible to be sure.

'Quite a feat of engineering,' I said. 'Must have been tricky doing it all without anyone noticing.'

'Six months' construction,' Bunny said. 'Three months digging, three months outfitting. A whole division of Canadian troops working around the clock.'

After ten minutes we reached a vestibule, two doors leading from it, one on each side. To our left, a grey, metal door with a terse sign:

High voltage.
No entry.

The other door was like something from a submarine. A metal oval, set into a solid metal plate, sealed tight with a circular mechanism that looked like a steering-wheel. The door had a small glass window, and the woman peered through it. She looked back at Bunny.

'We're late,' she said.

'You go ahead,' Bunny replied. 'I'll give our man the grand tour.'

Bunny gestured to the door with the sign. High Voltage. No Entry.

★

'This is the power plant!' Bunny had to yell over the noise of the large diesel generator, easily the size of a London bus.

Ductwork criss-crossed the concrete ceiling, presumably carrying away the exhaust, and cables as thick as my wrist disappeared into the darkness.

'How far down are we?' I shouted.

'Four storeys! Over sixty feet, each storey constructed from blast-proof concrete reinforced with steel.'

The heat in the room was incredible.

'Don't touch it!' he said.

The warning was unnecessary. I could feel the power radiating off the machine. It was like being trapped in a stall with a bull.

★

The submarine door held even more of a surprise.

'We call this the cinema,' Bunny said, as we stepped through into a plush lobby that wouldn't have looked out of place in Leicester Square.

Adams pulled the submarine door shut behind us, as Bunny let me take in our surroundings.

'If you're going to spend your days underground, no reason why it has to feel like a bunker, eh?' Bunny said.

I looked at Adams, curious to know if he shared the sentiment. He shrugged.

In the middle of the foyer, exactly where the entrance to the theatre would be, double doors beckoned us.

'You'll like this,' Bunny said, as he led the way. Adams caught my eye. 'Humour him,' the look said.

★

Two technicians sat at a desk, monitoring a bank of what I assumed was broadcasting equipment. A large window separated the booth from the next room – the studio – where the Germans took their places at two chromium microphones.

In the booth, a third technician was rifling through a wall of records.

There was a speaker on the wall, and the room was filled with opera music.

'It's Wagner,' one of the technicians said. He was in his shirtsleeves and waistcoat, his jacket over the back of his chair. He tapped his cigarette into a mug as he watched his colleague searching the records.

'I know it's bloody Wagner,' his colleague said.

'*Götterdämmerung*,' the other engineer said, leafing furiously through a well-worn reference book. 'New recording.'

'We haven't got a new recording,' Shirtsleeves said.

'We have, it came in last week from the Foreign Office,' the man searching the records said, as he pulled an album from the wall with a flourish. 'Gentlemen, I give you Wagner's *Götterdämmerung*, Berlin Symphony Orchestra, April 1940.'

Bunny nodded at the speaker.

'That's Radio Berlin. It's their equivalent of the BBC evening concert, broadcast across the entirety of the Reich. From Warsaw to Paris.

'Hitler's an absolute radio nut,' Bunny continued. 'He's got speakers on every street corner in every major town and city across his empire. Can you imagine, wherever you walk, there's a bloody radio announcer telling you what to think about how fantastic the leader is, and how quickly the war will be over once the English are subdued.'

The song finished, and a German voice started talking urgently.

'He's saying he hopes all the troops enjoyed the music, and that they should stay tuned for a special bulletin coming in a minute.' Bunny looked at his watch then caught the eye of the engineer in shirtsleeves.

'How are we doing? Ready?'

A woman's voice came on. Whatever she was saying, it sounded soothing. Her voice sounded familiar.

Bunny saw me listening.

'They're a double act. He gives the hard news and she makes you forget how worried you should be. She's very good.'

'Quiet!' Shirtsleeves snapped. He listened to the woman on the radio.

'They're going to play one more piece of the opera before the news,' he said.

His colleague was fumbling with the record he'd pulled from the stacks. He got it on a turntable and squinted at it, counting to himself.

'They're going to play the immolation scene,' Shirtsleeves said.

The third technician scoured the sleeve notes.

'Track three, side one,' he said.

The man at the turntable picked up the stylus arm with trembling hands and counted in.

'Track three?' he asked.

'Track three,' the technician confirmed.

'Wait for it,' Shirtsleeves said. 'Let them play five seconds, let's make sure.'

The woman stopped talking, and there was a brief pause. Opera music filled the booth again.

'Is that it?' the man holding the stylus asked.

'I don't know, you're the bloody Wagner expert,' Shirtsleeves snapped. 'Do it.'

The technician lowered the stylus onto the record, and a smaller speaker on his side of the booth started to play music.

It was the same track, slightly out of sync with the version being broadcast from Germany.

The three technicians looked at each other with wide grins. They looked like schoolboys about to play a prank on the master.

'Do it,' Bunny said.

Shirtsleeves reached across the control board to a large control knob. Two strips of paper, with neat type, were stuck onto the control board. The knob currently pointed to *THEM*. The other available setting was *US*.

Shirtsleeves looked at Bunny, who nodded, then he turned the knob.

There was a moment of static from the large speaker, and the music returned. Now it was perfectly in sync with the smaller speaker.

The piece of music finished, and Shirtsleeves moved a slider on his equipment, fading it out. He held up a hand to the man and woman the other side of the glass. He counted down with his fingers. Five, four, three, two, one, then he pointed at them.

'*Guten Abend,*' the man said, leaning into the microphone. He sounded exactly like the newsreader from Berlin we'd been listening to only minutes before. He continued talking in German. The woman joined in, a soothing conversation for the listeners, late in the evening as they listened to their wireless, all across the Reich, in quiet farming towns no different from mine, in big cities, with people hurrying home after a late shift at the office. Loudspeakers broadcasting, part of the wallpaper of sound that people heard but didn't think about.

Bunny motioned to me to follow him out of the booth. I joined him in the lobby he'd called the cinema.

'Surely the German broadcasters know you've taken over as soon as you do it,' I said to Bunny.

'Oh they hate it,' Bunny said. 'I've got it on good author-ity that Hitler had a tantrum about it last week. Smashed a nice Etruscan vase and had the man responsible for their radio network thrown into prison. The man *formerly* respon-sible for their radio network, I should say.'

'Why don't they stop you?'

'They can't!' Bunny was gleeful. 'This facility's the most powerful radio transmitter in the world. Five hundred megawatts! It was built for a station in America that wanted to drown out its competition but they got cold feet, so we snapped it up. We call it Aspidistra. Like the song.'

I wasn't a devotee of music on the wireless, and I certainly didn't visit the dance halls, but even I had heard of the song. It had been difficult to escape. A breezy tune with nonsense lyrics about the biggest aspidistra in the world.

Besides the song, it wasn't the first time I'd heard about Aspidistra. Washington, the butler, had mentioned it. He'd been testing me. Was he working with Bunny? I thought about telling Bunny I'd met one of his men, but I stopped myself. I was out of my depth, and it wasn't my secret to give up.

'You're hijacking the Germans' airwaves from a top-secret facility,' I said, 'but you send your agents out to local pubs to look suspicious. You identify the local fifth columnist and you lure him in. You give me the guided tour. Hitler's on the French coast and the invasion's probably weeks, if not days away. I'm assuming there's some kind of a plan?'

'I've got one more thing to show you,' Bunny said.

I expected him to turn back to the submarine door, but instead he led me to the far corner of the cinema lobby. A metal ladder was fixed to the wall, leading up to a hatch in the ceiling. It looked precarious, but Bunny took to it like a rat to a drainpipe.

'Hitler's ready to invade,' Bunny shouted down to me, as I climbed after him. 'He's been commandeering every barge and fishing boat he can lay his hands on. He's got an armada, ready to bring his troops across. There's only one problem.'

'Air power,' I shouted. 'As long as we've got fighters aloft, his boats will be sitting ducks.'

'Precisely,' Bunny said. 'Phase one of his invasion will be to take out our air force. He'll start with a massive wave of bombing our airfields. All those bombs we thought would be dropped on London back on day one, he's been saving them all up for a rainy day. Well, it's about to get very rainy. He's got his bombers lined up. Even got a code name. Eagle Day. *Adler Tag* in German. The day the glorious Luftwaffe destroy our ability to defend this little island.'

Having reached the top of his climb, he took one hand off the ladder to open a hatch above him. It swung up and out, letting in a waft of pine-scented air.

'Come on!' he shouted.

54

We were inside a ring of towering pine trees. Through the trunks I could see sky on every side.

Bunny led me through the trees. Metal girders sat on concrete pads, reaching up into the treetops.

Bunny slapped one of the girders. It made a dull ringing sound.

'Radio towers,' he said. 'Hidden in plain sight. Beaming our little radio show across Europe, as far as Prague apparently.'

'You said the Germans are going to invade,' I said. 'But you don't seem as worried as you should be.'

'Oh I am worried. Our boffins have modelled it all out. We've got theoretical mathematicians who can express it all in a formula. They're confident to within two standard deviations that the Luftwaffe will win, paving the way for the invasion. We'll all be citizens of the Reich by Christmas.'

'Unless?' I asked, hoping there was more.

Bunny tapped the side of his nose.

'Top secret,' he said, with a wink. 'Can't tell you any more about it. What I can say is it requires a number of rather tall radio masts, like these ones here. In fact, specifically these ones here. If the Germans have got any nous whatsoever, first thing they'll do is bomb these radio masts, and they'll have a free playing field. Game over. Mathematicians proved correct.'

At the edge of the ring of trees, we looked out across the Forest.

'If this place is so vital, why are you drawing attention to it with your radio programme?' I asked.

'The radio stuff's a bluff,' he said. 'We need these towers, and we need to give the Germans an explanation of why we've put them here.'

'That's insane.'

'I prefer the term creative. We've got some of the best screenwriters from Elstree working on it. Drafted it all out. All the way to the happy ending.'

I could imagine smoky rooms at the film studio. Enthusiastic young men drafting scripts. Men who didn't know the first thing about war. Men who thought their make-believe stories could help us defeat the most mechanised army the world had ever seen.

'Why the secrecy?' I asked. 'Why not lay on tours, show people the magical radio transmitter? Feature articles in the weekend paper?'

'Too easy,' Bunny said. 'The Germans wouldn't believe it. No, the only way they'll take the bait, hook, line, and sinker, is if they feel they've found it out for themselves. We know they've sent a parachutist, and we know they've got local help. Now we're sitting back, waiting for them to make their move.'

'How's it working?'

Bunny paused.

'Well, that's where you come in.'

*

We took the underground passage back to the house.

'Something's gone wrong,' Bunny said. 'We think something happened to the man they sent, and now they're scrambling. They're going to send another man but they need the right conditions. Meanwhile, the clock's ticking on the invasion and Hitler's getting impatient.'

'What do you want me to do?'

'I want you to lead their sightseeing mission,' he said. 'Infiltrate their unit. Bring them in. Give them the tour. Have them report back to Berlin so they can tell Hitler what we're up to, playing silly buggers with radio shows.'

'You want me to lead a team of fifth columnists into a secret military establishment, let them see everything, then get them out again safely,' I said.

The words hung in the air. I'd hoped it might sound less insane said out loud, but I was wrong. This wasn't a plan, it was a fantasy.

'Good man,' Bunny said. 'I knew you'd catch on.'

'What if it goes wrong and we end up shooting?' I asked.

'We've thought of that,' he said. 'We've set up a dead-letter drop. A place on the Forest where you can leave a message. We check it every odd hour. One, three, five, and so on. Leave a message when you know the date and time, and we'll dial down the security.'

We climbed the stairs and found ourselves back in the art deco house.

'I'm sure it doesn't need saying,' Bunny said, manufacturing an off-hand air, 'but everything I've just shown and told you is strictly between us.'

'Of course.'

'I mean it,' he said. 'Anyone at all. Friend. Family. Lover.'

I opened my mouth to ask if he knew about me and Margaret, but kept the words to myself. When it came to deciding which of the two I'd trust, Bunny or Margaret, I knew which side I was on. Besides, Bunny had recruited her just as he'd recruited me, sidling up to her in a London club, asking if she'd like to serve her country.

'She might think it odd if I suddenly suggest attacking a military installation,' I said.

'You'll think of something. I've read your file, Cook, all that stuff in the Himalayas. Quite imaginative.'

★

I kicked a croquet ball towards a hoop as I strode across the lawn. The ball hit the hoop but didn't go through.

'Cook,' Bunny called out after me. 'This has to work. Our ability to repel the invasion depends on it.'

I kept walking, to the edge of the lawn, and the trees beyond.

'Whatever it takes to get the job done, Cook,' he said, his voice coming out of the darkness like one of Scrooge's ghosts.

'Whatever it takes.'

55

Margaret was in my armchair, in the snug, her feet up on a wooden stool. She was asleep. The fireplace smelt of hundreds of years of smoke, even in the midst of summer. Stacks of books and seed catalogues covered the table under the window. She had a paperback on her lap, and an oil lamp glowed on the side table.

I kissed her, and she opened one eye.

'Change of plan,' I said. 'Infiltrate Vaughn's Nazi club.'

'Why?' she asked.

'Bunny,' I said.

I sat in the opposite armchair and took my boots off.

'Do I get the full story?' she asked.

'Top secret,' I said.

'I thought we told each other our things.'

'Do we?' I asked.

She opened her other eye.

'Miriam likes you,' she said. 'We could use that to our advantage.'

'I'm not that charming.'

'I've seen the way she looks at you. If she thought there was a chance to steal you away from me she'd jump on it.'

'Speaking figuratively,' I said.

'Or literally.'

'Are we talking about me and Miriam? Or you and Vaughn?'

'I've got no interest in Vaughn. Quite the opposite.'

'I couldn't do it,' I said.

'Why not? I'm not the first woman you've been intimate with,' she said, 'and I won't be the last.'

'You might be.'

'The Germans might not invade, you know,' she said. 'You might still have a few years left in you.'

'Even so,' I said.

She leant forwards and took my hand.

'John, there's a lot you don't know about me.'

We sat quietly.

'You'd seduce Vaughn if it gave us a tactical advantage?' I asked.

It made my skin crawl to imagine Margaret with Vaughn, no matter how useful it might be.

'Is what Bunny asked you to do important?'

'Vital,' I said.

'Make or break? Do or die?'

I nodded. Margaret's logic was always impeccable, even if I didn't like the direction it took us.

'So. Whatever it takes,' she said.

The same words as Bunny. The same cold logic. The two of them cut from the same cloth.

Whatever it takes.

56

'What's the plan? Ring his doorbell and say we've come to sign up for goose-stepping and Heil Hitler?' Margaret had to shout over the buffeting wind as we sped along the road on top of the Forest. There was a thick mist, and the air smelt earthy. I kept my eyes on the disappearing road in front of us. Margaret was driving faster than we could see.

'That's about it,' I shouted.

I'd told Margaret the minimum. We needed to get closer to Vaughn and Miriam. Get inside his organisation. I'd kept the whole 'secret radio station' story to myself. Even thinking about it in the cold light of day felt crazy, as if it were the product of a dream.

'He'll smell a rat,' she said, as she swerved to avoid a squirrel that darted out from the long grass by the side of the road. The squirrel froze in the middle of the road, courting death, then came to his senses and ran back the way he'd come.

'You'd better leave it to me,' Margaret said, with a grin.

★

The doorbell echoed through the house. I looked up at the black stone and thin, leaded windows. Footsteps echoed from deep within the house, getting closer. Washington, the butler, answered the door with a frown.

'We're here to see Vaughn,' Margaret said, and pushed her way past. Washington glared at me, his meaning clear. This wasn't what we'd agreed.

'Are they up?' Margaret asked, as Washington and I caught up with her in the grand entrance hall.

★

Vaughn was at breakfast. He shoved his newspaper aside and rose to greet us as Margaret hurried into the dining room.

'Mags! Fantastic to see you!'

He gestured to the remnants of the breakfast buffet.

'Join me. Miriam will be down soon I'm sure. What are you drinking? Tea?'

'Coffee,' Margaret said to Washington.

I sat at the table while Margaret took a plate and piled it with scrambled egg. How much did Vaughn spend on the black market in a week? Probably had a non-stop parade to the back door, like a trail of ants.

'This is jolly,' Vaughn said.

Margaret put a plate in front of me and flashed Vaughn a smile. She took a seat between the two of us and bit a triangle of toast with a crunch.

'We're here to join up,' she said to Vaughn, 'and we're not going to take no for an answer.'

Vaughn let the offer hang while he thought it through.

'I'll connect you with Constance,' he said. 'Cook, I think you sat next to her at dinner. She handles our membership list. It's half a crown subs. She'll be happy to put you to work. How do you feel about pasting up leaflets?'

'Cook can offer a more relevant set of qualifications,' Margaret said. 'As can I. I'm not just a pretty face, Vaughn.'

'Qualifications?' Vaughn asked.

'Hand-to-hand combat,' she said. 'Explosives. Principles of guerilla warfare and sabotage. Destruction of enemy posts. Countering enemy information systems.'

She took another bite of toast.

'We can paste up leaflets if you want,' I said. 'But I think you've got grander ambitions.'

'I had you two pegged as Churchill fans,' he said.

'I've got nothing against Churchill,' I said. 'It's the rest of his team I don't like. Far too many international financiers for my liking.'

Vaughn nodded. He gathered the teacups from in front of me and Margaret, carefully filled them, then passed them back.

'What you're saying is treason,' he said. 'As soon as you leave here it's my duty to phone the police and have you arrested. Defence Regulation Eighteen-B. Neither of you will ever be seen or heard of again.'

'Treason is betraying your country,' Margaret said. 'I love my country and I'm willing to do whatever it takes to save it from a war that will destroy another generation.'

'He's all talk,' I said. 'Easy to stand on a stage in a village hall and talk about peace. Let the others do the dirty work.'

Vaughn sipped his tea. Margaret gave me a worried glance. Perhaps I'd pushed too hard.

'Talk with Constance,' he said. 'Start at ground level. See how you like it. A lot of people talk about getting involved. But doing's a lot harder than talking.'

57

We sat on the upper deck of the bus. Six of us, mixed in with the rest of the passengers, all of us studiously avoiding each other's gaze. The bus slowly motored along the back lanes between Ringmer and Lewes, knocking overhanging branches and scratching against brambles growing exuberantly from hedgerows.

It was stifling. I opened the window as far as it would allow, but the air it admitted was as hot as the air already inside. If anything, the outside air was worse, filled with oily smoke from the engine.

We staggered our dispersal from the bus. Freddie and Kay rang the bell and got off at the Ringmer road. They'd have a ten-minute walk into town. Margaret and Miriam got off at the bottom of the hill, by the brewery. That left me and Constance. Vaughn had stayed behind. It was agreed by all that he was too high profile. If Lord Matheson were arrested with propaganda leaflets stuffed up his shirt the press would have a field day. Comparisons with Mosley would be unavoidable.

I watched from the upper deck as we threaded our way through the town centre, turning right to make the steep ascent of the high street. We got off by the castle gate, across the road from the records office.

My waistcoat felt stiff against my body. Constance had unpicked the liner to create a set of inner pockets. On my right, the pocket held a thin sheaf of leaflets. 'A Jews' War'. The same leaflet I'd seen at the pub. The left pocket bulged slightly. A waxed packet filled with wallpaper paste, and a thin brush. I wore a jacket over the waistcoat, despite the hot day.

It was late afternoon, and the crowds were thinning. People were on their way home, looking forward to their tea. The day's market was over, and the road was littered with discarded leaves from grocer's stalls, and straw and dung from now-dismantled animal pens.

The policeman who'd accosted me and Margaret on my last visit approached me, but thought better of it. I wasn't with Margaret this time, but perhaps he didn't want to risk a dressing-down from the unknown woman by my side.

I'd expected Constance to be furtive. We were committing treason. If we were caught, we'd spend the rest of the war in prison at the least. They were cracking down, that was the word. Before long, there'd be an execution. Keep people in their place. But Constance looked like every other woman striding along the pavement. Nothing out of the ordinary. No worried looks around. She wasn't even sweating, despite her large cardigan.

If anyone was going to give the game away, it was me. My heart was pounding, and I imagined everyone's eyes on me. This was new territory. I've been over the top into the hell of no-man's-land. I've been ten miles behind enemy lines in remote Waziristan. I've walked into a gang headquarters in Hong Kong and walked out the only man standing. But committing treason in my home country was beyond the pale.

We took a side street, a steep hill down towards the railway station. A man walked ahead of us, but he took out his key and let himself into a house. The door closed, and we were left alone.

'The post box,' Constance said.

A red post box, built into the wall, beckoned. I approached it. I was sweating heavily. I could smell the stink rising from my armpits. I was the picture of guilt.

'I'll whistle if anyone's coming,' she said, dropping back.

I reached into the right-hand side of my waistcoat and pulled out a leaflet. 'A Jews' War'.

'Not too much paste,' she said, keeping her voice low. I remembered the leaflets I'd seen in the toilets at the pub, sliding down the painted brickwork. Someone had rushed the job.

From my left inner pocket I pulled out the brush. I held the leaflet back to front against the bulging royal crest on the post box, painted and repainted every ten years. Victoria Regina. Thirty-nine years dead and her ghost still lingered on every street. I smeared paste on the leaflet, turned it round, and pressed it onto the red paint, covering the royal crest, the dead queen watching with disapproval.

Constance whistled. I hurried away from the scene of the crime.

'Walk normally,' she hissed, catching up with me as a young couple passed us in the opposite direction. I tensed as they passed. Were they undercover police agents? I felt the handcuffs on my wrists and imagined the shame Mum and Nob would feel seeing my picture in the paper. Traitor, it would say.

Ten leaflets took two hours and twelve attempts. Two abandoned after too many whistles. We went as far as Anne of Cleves' house, back past the priory, towards the station, finishing up with a loop along the railway. The others had their own sections of town. I listened for police whistles that would tell us someone had been caught. If that happened we were to dump our materials and make our own way home.

By the time we got back to the bus station my neck and shoulders were solid, the stress of the afternoon reaching far into every muscle. I had a splitting headache, and I stank to high heaven.

'It gets easier,' she said to me, from five yards behind, as we hurried across the parking area towards our bus. I made sure nobody was watching and dropped the remains of the waxed paper and the brush in a litter bin. Finally, I felt a lightness I hadn't felt since we'd set off earlier that afternoon.

'Whatever it takes,' Bunny had said. This kind of thing would presumably be a footnote to the kind of things he was up to. If this was his way of waging war, he could keep it. Give me a gun and an enemy who's sworn to kill me, and let me get the job done.

We sat on the bus as it threaded its way back through the country lanes. I risked a look at my co-conspirators. Margaret's hair was blowing in the breeze from her open window. She was as cool as a cucumber. She caught my eye and smiled. She was clearly a lot better at this kind of thing than I was. But that didn't surprise me. Margaret was my better in most ways.

58

Vaughn put a tray of drinks on the table. Pints for the men. Glasses of sherry for the women. We had the saloon bar to ourselves in the early evening. The public bar on the other side of the wooden screen was busier with the usual crowd of farm labourers and Tommies.

Freddie passed out the drinks.

'What's your assessment?' he asked Constance.

'A bit nervy, but we'll make a poster-sticker of him yet,' she said.

I took a deep swallow of beer and for the first time that day felt a settling, a return to reality.

'Will it be in the paper tomorrow?' Margaret asked.

'No,' Vaughn replied. 'They keep it quiet. Doesn't fit in with their version of reality.'

'The news is controlled by the people in power,' Freddie said. 'Don't ever believe anything you read in the paper or hear on the radio.'

Margaret knocked back her sherry and reached across the table for my pint, taking a deep swallow before returning it. I knew how she felt. I finished the beer and rose to get more.

'Anyone else?' I asked, but they ignored me. Freddie was getting onto his high horse, ready to win another debate.

'Every time you hear something on the radio, ask yourself why they're letting you hear it,' Freddie said. It sounded like a well-rehearsed pitch. I stood at the bar waiting for the landlord, and watched Margaret listening to Freddie's lecture. She was glowing. They all were. I knew the feeling well. Returning from a mission, that feeling of having beaten the odds, returning unscathed. The conquering heroes.

I ordered two pints of best, and two shots of whisky, and listened to Freddie while I waited.

'Every news story, ask yourself, if this is true, why do they want me to know it? What do they want me to think, or feel, or do?'

There was a noticeboard behind the bar. A community service, a place for announcements, job postings, government warnings about keeping mum. What to do in the event of an invasion. A new poster stood out.

Behind me, Freddie was getting into his rhythm.

'Imagine it's not the truth,' he continued. 'Why are they lying to me? Either way, with the limited time to tell you what's going on in the whole wide world, why are they choosing these things? What kind of picture of the world are they trying to conjure up? What do they want of me?'

The new poster was a land agent's notice. Sale of property. Victorian villa. Superior craftsmanship. Priced for a quick sale.

At the far end of the bar, someone was watching me. Horace Knight. The land agent. Like a spider, watching his lines for tremors.

He joined me, and paid for my drinks. He could afford it. He'd done well enough out of me in the past, each time I'd added land to my farm.

'Interesting opportunity,' he said. 'Not sure how it would fit in with your operation, but I try to leave the strategic thinking to my clients.'

'An investment,' I said. 'I hear the rental market's heating up. People want to get out of London, avoid whatever's coming.'

'You're telling me,' he said. 'Rents are double what they were a year ago. You could let that place for a pretty penny.'

'Who's the seller?' I asked.

'Davidson's boy.'

'How much do you reckon he'd let it go for?'

'He's motivated to sell. Gambling debts.'

'How motivated?'

Knight sipped his drink. He had to be careful. He was representing the seller, and wanted to get as much for his client as he could. But his main incentive was to sell the place quickly and pocket the commission. If they sold the place for twenty thousand, his one per cent commission would be two hundred. A nice fee but not likely to make or break his year either way. If a buyer knocked him down to fifteen thousand, the sellers would be out by a fortune, but Knight's fee would only be cut by fifty pounds.

'I think he'll go for sixteen,' he said. My estimate had been close to the mark. Kate's father would have spent as much to build the place at the turn of the century, but the economy had been on a wild ride since then.

'When did he take you on?' I asked.

'The day after the mother died,' he said. 'Life goes on.'

'I'll think about it,' I said.

'He said you'd come around,' he said. 'Gave me a message to pass on.'

He smirked as he rummaged in his coat pocket. He'd been holding back, enjoying the power. Treating me like a fool.

He handed me an envelope. Nice paper. Expensive. A relic of the family's past. Grandfather sitting in his study writing important letters to important clients. I opened it. The letter was written in a barely legible scrawl. Three generations, they say, to go from rich man to poor.

The note was a threat. Not particularly intelligent. I could take it to Neesham and it would give him all he needed. But that would be the coward's way out. If a job's worth doing, Blakeney used to say, do it yourself. And this was a job that was well worth doing. The note read:

Your next

The grammatical error blunted the message. Harder to take a man seriously when he lays his lack of intelligence in front of you.

Someone was next, that much was true. But it wasn't going to be me.

Margaret gave me a quizzical look as I took the drinks back to the table. I passed her a pint and a shot and took my place between Constance and Miriam. There was a pregnant pause.

'What did I miss?' I asked.

Everyone looked at Vaughn. He was clearly the one pulling the strings.

'The thing is, Cook,' Vaughn said, talking in a low murmur, 'we reckon there's a higher than fifty per cent chance you're a plant. Sent to egg us on until we're in it up to our necks.'

'Margaret gets a pass, I suppose.'

'We know Mags,' Vaughn said. 'We don't know you.'

'Difficult to prove a negative,' I said.

I drank my beer and looked each of them in the eye, ending with Vaughn.

'You're right not to trust me,' I said. That got Vaughn's attention. He exchanged a look with Freddie.

'People look at me, they see a farmer,' I said. 'Suits my purposes nicely, let's me move about the countryside, talk to people. Keep my finger on the pulse.'

I leant in, and everyone else around the table followed my lead.

'A month ago I was up in London to see an old friend for a pint. Army man. Knows what's really going on. Knows how tenuous the whole thing is, especially since they locked up Mosley.'

I sipped my pint, gave it a long pause for dramatic effect.

'I've been given a job,' I said. 'Keep an eye out for agitators. Report back to the authorities. It gives me access.'

Vaughn nodded.

'I was told to infiltrate your unit,' I said. 'Margaret was the way in. Seduce her, get her to introduce me to you.' I looked at Vaughn. 'There are a lot of people high up in the War Office who'd like to see you brought down a peg or two. You've got them worried. They know if the invasion starts and you're here, you'll be a rallying point for right-minded people.'

Vaughn looked at Margaret.

'She doesn't know,' I said. 'Like I said. I've been using her. Not such an odious task, as you can imagine.'

Margaret got up from her chair. She looked shocked. I doubted she was buying my story. I hoped she wasn't. Hoped this was her acting. If it was, she was doing a decent job.

She slapped me. The crack of it silenced the pub. Acting or not, it hurt like hell.

'Margaret,' Miriam said, getting up from her chair in support. Margaret rushed out of the pub, and Miriam followed.

I watched them go. When the door closed behind them, and the evening's chatter resumed around them, I looked back at Vaughn and Freddie.

Vaughn was hooked. I could see the part about me using Margaret had got into his head. Probably imagining us together. Realising that was over, and she was available.

'We've got an opportunity,' I said. 'I've got no love for the Germans but if it's them in charge instead of us going through another four years of war, that's a price I'm willing to pay. I was there last time. I've seen what war looks like.'

Vaughn leant back, thinking. I had him interested. He'd seen the bait, but he hadn't decided whether or not he was going to bite.

'I know about Aspidistra,' I said.

Vaughn couldn't hide his reaction. He was hooked. Now I just had to reel him in.

Freddie still had his doubts. 'And we're just meant to believe you're willing to turn traitor?' he asked.

'I'm not a traitor,' I said, giving it some edge. 'I'm a patriotic Englishman. I love this country and I'll do what it takes to protect it. Like I said, I don't care who gets to sit in Downing Street, but I'll do whatever I can to stop my farm and others like it turning into wastelands like the Somme. If you want to get into Aspidistra, you've got a decision to make. Keep listening to fences, or take a punt.

'You know where it is?' Vaughn asked.

'I've been inside,' I said. 'I can show you.'

59

Kate's house was dark. The barns round the back sagged under blackened thatch. I forced the door into the smaller barn.

There was an abandoned log pile in a dark corner. It smelt of mildew. I kicked a log and my foot sunk into it, like pressing on a sponge. A thick rat's tail disappeared into the darkness. I was about to give up when I found what I'd been looking for. An ash handle, a foot long, grey with age. I grabbed it and pulled. The hachet came away from the log without any resistance. The blade was brown with rust. It would do.

I left the note on the front door at eye level, held up by the hachet, buried an inch deep in the oak door. A promise, and a challenge.

Your next.

★

I stopped on the way home, outside a small, dark cottage on Snatt's Road. I sat in the van. Kate's housemaid was as much a victim of Victor as the Leckies were. It would be wrong to involve her.

While I wrestled with my conscience, the front door opened. The maid ran out, pulled at the passenger door of the van, and climbed in.

We sat in silence. I turned off the ignition and the engine ticked as it cooled.

'He's coming for me,' she said. 'After he's sorted you out. We're going north. He's got a friend in Letchworth. Says he can get him a job in a factory.'

'Why?' I asked.

'Money,' she said. She thought more. 'Pride.'

'Do you want to go with him?'

She shook her head.

'I've been looking for someone to do for us,' I said. 'Know anyone?'

'What's the pay?'

'Board and lodging. Two bob a week.'

'Three.'

'Two and six. If you're a good worker we'll see about a raise at Christmas.'

'All right.

The silence returned. It didn't bother me, and I got the sense it didn't bother her either. She was used to living quietly.

'What about him?' she asked.

'You won't hear from him again,' I said.

'How do you know?'

'I know,' I said.

60

I sat in the kitchen, watching the clock. Half eleven.

I'd known countless men like Victor. Behaviour determined by their experience. I knew exactly how the evening would play out, down to the minute. I could have written it out in a script, like one of Bunny's Elstree screen writers.

It went back to a domineering grandfather. A man whose intellect and sense of control over his surroundings had allowed him to claw his way up through the hierarchy. From a slum in South London to a custom-built villa in Sussex. A solicitor. A man of means, recognised as such.

A daughter brought up to inhabit the new position. Educated in the new fashion. Married well. As shrewd as her father.

Two sons, in a house without a father, shouldering a grandfather's constant disappointment. A childhood of never living up to expectation. Never understanding the quips. Grandfather's books in the library untouched. The end of the line. Great expectations unmet. The only consolation being bigger than the other boys in the playground. A sense of power.

An easy life after school, riding out the remains of grandfather's money. Drinking away the inheritance every night. Cock of the walk amongst the old schoolmates who started their working lives at the bottom of a slippery ladder.

Watching those mates climb their ladders. No longer apprentices. No longer impressed by grandfather's money, making their own way in life.

The grandson finds a woman he can dominate. He looks for a shortcut to money. It doesn't go as he expects, and now he's in the hole to people who don't care about his grandfather's name. The power he felt when dominating the weaker boys in the playground a distant memory.

The clock ticked on.

He'd spend the night in the pub, the place he felt safest, but surrounded by men he resented. Drinking more than usual. Working up the courage to take action. His gambit had failed. He'd scraped together money to pay a deserter to do his dirty work, but the work was left only two-thirds complete. The man was still out there, the one who hurt him, who put his arm in a cast. The farmer who thought he was better than everyone else. The farmer who'd got above himself. Made money off everyone else's misfortune, while honest hardworking men were sliding backwards.

Twenty to eleven, the bell for last orders, he'd get a couple more drinks. Dutch courage.

Closing time at eleven. The landlord going through the motions, turning the lights on, sweeping up the cigarette butts. He'd nurse his drink.

Twenty past, they'd kick him out, not bothering to hide the exasperation. Ten years of this, the camaraderie long gone.

Eighteen minutes' walk from the pub to the farm. He'd take a wrong turn after The Rocks, that path that leads off towards the lake. He'd realise his mistake, the humiliation and rage building.

Twenty to twelve, crossing the field, the farm in his sights. Give it 'til midnight, he'd think to himself.

A siren started up, its long wind-up by now a familiar part of the night. A change to the script.

Hurried footsteps on the stairs heralded Frankie's arrival, bursting into the kitchen, his hair tousled from sleep. Elizabeth followed behind. Frankie reached for the shotgun but Elizabeth, the taller of the two, got to it first.

'In the cellar,' I said. 'I'll get Mum.'

Uncle Nob lay in his bed, eyes screwed up tight. Mum held his hand.

'I'll stay with him,' she said.

Pom pom pom pom. The Bofors gun fired. It wasn't a drill.

61

The farmyard was dark. No moon. No stars. I pulled the kitchen door closed behind me, fastening the latch as quietly as I could.

The siren was louder outside, carrying across the fields from its position on top of the telephone exchange.

I'd left the family undefended. If Victor got his own way, I'd be dead in minutes and they'd be vulnerable. The odds of that outcome, though, were one in a million. Me against a drunk man with a broken arm.

I crossed the yard, almost completely dark, and took up a position with my back to the barn, where I could watch the house and the main approaches. If he came from the road, he'd come into the yard from my left. If he came across the fields, he'd come into the other end of the yard, to my right. He'd have his eyes on the house, and I'd be behind him.

Pom pom pom pom, the gun firing again. I heard the tell-tale distant rumble of a bomber, not yet visible on the horizon, where the South Downs stood guard.

I slapped my cheek. It felt like a bee sting. A long splinter, jagged wood protruding an inch from my face. The crack of the rifle shot caught up with the bullet, and I dropped to the ground. He'd missed, but only barely.

I rolled to my left, movement essential now he'd had a chance to calibrate. The second shot thumped the oak door where I'd been only a second before.

Fast fire, calm, professional. Someone who'd been trained with the rifle. Someone whose pulse wasn't raised by the prospect of another killing.

I'd miscalculated. Victor had come to finish things. But he hadn't come alone.

Pom pom pom pom. The Bofors gun again. The women getting faster at their routine. Aim, fire, reload.

A metallic crack from the concrete – another near miss. If I didn't move, I was a second or two away from the end of my life. I've seen men freeze. Pretend it wasn't happening. But not me. Something I've learnt about myself. The greater the threat, the greater the pressure, the calmer I get.

The next shot was even closer. I rolled to the protection of the water trough, in the middle of the yard. As I rolled, I saw Victor, standing by the front gate, watching his hired hand do the job he'd paid him to do.

If I was going down, I'd take Victor with me. I pulled myself to my feet and ran towards him, towards the front gate. I was in the open, a clear black shape against the yard and the road. The air beside me fizzed as a bullet whipped past. Close. Victor ducked and yelled. His hired man was now shooting towards him.

I could hear the bomber now, quite clearly, this side of the Downs, heading north. Towards my farm.

A crash of old milk pails told me the shooter was on the move, trying to get a diagonal so he could shoot at me without taking out his paymaster.

Victor pulled out a revolver. I was still ten yards from him, running. Every step closer to him I was a bigger target. He held out the gun, hand shaking, cocked the hammer. A sequence he'd seen in the flicks. *Gunfight at the O.K. Corral* and all the rest. If he did it fast enough, and held his aim, I was a dead man.

I lunged at him, towards the gun. I swiped the gun from his hand and it clattered away on the concrete, his arm bending outwards, the break giving way entirely. He screamed in pain and rage and swung at me with his left hand, knife blade flashing in the dim light.

I darted back. He came at me, and I moved back further, my foot tripping on something. I went down, and he took his chance, dropping onto me and raising the knife to plunge into my heart.

Heavy boots, running fast, echoed across the yard, closing the distance to me.

It was Milosz. He had a weapon in his hand. A wood axe from my log pile.

Behind him, filling the sky, the bomber cleared the trees at the far end of Dadswell's Flat.

Milosz swung the axe. It took Victor in the chest with a wet crunch, and he went down, falling to my side.

The bomber roared overhead, on the same path as before. South to north, heading for the Forest.

A bullet cracked past us. Now the paymaster was down, there was nothing to stop the sniper from firing. But he was shooting too far left. The next shot was closer, hitting the gatepost, a yard from my left.

We were exposed, with a skilled sniper zeroed in on our position. A matter of seconds. I nodded my thanks. Milosz had saved my life. Now we'd die together.

The next shot rang out. A different sound, familiar on the farm. A shotgun. Followed by another blast. The second barrel.

Then it was quiet, the roar of the bomber subsiding, the air-raid siren winding down.

I walked to the middle of the yard, where I had the best view of the northern sky. Just in time to see a parachute drop from the plane.

'You brought help,' I said, nodding towards the source of the gunfire.

'No,' Milosz said. 'Just me.'

★

I found the sniper on the ground by the milking shed. He was dead. A shotgun blast to the side, and one to the head, point-blank range, just to be sure.

Elizabeth was in the kitchen, the shotgun back in its place. She had her back to me, but I could see she was shaking.

'Well done,' I said. She stood in the doorway. A girl who'd had her childhood stolen from her.

I knew I should go to her, but I didn't know how. Margaret would have comforted her, but Margaret was with Vaughn.

She hurried upstairs.

★

Milosz stood by Victor's body, smoking a cigarette.

'We can bury him in the woods,' I said.

'No,' he said. 'Look after the girl. Besides, better you don't know where, in case anyone ever asks.'

'What if they ask you?'

'I'm not here,' he said. 'I'm not even in this country.'

Victor moaned. The wood axe protruded from his chest. It swayed as he shifted on the ground. I knelt by him, in a lake of blood and dust.

'Why the Leckies?' I asked.

'Paid,' he said.

'You paid?'

He shook his head.

'Vaughn Matheson. Paid.'

62

I drove up to the Forest, once again following the path of the bomber. This time, though, I knew where I was headed.

I parked under the old redwoods. Vaughn's house was dark from this side, but I heard voices. Vaughn and Freddie.

I walked round to the back of the house, overlooking the Forest.

'Stop,' Vaughn said, laying down his end of what looked like a coffin. They were halfway up the steps to the terrace.

'Who's there?' Freddie asked. He was at the bottom of the steps, and had the view up towards the house. He had a bundle of silk over his shoulder. A parachute.

'Looks like you could use a hand,' I said, stepping out of the shadows of the house.

★

We laid the casket on the terrace. It was metal. Its corners were rounded, and it had several loops on the upper edge. Each loop was connected to a metal clip, and each metal clip was fastened to a length of rope. Some kind of harness. The ropes had been cut several feet from the ends.

The underside of the coffin was crusted with sand, from where it had bedded itself into the ground.

'Father Christmas come early?' I asked, as Freddie busied himself undoing the clasps. He looked like he knew what he was doing.

'Gift from the gods,' he said, looking up at the dark sky.

Freddie busied himself unbuckling a set of clasps along the side of the coffin, giving a grunt of effort with each one. It was well engineered. Designed to withstand a hard landing without springing open.

'You had the Leckies killed,' I said to Vaughn.

'What's it to you?' he replied.

'She was my first teacher,' I said. 'A long time ago. And I liked her.'

'I hated my teachers,' Vaughn said.

'Does that tell us more about them, or about you?' I asked.

Freddie looked up at us, but kept going with his work. He unclipped the last fastener, and the lid of the coffin rose slightly. It had been tightly packed.

Freddie pulled open the lid with a flourish. He picked up his oil lamp so we could see what was inside.

'What do you think?' he asked.

'I think Vaughn owes me an explanation,' I said.

'I thought you were with us,' Vaughn said. 'All that stuff about turning double agent. But you keep on about the blasted Leckies. Makes a man think you're not on his side.'

The coffin lay open like a clamshell. Both sides were full. The top half was guns. There must have been a dozen automatic weapons, packed head to toe like sardines in a can. I didn't recognise them. That in itself wasn't remarkable – it had been sixteen years since I'd left the army. A lot had changed. But I didn't think these guns had come from one of our factories. Next to the guns were a set of grey, metal canisters, printed with dense text that I couldn't read. Ammunition, I assumed.

The bottom half was covered with canvas, kept in place with studs. A couple of the studs were opened, and Freddie grabbed the canvas and pulled it up. The rest of the studs popped loose, and Freddie peeled the canvas back. Underneath, the coffin was packed with what looked like cloth-wrapped bricks. Each one was the size of a small bag of flour. Freddie took one out and threw it to me. I caught it. It was a dense material with a slight give. It made a crinkling sound as I squeezed it. I peeled back the cloth. Inside the cloth was another wrapper made up of some kind of waxed paper. I ripped the paper. It was what I'd expected. Yellow putty. TNT.

'What's this lot for?' I asked. Safer to talk about guns and explosives than about the Leckies.

'The fight for peace,' Vaughn said.

'You could make a fair amount of peace with that lot,' I said.

63

The squirrel sat on the stone balustrade, eating an acorn. Twenty yards from our party. He didn't seem bothered by us.

We made quite a shooting party. Me and Margaret, Vaughn and Miriam, and Freddie.

I'd shown them how to load and fire a revolver. Freddie was waving his towards the squirrel.

'Don't!' Miriam said, putting her hand on his arm.

'Nothing to worry about,' I said. 'The thing about a hand-gun, it's useless for accuracy, no matter what the gunfighters do in the pictures.'

'Useless for you perhaps,' Freddie said, fancying himself a marksman.

'Freddie . . .' Miriam said. I shared her feeling. This was a mistake, letting the training session become some kind of social affair.

Freddie stood sideways, the way he'd seen gunfighters stand in the movies. Billy the Kid. Annie Oakley. The kind where the sharp-shooter could hit a coin at a hundred yards.

'Don't, Freddie,' Miriam pleaded. She was excited, though. It was the guns. I'd seen the effect before, on people who hadn't been on the receiving end, who hadn't yet learnt that the world would be a better place if all the guns were melted and turned into plough shares.

'Don't worry,' Vaughn said. 'He's got as much chance of hitting that as I have of becoming King.'

Freddie squinted. I'd taken him through the basics. Squeeze the trigger, prepare yourself for the recoil. I'd laid it on a bit thick. Wanted to let Freddie know that this wasn't a toy. He was probably expecting his arm to fly backwards, the kind of kick you'd get from a shotgun.

He fired. The squirrel, unmolested, dropped its acorn and ran along the balustrade, leapt into a tree and disappeared.

'Let's see you do better,' Freddie said to Vaughn, who took the gun and checked the chamber.

'What am I aiming at?' Vaughn asked, squinting into the morning sun. In his shirtsleeves and braces, he looked like he'd rolled out of bed.

'As I said, with a gun like this, aiming is going to get you killed. I want you to practise drawing the gun, and firing forwards as soon as you can. The only way to make sure you kill a man with a handgun is to stand so close you're touching him, and make sure you get your shot off first.' These were things I'd learnt through experience, in the trenches, and in the crowded alleys of Hong Kong.

Vaughn ignored me. He strolled over to the balustrade and put down his teacup.

'That's Mummy's best china,' Miriam said.

'It's all right,' Freddie said. 'He won't hit it.'

Vaughn didn't comment. His standing as lord of the manor was suddenly at stake.

He fired. A stone chip flew off the balustrade, and I winced, anticipating a ricochet.

'Nice try,' Freddie said.

Vaughn wasn't finished. He cocked the gun again, aimed and fired. No stone chip this time. He was rattled, and his aim was only going to get worse. He fired again, and again, but the family china was safe.

Margaret stood up, exasperated.

'Give it here,' she said to Vaughn. He handed her the gun carefully, making sure to point it away from her.

'The bullets come out the other end,' Freddie quipped, as Margaret took the gun.

She ignored him, and cracked open the gun, peering down the barrel. She flipped open the chamber and emptied the shells into her hand, then flipped it closed again. She pointed the gun into the air and dry fired it three times. Click click click.

'It helps if you put the bullets in,' Freddie said.

'Thanks,' Margaret said, as she opened the chamber again and fed in one shell. She closed the chamber and aimed at the cup.

She fired, and the cup disintegrated. She winked at me, and turned to Freddie.

'Bombay shooting club,' she said. 'Gold rosette, three years in a row.'

'Miriam, get another cup,' Freddie said excitedly, now the gauntlet had been laid down.

While the others played with the gun, Vaughn nodded to me and strolled away from the group. I joined him at the far end of the terrace. He looked out across the Forest.

'We've got a job to do,' he said, keeping his voice low. 'Aspidistra.'

"When?' I asked.

'As soon as possible,' he said. 'I'm getting pressure from the top. If I don't show some results soon, they're going to send someone to get things moving.'

'Who would they send?'

'Let's not find out.'

64

Vaughn crawled to me through long grass, keeping his head down. His face was blacked, and he wore a black outfit.

He held up one finger – one sentry – and pointed towards the trees. I made a circle with my thumb and forefinger. OK.

I'd spent the afternoon teaching them how to approach a building in the dark, communicating silently. Eventually I'd relented, said they were ready.

I pointed to him, and made a lateral gesture, ordering him to move out to the side. We would flank the sentry.

As Vaughn crawled away, I listened carefully for signs of the rest of the group. The wind was loud in the trees, coming from the south, instead of the west. Rain on the way.

I crept forwards, moving as slowly as I could. I'd impressed upon each person that in the pitch dark of a moonless sky, the only way we'd be discovered was by making a sound while moving.

I froze. A sound from twenty yards ahead. A branch, pushed aside, leaves swishing as it sprung back. Possibly a deer, picking its way through the undergrowth. Most likely the sentry Vaughn had seen. I'd have to be careful. I'd told Vaughn to go around, then gone straight forwards myself. A certain level of hubris, I had to admit to myself. A feeling of invulnerability. I was the expert in this situation, and I was on home turf. But that was the kind of thinking that got men killed. And if I was going to get taken out, I'd be damned if it was in front of Vaughn and chums.

I pushed through the grass, an inch at a time, pausing every second to listen. Vaughn was on my right. He was doing his best impression of stealth, but it still sounded like a man trying not to make too much noise. He'd brought me into the unit to teach them, he'd said, but he didn't want to learn from me. Generations of breeding and behaviour had given him the rock-solid assurance that a gentleman had nothing to learn from a farmer.

Vaughn was master of his own destiny. I'd given him the information, but only he could decide what to do with it. If it got him killed, that was up to him.

There was something ahead. A patch of darkness below a tall pine changed shape. A subtle shift. I froze, watching the darkness with my peripheral vision, where the sensitivity to light is greatest. Vaughn made another sound, and the shadow shifted again. If nothing else, Vaughn was going to be useful as a decoy.

I waited for the shadow to move from the safety of the tree. I got to my feet but stayed in a low crouch. If the sentry turned, he'd be less likely to see me if I was close to the ground.

The sentry moved quickly. There was a quiet snap of a holster guard being undone. The whisper of metal on leather, a gun being drawn.

I hurried behind the sentry, and as I did Vaughn moved in the far undergrowth. I pulled my knife. Saving Vaughn wasn't my primary consideration, but if I could reach the sentry before he pulled the trigger I'd keep the advantage of silence.

Vaughn saw the sentry. He broke cover and ran towards the house that loomed beyond the trees. The sentry sprinted after him, and I followed them both.

244 *Stephen Ronson*

I gained ground on the sentry and went with a rugby tackle. Unsubtle, and noisy, but the best way to make sure. Arms wrapped around legs, no further movement possible, we crashed to the ground.

Vaughn reached the house unharmed.

'I did it!' he shouted.

The sentry rolled over. She pushed me off.

'You should have let me get him,' Margaret said. 'Would have taught him a lesson. He'll be unbearable now.'

Our final training exercise. I wanted everyone to try their hand at penetrating a target at night, using stealth and the cover of darkness.

'We'll take him down a peg or two tomorrow,' I said.

'I heard you, by the way,' she said, as she picked herself up, brushing pine needles from her knees. 'You breathe like an elephant.'

'How do elephants breathe?'

'Loudly.'

'Any of the others make it through?'

'Just Vaughn.'

Vaughn made his way over, the conquering hero.

'Good job,' I lied. If this had been a real mission we'd all be dead, or captured. Nobody was ready. We weren't operating as a team, we were a group of individuals out for a lark.

'Does the victor get a kiss?' Vaughn asked Margaret. He pulled off his balaclava and wiped his face, smearing the blacking.

'You'll be lucky,' she said.

'I'm going to win you over, Mags, you see if I don't,' Vaughn said.

He slapped me on the shoulder.

'We're ready,' he said. 'I can feel it.'

'One more thing,' I said. 'Tomorrow. First thing.'

65

The sky was black over the Downs, a solid line as if an artist had slashed a paintbrush across the canvas. Alarms rang out. Church bells rang. Codename Cromwell – the day we'd all known was coming. The invasion was happening.

I sprung from the bed, heart pounding, sweat pouring from my body. It was pitch-black. Only the alarm remained.

I slapped the clock, and sat on the end of the bed, trusting that the panic would pass. I breathed, slowly, in and out. In and out.

There was no invasion, I told myself. Not yet. I still had time.

'What time is it?' Margaret asked. She didn't sound put out at all. Had she even been asleep?

'Four,' I said.

'I'll drive down the road and come back,' she said. 'Don't want Vaughn thinking we spent the night together.'

She kissed me, her hand on my cheek where she'd slapped me.

'You didn't hold back,' I said.

'If a job's worth doing . . .' she said, with a grin.

★

A pair of headlights wobbled in the distance as a car made its way along the lane to the farm. I stood in the cool morning air, waiting. Bill Taylor joined me. He'd gone home for the night, liked to sleep in his own bed, but now he was here, ready for the day. It would be the most important day in our year. Make or break.

After months of dry weather, the forecast had suddenly changed. A storm was blowing in from the Atlantic. Twenty-four hours before it arrived, if we were lucky.

Two hundred acres of wheat needed harvesting. Yesterday had been too early. Too much moisture in the stalks. Many of my neighbours had blinked in the face of the oncoming storm, cut their corn even though they knew better. Give it a day and their stooks, bundles of wheat gathered together across their fields, would be steaming, generating enough heat to destroy what had taken half a year to grow. But at least they'd got it harvested, they'd be telling themselves as they rode out across their fields, watching the tell-tale wisps of smoke and praying for rain. Maybe they'd get lucky. Maybe their moisture content was all right. Today they'd be watching the sky as the clouds rolled in, hoping it would arrive before I could get the harvest done. Nothing more pleasing to a man who's made his own mistakes than seeing his neighbour getting his comeuppance.

The peaceful morning was broken by the throaty cough of the tractor turning over. It fired, then roared. Seconds later, it rolled out of the barn, cracking pebbles under its thick tyres, Elizabeth at the wheel. Bill Taylor had tied a cushion onto the seat so she could see over the steering-wheel. I saluted her, and she nodded. If you'd told me back in November when we planted the seed that come harvest I'd have a twelve-year-old girl in the driving seat, I'd have said you were crazy.

The car pulled into the yard, Vaughn at the wheel, excited as a schoolboy on his way to the beach. Miriam climbed out.

Her walking stick was gone, and I hoped her recovery was complete. A long day in the fields would test her, and the last thing I needed was to lose a pair of hands halfway through the day. Freddie slumped in the back seat, asleep under a pile of coats.

Behind them, the lane was filled with people, here to help. Bill Taylor had put the word out that we were paying twenty shillings a person for the day's work. Good money that for many would help keep the wolf from the door.

Margaret's car threaded its way through the labourers. Vaughn saw it. He smirked.

It would be a long day, but if the weather played along, we'd get the job done.

66

We put in three hours before breakfast. Elizabeth drove the tractor, towing the binder with its big wheel of cutting blades. Each blade cut and scooped up an armful of wheat, and dropped it onto a chute. Inside the chute, the machine bundled the wheat and tied it, before spitting it out. One of Bill Taylor's inventions. I kept a close eye on Elizabeth. Letting her drive at this critical time was a risk. Bill Taylor had argued she was ready. Watching her now, I realised he was right. She did a fine job, kept to straight lines a veteran ploughman would be proud of. The rest of us followed behind, picking up the bundles and stacking them into stooks – small pyramids, six feet across, ready to be carted away.

Most of the day-labourers from Uckfield knew what they were doing. It was all new to Vaughn and his lot, of course. Not on the syllabus at Eton, or whatever Swiss finishing school Miriam had been sent to. But they were quick learners, give them their due. Bill Taylor had given a tutorial – shown them all the technique, hold the wheat upright, slam it into the ground, build the stooks every ten yards until the whole field was covered with them. Even if the rain arrived tonight, once the corn was in stooks, it would weather the storm. We could stack it later on, once it had dried again.

The first field was rough around the edges. A lot of stray wheat on the ground from bundles that broke apart under inexpert handling. A number of stooks falling over. Bill Taylor followed behind, always ready with another lesson or a sharp word, each as required. If the man from the War Ag had been there, he'd have given us a black mark. But we were moving along at a good clip. Not letting perfection get in the way when good enough would do.

Breakfast was at eight, and everyone was ready for a break. The novelty had long worn off. Freddie was in short sleeves already, and his arms were a mess of scratches from the unforgiving stalks. Bill Taylor drove the van out into the field, loaded up with provisions. Everyone settled into their own groups, eating and talking. I sat with Vaughn, Miriam, Freddie and Margaret, on a blanket set out on the headland, the grassy piece of ground next to the hedge that had been left unplanted. No point wasting good seed where the tractor would be making its turns. Frankie poured us tea, doing the rounds. It was good to see him at home in the fields, doing his bit.

Elizabeth ate her breakfast in the driving seat, up in the tractor.

'How much more?' Vaughn asked.

'Eight or nine hours, if the rain holds off,' I said. We'd been working for three. I watched them as it sunk in. I wanted to see their reactions. If I was going into any kind of action with this lot, I wanted to see how they handled a bit of adversity. Nothing like farming to tire a man out, and test his endurance, mental as well as physical.

'The rain will delay the invasion,' Vaughn said. 'Their first step will be to bomb our airfields. You can't do precision bombing if you can't see the targets through the clouds.'

'What does the forecast say, Bill?' I asked. I wanted to remind Vaughn that he wasn't surrounded by fellow travellers. He'd have to watch what he said.

'Two days of rain, then the clouds pass and a week of fine weather,' Bill Taylor said.

'Two days,' Vaughn said. 'Then it's *Adler Tag*.'

'Adder Dog?' Frankie asked, spilling tea on the ground as he looked up. I'd been teaching him about some of the local wildlife. He was desperate to see an adder, the only poisonous snake in Britain. I'd told him its bite wouldn't kill him, but I could tell he didn't believe me.

'*Adler Tag*,' Vaughn repeated, relishing his role as school master. '*Adler* means eagle. And *Tag* means day.'

'What language?' Frankie asked.

'German,' Vaughn said.

'Lord Matheson's been listening to too much of our friend Lord Haw-Haw,' I joked, but Frankie wasn't convinced. He backed away, keeping a wary eye on Vaughn.

*

The day went as days do when you have a seemingly insurmountable task in front of you, but you keep at it slowly and steadily. After breakfast we moved on to Dadswell's Flat, the largest field. Elizabeth, sitting regally on her tractor, cut down the golden wheat one strip at a time, and we followed behind, bent to our tasks. Conversation dropped off, and every man and woman found their rhythm. Each one of us found the satisfaction of doing a worthwhile job that needed doing.

I'd been worried about Margaret and Miriam, society women who'd been raised to believe that everything they ever wanted would be brought to them on a silver platter, but they were doing their bit. Margaret worked in a slow, steady manner, every sheaf impeccable with hardly any loose straw left in her wake. She caught my eye, realising I was watching her, and grinned. Miriam had a different style. Every step was hurried, and she zigzagged across her patch like a spaniel hunting a bird. She left quite a trail of missed corn. We'd be down a sack or two of grain by the end of the field. But still an invaluable pair of hands. Miriam had discarded her cardigan as soon as the sun had cleared the trees, and her shoulders were getting pink. She'd unbuttoned the top few buttons of her blouse, and as she bent to pick up the corn I realised I was far from the only man in the field watching her.

Freddie joined me, lighting a cigarette.

'Uncanny, isn't it?' he said. 'They could be sisters.'

Miriam and Margaret shared a joke as they crossed in the field. Margaret sensed us watching, and she gave a wave.

Freddie was right. I'd noticed it the first time I saw them together at Vaughn's party, but since then I'd got used to it and stopped seeing it. Margaret and Miriam moved differently, and came at their work in their own unique ways, but when it came to physical appearance they were like peas in a pod.

'Makes you wonder what's going through Vaughn's mind,' Freddie said, 'the way he goes after Margaret like a dog after a bone.'

I ignored him, and looked away from Miriam and Margaret. I had a whole field of people to keep an eye on.

'I reckon you could get them both in the sack at the same time, if you played your cards right,' he said.

I started to tell him to keep his foul mouth shut, but he grinned. He had a disarming way of being insulting while not being hateful. It made it hard to take against him.

'No smoking,' I said. 'This whole field could go up.'

Freddie weighed the ups and downs of picking a fight. He flicked his half-smoked fag into the stubble.

'Yes, sir,' he said, giving me a wink.

I followed the arc of the cigarette and ground it out. I turned back to him, ready to tell him off for being a fool, but he was already ambling away, back to his place in the line.

67

The river snaked its way through the lower meadow. At some points it was only ten feet across, the cow parsley growing on either bank almost touching in the middle.

Here, at a broad oxbow, it widened. The far bank was twenty yards away, shadowed by a willow that leant over the water.

Freddie landed with a splash and a yell. He surfaced with a whoop, entirely unabashed about being naked in front of a mixed crowd.

'Beautiful!' Freddie yelled. 'Come on in!'

The day had gone well. Bill Taylor was paying off the locals, many of whom would be heading straight for the pub. Freddie had hit on the idea of jumping into the river and wouldn't let up until I relented. If he wanted to act like a pup, I couldn't see the harm in it.

Vaughn pulled off his shirt.

'Look away, ladies,' he said, as he pulled off his trousers and underwear. He picked his way through a patch of nettles on the bank and launched himself into the water with a shout.

'You're next, Cook!' Freddie shouted, as he trod water in the middle of the channel. Vaughn swam across to the far side, disappearing under the canopy of willow.

I didn't fancy the nettles, so I walked upstream twenty yards to the bridge. In former years we used it to get the cattle across to the meadows on the other side. We'd got rid of the herd last year, on government orders, but the bridge was still caked with dried cow dung. I pulled off my shirt and draped it over the railing, giving the sweat-soaked back a fighting chance of drying out while I was in the water.

'Cover your eyes, Miriam,' Margaret said, putting her hand in front of Miriam's face. I stripped off quickly and leapt from the bridge. Too late, I hoped the river was deep enough. The last time I'd done this was as a boy, more than thirty years ago.

The water was cool and clear, colder in the depths. I surfaced to laughter and applause from Margaret and Miriam.

'You've got quite the following,' Vaughn said, swimming back to the middle of the channel.

'Don't mind him, he's jealous,' Freddie said, floating further downstream. 'Cook, this is glorious. I feel like I could swim for miles. Where does this go?'

'Where all rivers go,' I said.

'You mean I could swim to the sea?'

'You might draw a bit of attention swimming through Lewes like that,' I said.

I looked up to Margaret but she and Miriam were gone. I could hear them, giggling and shushing.

'Keep still, you'll have us over!' Margaret snapped. I swam upstream to the shadow of the bridge. The women were negotiating the rather tricky process of getting into the rowing boat we kept moored to a rotting old dock on the far side of the bridge. Bill Taylor sometimes used it for fishing, or to inspect the inlets to our drainage ditches where wooden boards kept the river out until we wanted to flood the meadows.

Margaret was already on board, and Miriam had one foot on land, one in the boat. She hopped in, and collapsed on the seat, as the small craft settled.

Margaret tried to use the oars in the rowlocks, but it was clearly a new experience for her. She pushed on the right oar and the boat started to rotate.

As the boat drifted downstream, Vaughn circled it.

'That's no fun, girls,' Vaughn said. He grabbed the left oar. 'You'll never cool off up there.'

His weight pulled down the left side of the boat, eliciting a scream from Miriam and a glare from Margaret, who had the look of someone trying to master a new skill. She waggled the oar, but Vaughn wouldn't let go.

'No, Vaughn!' Miriam cried.

'Come on, Cook! Help me get these nymphs into the water!'

Vaughn let go of the oar and circled the boat. He darted in, reached up and grabbed the side, two feet above the water. As he settled back into the water, the weight of his body pulled the side of the boat down, close to capsizing.

I swam backwards, putting some distance between me and the horseplay. If the boat went over, it would flip with a lot of momentum.

'Vaughn!' Miriam cried again. I couldn't tell if she was enjoying herself or not. If she hadn't been Vaughn's sister I would have intervened. Ungentlemanly conduct. As it was, it felt like a private joke, best kept out of.

Miriam stood up. Not the best move in terms of improving her balance.

'Wait!' she said. 'Let me get ready!'

She reached down and grabbed the hem of her dress. With a deft movement, she pulled it up, over her head. She waved it with a flourish, and I looked away as the setting sun shone through her slip, showing every detail of every curve.

'In you come!' Vaughn shouted, as he pushed up on the boat, counter to the way Miriam braced herself. For a second it looked like she might regain her balance, but Vaughn pulled the boat down, and Miriam went over. As she fell, her head hit the side of the boat with a heavy thud. She hit the water with a splash. Then there was silence.

Vaughn swam backwards, putting distance between himself and the boat. He had the decency to look sheepish, ready to receive an earful from his sister the moment she surfaced.

But she didn't surface. Margaret looked at the side of the boat, and held up her hand. It was red with blood.

'She's hurt,' Margaret said.

'What's going on?' Freddie called, swimming back from around the corner, powerful strokes bringing him closer by the second.

'Miriam's playing the fool,' Vaughn said.

'Cook,' Margaret said.

I was already filling my lungs, blowing out until they were empty, until they wouldn't expand any further. I did it again, partly for the oxygen, partly to ready myself for what I might find. I dived.

The water was cloudy. Vaughn's splashing around had stirred up the silt and it was hard to see more than a few feet. The shade from the bridge made it gloomy, and the boat above made it even harder. I swam to the bottom with my hands outstretched, heading for where I guessed she'd gone in.

I felt in the reeds, expecting to see her any second. My lungs were telling me to breathe, and I gave it a count of twenty, before I gave in.

I surfaced as Freddie joined us.

'Where is she?' Margaret asked.

'She's fine,' Vaughn said. 'Swims like a bloody conger eel.'

'Miriam?' Margaret shouted.

I dived again. The shadow of the boat and the cloudy water made it impossible to see. I pulled for the bottom, heading downstream this time. There was a flash of white. I swam towards it and grabbed it, getting a handful of mud along with the fabric.

I slung the sodden material into the boat as I surfaced. Margaret held it up.

'It's her dress,' she said.

68

Vaughn surfaced with a gasp for air. He'd been under the water for an eternity. He looked at us, frantically.

'Bloody girl,' he said. 'Cook. Freddie. With me. We'll start where she went in and work our way downstream. If we're side by side we can't miss her.'

With Vaughn in the middle, anchoring the line, Freddie and I filled our lungs and dived. Our activity had stirred up the silt on the bottom and the water was a soup. I swam to the riverbed, feeling the pressure of the water building as I got deeper.

I ran my fingers in the mud and silt, and let the current carry me downstream. A shape loomed in front of me. Lighter than the mud, catching dull glimmers of what sunlight penetrated down here. My heart pounded, and I fought the desire to shoot to the surface.

I closed the distance to the shape and reached out to touch it, prepared for cold flesh.

Rough stone scraped my fingers. A rock, lighter than the silt, lying there underwater since the beginning of time.

I broke the surface. Freddie and Vaughn were already up, readying themselves for the next dive.

There was a whistle from the reeds downstream. An approximation of birdsong, but not a bird.

'Ready?' Vaughn asked, no longer hiding the desperation in his voice.

'Quiet,' I said.

The whistle called again, and I saw her. Head and shoulders bobbing above the surface, partly hidden by thick reeds, by the river's edge. Vaughn's head snapped around, following the sound.

'You bloody idiot,' he shouted.

Miriam swam out from the reeds, her translucent slip billowing behind her like a parachute.

'Got you,' she said.

'For Christ's sake, Miriam,' Vaughn said. His voice was cold. The game was over.

'What?' Miriam asked.

Vaughn swam to the dock, upstream of the bridge.

'You're a bloody fool,' he shouted.

Margaret was tying up the boat. Vaughn pulled himself out of the water and stood, naked, in front of her. He shook his head as she asked a question. He looked back at Miriam then said something to Margaret. Margaret threw Vaughn his clothes and stood up.

From my position in the water, I couldn't hear what Margaret said to him, but I could see her lips. She was telling him it was his fault. Or was she saying his name? Vaughn, Fault. The same 'f' shape of the lips.

'Fault,' Kate had said as she lay dying. Her last word to me. Except it wasn't my fault, that was my guilt over getting involved in the situation inserting itself into my interpretation.

Freddie swam up to me.

'I'm going to swim down the river,' he said, his teeth chattering in the cold. 'See how far I can get. You with me, Cook?'

'You go, Freddie,' Miriam said, swimming towards us. 'Cook can stay here with me. Make sure I don't drown.'

69

'You've got a nasty cut,' I said to Miriam. She winced as I touched her forehead. Blood flowed from the wound, two inches across. It looked deep, probably needed stitches. 'We need to get something on it. Apply pressure and keep it there.'

I looked around. My shirt was hanging over the railing on the bridge. It was filthy, but it would have to do.

'I've got it,' Miriam said. She'd been treading water, but stopped, and slipped below the surface. When she came back up she had a ball of fabric in her hand. Her slip.

We swam to the shallower water near the bank. I wrung out the slip, and folded it. I pressed it against her forehead and it instantly bloomed red.

'Hold it firmly,' I said. She put her hand on top of mine, trapping it.

'He gets like that if he doesn't get his own way,' she said.

'Vaughn?'

'My darling brother,' she said. 'It's my job to take him down a peg or two. It's the only thing he understands.'

She was shivering.

The cold water had blanched her skin, taking away the sunburn, albeit temporarily. Her shoulders were bruised. I touched them.

'What happened?' I asked.

She lowered herself into the water.

'Nothing,' she said, 'Freddie had me carrying his art supplies across the Forest. Doesn't like to do his own work.'

Her teeth chattered as she talked.

'We need to get you dry,' I said.

'Not yet,' she said, moving closer. I felt her breasts against my chest, her nipples brushing my skin. 'Hold me.'

I put my arms around her and pulled our bodies closer. I was a useful heat source, and nothing more, at least that's what I told myself. Not every part of my body got the message, though, as I responded to the feel of her soft body against mine.

'You *do* want me,' she said. 'A girl does wonder, you know.'

'Don't take it personally,' I said, as she moved against me.

'I intend to take it very personally,' she said. She moved her hands to my bottom and pulled us closer together.

'You know I love Margaret like a sister,' she said, 'but she's not right for you. Not for the long run. She doesn't look at you the way you look at her.'

She kissed me, and moved her hips gently. I lowered my own hands, down her back, letting them slide over her bottom, pulling her close.

She put her hand on my shoulder, and braced herself, then wrapped her legs around my waist.

'Miriam,' I said.

'Our secret,' she said, reaching down to position herself.

I tried to be dispassionate, to weigh the pros and cons.

The pros were immediate. Short-term pleasure, no doubt. A beautiful young woman, an idyllic spot, our secret, nobody would know. And Margaret had practically told me to seduce her. The cons were more abstract. Disappointment with myself, losing control. But disappointment and I were old friends.

'Margaret's with Vaughn,' Miriam said, as she tensed her legs behind my waist, pulling herself onto me. She was warm inside.

She slid up, then down, clenching her bottom, the water allowing her a freedom of movement she wouldn't have on land. She leant back, looking up at the sky, her chest rising to the surface. I bent to her breast, and I saw the bruises again, circling her shoulder. A pattern, like a strap, more defined under her arm.

I remembered Doc pulling back the shirt of the man I'd killed at Kate's house. Checking the shoulder and shaking his head at Neesham. A moment of understanding between them. An important detail.

'How's your leg?' I asked. When I'd first met her, she'd been using a cane.

'Fine,' she said, 'especially with you taking the weight so manfully.'

'What was it like?' I asked. 'Jumping out of the aeroplane, into the darkness?'

Miriam froze, her legs wrapped around me. She looked at me, trying to decide.

She restarted her movements, the decision made, it seemed. She kissed me.

'I don't know what you're talking about,' she said.

'They sent you to find the source of the radio transmissions, but your equipment was destroyed when it landed,' I said. 'So you were stuck listening to fences.'

'It's an interesting theory,' she said. 'But I'm not that exciting.'

She kissed me.

'Lucky you found me,' I said. 'I'll show you Aspidistra, and everyone gets what they want.'

'Except me,' she said. 'You'll go back to Margaret, I know you will.'

*

We walked barefoot across the fields, keeping to the grassy headlands. Fat raindrops plopped to the ground. Black clouds rolled in over the Downs.

'Our secret,' Miriam said, as a distant rumble of thunder gave us notice of the coming storm.

Margaret stood on the horizon, the farmhouse beyond. Vaughn joined her. They watched us. We obviously weren't quick enough for their liking, because Vaughn ran towards us. He held a slip of paper in his hand, and he waved it like it was a winning raffle ticket. A telegram.

There was a boom of thunder, louder than a salvo of artillery, and the rain came on in force. By the time Vaughn reached us, halfway along the hedgerow flanking Dadswell's Flat, it was like we were standing under a waterfall.

'We've got a problem,' Vaughn said, trying to catch his breath.

'What?' Miriam asked. A flash of lightning lit the black cloud from the inside.

'The old man's coming. Tonight.'

A jagged shard of lightning pierced the gloomy sky, reaching down to the tallest oak at the far end of the field. The same instant, a deafening crack, and the lightning branched out, across the line of trees.

'Cook can take us in,' Miriam said. 'He's one of us.'

There was a boom of thunder, and more lightning, multiple flashes building on each other. Vaughn twitched at each boom. I felt it too. We'd survived the trenches, but we hadn't left them behind.

'We'll go in tonight,' Vaughn said, in his best attempt at a command voice. It came out like a man trying to convince himself he knew the right way forwards. I'd heard that tone all too often. Invariably, it meant my men and I were heading into trouble, our lives subordinate to an officer's need to show the world he was a man to be reckoned with.

70

Elizabeth was glowing after her day in the driving seat. She sat taller in her chair.

'You did all right on that tractor,' I said, as Mum handed out plates of sausages and mash. 'Think you might be able to give Bill Taylor a hand ploughing all those fields, now we've got the harvest in?'

Elizabeth shrugged, but her eyes met mine and there was a smile in there, beneath the darkness.

'What about me?' Frankie asked.

'Give it a year,' I said, 'and we'll get you up there too. You both did us proud today.'

Big Ben tolled eight on the wireless, and Mum turned it up.

'Good evening,' the BBC newsreader said. 'Today, Marshal Pétain, the premier of France, signed an armistice with Germany ending all hostilities. We go straight to Number Ten for an address by the Prime Minister.'

The mood in the kitchen changed. For a minute we'd let ourselves forget the war, celebrating the harvest the way farming families had for hundreds, if not thousands of years. Reality came back, through the hissing static of the radio broadcast. I pictured a room of technicians, flicking switches to connect us to Downing Street. Incredible that in a second we would have a direct line from the Prime Minister to our farmhouse kitchen.

'It has come to us to stand alone in the breach and face the worst that the tyrant's might and enmity can do,' Churchill said. 'We await undismayed the impending assault. Perhaps it will come tonight. Perhaps it will come next week. Perhaps it will never come.'

I put my hand on Elizabeth's, expecting her to flinch, but she let it rest there, as we listened to the Prime Minister telling us our world was about to end.

'We must show ourselves equally capable of meeting a sudden violent shock,' he continued, 'or – what is perhaps a harder test – a prolonged vigil. But be the ordeal sharp or long, or both, we shall seek no terms, we shall tolerate no parley; we may show mercy – we shall ask for none. But all depends now upon the whole life-strength of the British race in every part of the world and of all our associated peoples and of all our well-wishers in every land, doing their utmost night and day, giving all, daring all, enduring all – to the utmost – to the end.'

There was a hiss of static, as the radio technicians waited to learn if there was more to the speech. I nodded to Mum and she turned the radio off.

'Well,' I said, 'whether the Germans invade tomorrow, or next week, or not at all, those stooks will have to be brought in and stacked, and the land will have to be ploughed and seeded for next year.'

Elizabeth squeezed my hand, and Frankie nodded. I'd sounded more confident than I'd felt, but I believed what I said. One of the great comforts of farming, compared to soldiering, farmers come and go, but the land remains.

71

The dead-letter drop was a stone next to a small waterfall. One of the many streams that threaded through the undulations of the Forest, running through wet weather or dry, fed by seemingly inexhaustible springs. The locals called the place the Garden of Eden. On a hot day, a pretty place to bring your family for a picnic, sit on the heather and listen to the burbling water. On this stormy night, the swollen stream gushed over the short drop and churned in the receiving pool, making drifts of white foam that clung to the banks.

Bunny had told me to alert him to our coming. It was a critical part of the plan. A weak link. He'd promised they'd check the drop site every couple of hours, day or night, rain or shine. I looked around but didn't see anyone, and didn't fancy my chances. Perhaps they had someone surveilling it from a distance.

My note was brief:

Tonight

I'd rolled the paper and put it in a cigar tube, sealed with paraffin wax.

The rain beat heavily on my hat and my waxed coat. I sounded like a drum, announcing my presence to the whole of the Forest. I took one last look around, and put the cigar tube in the shallow hollow clearly created for the purpose, replacing the sandstone rock on top.

If the note got to Bunny, the plan would work. If it didn't, the whole thing would be over before it got going. I'd be leading a team of Nazi sympathisers into a sensitive military installation, after Churchill had broadcast to the nation that the invasion may come tonight. Everyone would be on the lookout.

72

Three cars sat next to each other, parked under the redwoods. Big, black, expensive.

The front door was open, and undefended, William Washington evidently elsewhere. Voices came from the library and I stopped to listen.

'Get this right and they'll give you Sussex and Kent.'

'What about you?' Vaughn said.

'Hitler's got something else in mind for me.' A different voice. Older. More confident. A man who lived his life with absolute certainty. 'I'll be the King's right hand. The power behind the throne.'

'The King?' Vaughn said.

'The *real* King.'

Footsteps behind gave me warning. I turned to see two men looking at me as if I were a mess the dog had made.

One of the men pulled a gun and levelled it at my chest. He was a giant. Seven foot at least, and thick with muscles. His nose gave him away as a boxer, and his face was vaguely familiar, in the way of someone you might have seen in the back pages of a newspaper. He was dressed in a stylised manner – tight black trousers, a well-fitted black polo-neck sweater, and a thick belt with an oversize buckle. He looked like a film designer's version of a man from the future. I'd seen the look in newsreels. One of Mosley's Blackshirts. Their uniforms a nod to Hitler's SS Stormtroopers.

The Blackshirts had travelled with Mosley to rallies around the country, acting as part bodyguard, part provocation. Every event had ended in violence, a predetermined part of the show.

The second man was dressed identically. He was smaller than me. Wiry. Dark-complexioned, from southern Europe perhaps. One side of his face was cross-hatched with scars, and as he stood in the hall a flick knife appeared in his hand like a magic trick.

'Nice costumes,' I said.

'Is that you, Cook?' Vaughn called from the library. 'Come in, man.'

I gave the Blackshirts a nod. Neither of them put their weapon away, but they didn't frighten me. I knew the type. Foot soldiers. If they'd been smart enough, they'd have been given more responsibility. But they weren't. They were smart enough to get out of bed in the morning and get themselves dressed, but it didn't go much further than that. If it came to it, I'd take them down as I'd taken down so many of their type.

What did they see as they looked at me, in the dusty hall? An aging farmer, dripping on the floor in his sodden rain gear. A nobody. That was fine with me. Under-promise, over-deliver.

Vaughn was sitting by a smouldering fire. Freddie, as usual, hovered in the background, fidgeting with the drinks at the sideboard. In the other armchair, opposite Vaughn, was the visitor.

I recognised him instantly, as anyone in the country would. Lord Lisl Howe, the Duke of Wessex, a vocal supporter of Mosley and the British Union of Fascists, before they were outlawed. A black sheep in the royal family. They said he refused to travel in the same car as his luggage. Not something a gentleman would do. Hence the three cars outside. One for him. One for his briefcase. One for the Blackshirts.

'Vaughn says you're ready to go in,' Howe said, matter-of-fact.

'It's now or never,' I said. In my experience, it was the kind of thing men like Howe liked to hear from their subordinates. Gave them carte blanche to authorise action that would give a rational man pause. It worked on the men as well. A multi-purpose saying. Said when you wanted them to put aside their better judgment. I'd seen it work in desperate situations, and it worked here. Freddie smiled.

'Now,' Vaughn said. 'I'm tired of planning.'

'Where do *you* fit into all this?' Howe asked me, giving me an appraising look.

Freddie hooked his arm around my shoulders. 'If it weren't for Cook, we'd still be pasting up leaflets.'

'What do you get out of it?' Howe asked.

'Same thing we all want,' I said. 'Peace.'

Howe smiled and nodded.

'Correct,' he said. 'But perhaps you want a prize once the dust has settled?'

'Big house like this wouldn't hurt,' I said.

'I'm sure we'll be able to come up with something,' Howe said, pleased he'd got the measure of the man in front of him.

73

Dinner was subdued, Howe's presence as much a dampener on spirits as the storm that lashed the windows. I knew how Vaughn would be feeling. It had happened to me on occasion. You have your unit, and every man knows the other, then a superior officer graces you with his presence, and all every man can do is to watch the minutes tick slowly by.

Howe regaled us with stories designed to show off his inside knowledge of the highest levels of government and royalty. To hear him talk, every time he left home he saw only imbeciles and sycophants. Clearly Howe didn't have any mirrors in his own house.

The war stories got us through dinner, but the tone changed as our plates were cleared for pudding.

'Talk me through the plan,' Howe said.

Vaughn sat up taller in his chair, finally his chance to prove his quality. I willed him to present himself well. The solidarity of the underling when faced with the heavy boot of authority.

'We go in at two,' Vaughn said. 'No moon. Full cloud cover.'

'Who goes in?' Howe asked.

'Me, Freddie, Cook. Miriam.'

'Of course.'

'Margaret.'

'No,' Howe interrupted. 'Lady Margaret can sit this one out. I'll leave one of my men to keep her company.'

'I don't need a babysitter,' Margaret said.

'This isn't a discussion,' Howe said, firmly. 'Margaret stays here. It'll help Sergeant Major Cook keep his head straight. You, too.' He looked Vaughn firmly in the eye. 'I've seen the way you look at her.'

'I insist,' Vaughn said.

'I don't think you understand your situation,' Howe said. 'You've fouled up every aspect of this operation so far. People have been killed. The police are sniffing around. You've got a self-confessed double agent in the midst of your team, a man you know nothing about, and you've left it to the last minute. I can assure you, there are people in Berlin howling for your head. It took all of my diplomatic skills to stop them from sending a team of SS troops to take over the operation. So, are you going to tell me the rest of the plan, or are we going to bicker about whether you get to take your girlfriend?'

As he spoke, the large Blackshirt appeared at the door. He caught Howe's eye, and Howe waved him over.

The Blackshirt whispered in Howe's ear and handed him something. Howe kept the object below the level of the table and looked at it. When he looked up, his face was pale, his jaw quivering with rage.

Howe whispered orders to the Blackshirt, who nodded and left.

'You leave at two,' Howe prompted.

'We've located a house in the woods near Nutley,' Vaughn said. 'We've got a source, telling us there's an underground passage from there to the towers. There's some kind of underground facility beneath the towers. We've traced the route of the passage on a map and we've found a way in halfway along the passage.'

'How reliable's the source?' Howe asked.

'I'm the source,' I said. 'You're right that it's a risk to trust me, but the upside outweighs the downside. If I'm on your side, I get you in. If I'm not, it all goes wrong. But if you don't use me, it'll go wrong anyway. So I'm all you've got.'

'I don't like it,' Howe said.

'We go in,' Vaughn said. 'Miriam confirms it's a radio transmitter—'

'Or not, as the case may be,' Howe interrupted.

'Or not,' Vaughn agreed, 'then we get out, and get a radio signal back to Berlin.'

Howe looked at me, then at Vaughn.

'I've got a couple of extra details,' he said. 'New orders from Berlin.'

'It's too late for new orders,' Freddie said.

Howe looked at Freddie as if one of his servants had offered a strategic opinion.

'I'll let you pass that insight on to Herr Hitler in person, when he's here in a week,' Howe said to Freddie. 'They don't want it going out on the radio. Too many people listening. They want a debrief in person.' As he said this, Howe looked meaningfully at Miriam.

'Impossible,' Vaughn said.

'It's all right,' Miriam said, putting her hand on his.

'There'll be a U-boat half a mile off the coast. You'll need a boat, and someone to row her out there.'

'No,' Vaughn said. 'It's insane.'

'It's war,' Howe said.

'I'll take her,' I said. 'I know the river. I know the defences.'

Howe nodded.

'One more thing,' he said. 'It's no longer a sightseeing mission. It's a demolition job.'

Freddie sat up straighter.

'If it's anything close to what we think it is, we can't risk leaving it operational.'

'We haven't trained with explosives,' I said.

'I'm ready,' Freddie said. 'I've been reading up on it.'

'That's settled then,' Howe said. End of discussion.

He raised his hands from below the table, and I saw what the Blackshirt had given him. A cigar tube. Sealed at one end with wax to keep the water out. The seal had been broken.

Howe put the cigar tube in his inside pocket.

'Ladies, you'll have to excuse us. Gentlemen, we've got an issue to attend to.'

74

The rain was deafening on the leaves, soaking us as we pushed our way single-file through the undergrowth. Me, Vaughn and Freddie, with Howe and the tall Blackshirt leading the way.

Vaughn and the Blackshirt carried battery-powered torches, the Blackshirt shining his on the ground in front of Howe. Freddie and I had to fend for ourselves.

The Blackshirt seemed to know where he was going. He held a rifle slung over his shoulder, like he was on parade. Useful for showing your sergeant major your arms, and nice to look at when you had a hundred men in formation, but not particularly effective in terms of readiness. If I ran, he'd have to swing the barrel off his shoulder, reverse the gun, get his finger in the trigger guard, then aim. I'd be long gone, with fifty feet's worth of ancient oak trees between me and him.

I should have run, but it would have meant abandoning Margaret, and the mission. I assumed one of the Blackshirts had seen me leave the message. They must have known about the drop site. Been watching, just in case.

After all the places I'd fought, all the life-or-death situations, I was walking to my execution in the Sussex countryside. They'd take me far enough from the house to be discreet, put me against a tree, and shoot me.

Perhaps they'd rough me up first. Try to get me to spill the beans on what I was up to. But they wouldn't get anything from me. Let them do their worst. I'd do my bit, even if doing my bit at this point was dying quietly.

We arrived at a clearing, and the Blackshirt pointed his torch to the far side. I assumed that was where he wanted me, up against an old oak. It took me a moment to realise what I was seeing, in the weak light of his torch, through the curtain of rain.

The butler, William Washington, was strung up against the tree, his arms behind him, wrapped backwards around the trunk. He was unconscious, and one of his shoulders was dislocated. His face was bloodied, both his eyes swollen. It looked like someone had used him for batting practice and hadn't held back.

'What's this?' Vaughn asked.

'You've got a mole,' Howe said.

'Impossible,' Vaughn said. 'This man's been with me for years.'

'Saw him going for a walk,' the shorter Blackshirt said, stepping out from behind a tree. He was cleaning a large hunting knife, the kind you'd use to gut a deer. Eight inches of steel.

'Going for a walk's not a crime,' Vaughn said.

Howe took the cigar tube from his inside pocket and passed it to Vaughn. Vaughn tapped it on his palm and a roll of paper slid out. He unrolled the paper. I knew what it said.

Tonight.

'What did he say?' I said.

'I didn't ask him any questions,' the shorter Blackshirt said. 'You hurt a man that much, he'll say anything to make you stop.'

Vaughn looked at Howe.

'What are we doing here?' he asked.

'Killing two birds with one stone,' Howe said. 'In a manner of speaking.'

Washington opened his eyes. He looked at me. I forced myself to meet his gaze. Turning away was a coward's way out. One way or another, this was going to end badly for him. A train of events that had been put in motion the second I'd put the note in the cigar case and left it in the dead drop.

'Cook,' Howe said. 'I'm sure you've been racking your brain trying to think of a way to prove your loyalty to Vaughn. Well, it's your lucky day.'

'Killing him doesn't prove anything,' I said. 'I've killed scores of men for all kinds of reasons. It doesn't give you any indication of my allegiance.'

The Blackshirt tossed me the knife. It spun in the air and I stepped away, letting it land in the leaf litter. I picked it up and cleaned the blade on my sleeve.

'What if I won't do it?' I asked.

'I'll get Vaughn or Freddie to do it,' Howe said. 'You'll be next.'

'Generally, we don't kill prisoners of war,' Vaughn said. 'It's bad form.'

Williams groaned. He shook his head. Nobody wants to die.

I was thinking furiously, trying to run through the options. I could kill Howe and the Blackshirts, overpower Vaughn and Freddie, and free Williams. The right thing to do.

Bunny's voice echoed in my head:

Whatever it takes.

Kill one man to save thousands, or save the man and worry about the thousands later.

'I'll do it,' I said.

I walked to Williams, forcing myself to look him in the eye. I could see confusion on his face. He was trying to work out what the angle was. How I was going to square the circle and get him out of this situation. He thought I was the hero of the story. He thought there'd be a twist. A way for us both to end up running through the woods, the villains hot on our heels, escaping by the skin of our teeth.

He was wrong.

'I've got a wife,' he said, looking into my eyes and seeing what was going to happen.

I could have said I was sorry. I could have told him he was dying for his King, making the world a safer place. I could have told him I'd get a message to his wife. Tell her he'd died bravely. But none of those things would have kept him alive any longer.

'All of you,' Howe said. 'Vaughn, Freddie, Cook. I want three hands on the knife.'

Vaughn and Freddie joined me. Vaughn looked like he was going to be sick. Freddie was vibrating with nervous energy. He smiled at me, his teeth chattering.

'Hands on the knife,' Howe ordered. The Blackshirt who'd led us into the woods took the rifle from his shoulder and cocked the hammer. A theatrical move, but it broke the deadlock.

Vaughn put his hand over mine, on the hilt of the knife.

Freddie didn't need persuading. He put his hand over Vaughn's.

The three of us held the knife, the blade vertical, like a candle, the tip half an inch below Washington's throat.

With three hands on it, the knife had a life of its own. I held it down, but it wanted to rise. Freddie's influence, I suspected.

'Please,' Washington whispered.

'On the count of three,' Howe said. 'One.'

'This isn't right,' I said, quietly. But Vaughn didn't reply. He'd gone somewhere else.

'We've met before,' I said. 'In France. You killed those farmers.'

That got him back. He looked at me as if seeing me for the first time.

'Margaret says you're a good man,' I said. 'I've seen it myself. You're not defined by the worst thing you did.'

'Two.'

Freddie's arm was quivering. I held the knife down. I could keep it there all night if it came to it.

'Wait for my signal, Washington,' I said. He looked at me, a wave of relief flooding across his face. He nodded.

'Three.'

75

The water ran clear from my hands, swirling in the sink. Fine cracks in the old porcelain stained red from the blood. I could let the water run all night and those cracks would still be stained.

The bathroom door opened behind me. I was expecting Margaret. She and Miriam had been kept in the dark. Howe may have been a murderer, but he had a fine sense of decorum.

It was Miriam. She closed the door behind her. It was a cramped space, a small bathroom, carved out of a bedroom when they'd installed indoor plumbing. The wall cut a window in half, a bad design, favouring function over form.

I turned off the tap but kept my back to her. She was as much a part of this as Howe was, as much a part as Vaughn was. As I was, if I was being honest with myself.

'The first jump was the hardest,' she said. 'That was in daylight. They made me do three practice jumps. Apparently, the rate of injuries drops off significantly after the first three. They've done a study. The most common injuries are twisted ankles, second most common broken ankles. Then injuries to the shoulders, when the parachute pulls you back.'

'Must be tricky in the dark when you can't see the ground rushing up at you,' I said. 'Hard to come down smoothly, I'd imagine.'

'Vaughn had a light,' she said, 'but that was for the pilot. Once I was in the air it was pitch black. If you hit open ground you're lucky. If you hit a tree, you're not. Like roulette. I got lucky.'

'Why?' I asked.

'They've got reconnaissance pictures of those transmission towers going up. All those lorries in and out of the place. Slap bang in the middle of the invasion zone. Would you want to be in charge of the invasion and have to tell Hitler it failed because of some secret thing in the middle of your drop zone that you hadn't managed to check out?'

'So you're the key to the invasion?'

'I wouldn't put it like that.'

I looked at my watch. It was half nine.

'When do we go?' she asked.

'Two,' I said. 'Get some rest in the meantime.'

I pushed past her and opened the door. Vaughn was outside, in the corridor, listening.

'Howe's gone,' he said.

I ignored him and strode along the corridor. I had things to do. Vaughn followed me like a puppy.

'Where are you going?' he asked.

'I'm going to sleep,' I said.

'How can you sleep after that?' he asked.

'I've done worse than that before breakfast,' I said. 'And so have you. You do it enough, you stop noticing.'

I left him, standing there in the corridor. He shouted after me.

'I don't believe that, Cook, and neither do you.'

76

I lay on top of the covers, dressed, boots on, wondering where Margaret was sleeping. One in the morning. There'd been lots of movement, stomping along corridors, flushing of toilets, but things had gone quiet. Everyone was trying to sleep, or pretending to.

I got up quietly, and went to the window. The rain had stopped but fat drips fell from the gutters above. I was on the second floor, and my window looked out onto the patio. I could smell honeysuckle, its thick vines covered the back wall of the house.

I had to get word to Bunny. If we went in without advance warning, the whole operation would be over as soon as we met the first sentry, and Howe's orders about it being a demolition job added even more urgency. I was about to lead a team of saboteurs into a site that Bunny believed was pivotal, a slim chance that we might defeat the coming wave.

I climbed onto the window sill. It was awkward, squatting there. The window was eighteen inches wide, not wide enough to get through comfortably. I grabbed a vine on the outside wall and tested its strength. It was as thick as my wrist, its woody fibres twisted like a rope. I tried to pull it away from the wall but it stuck firm. I hoped it took my weight.

I swung out of the window and clung onto the vine. There was a tearing sound. The thick vines were lined with hundreds of tiny roots, each thinner than a piece of string and shorter than a fingernail. A whole section pulled out of the old stone wall and I swayed backwards, putting even more pressure on the remaining roots.

I hurried down the vine, and landed on the patio as softly as I could, outside the glass doors to the library.

Standing on the patio, I had the long sweep of Vaughn's lawns and gardens in front of me, dropping away into the valley that separated his house from the untamed expanse of the Forest. The Forest mirrored the sweep, back up to the far horizon where the clump of trees hid the radio transmitters.

Behind me, a door creaked. I was exposed, on the moon-lit patio. Nowhere to turn.

It was Margaret. She looked behind her and pulled the door closed.

'What if you don't come back?' she whispered.

'Not exactly the confidence boost I was looking for,' I said, keeping my voice low.

'Hope for the best, plan for the worst, isn't that what Blakeney told you?'

She was right.

'Tell them I ran. Tell them you always suspected I was a traitor but you didn't want to believe it. You'll have to help them run the mission. They're amateurs. They'll shoot themselves in the foot before they get halfway across the Forest.'

'Vaughn won't let me go,' she said. 'You heard Howe. I'm the hostage. The princess in the tower.'

'Vaughn will do anything you tell him,' I said, giving her a kiss. 'You're the kind of woman a man likes taking orders from.'

She checked her wristwatch.

'I'll be back in an hour,' I said. A mile each way. Fifteen minutes brisk walk. Time to find Bunny and brief him. Barely.

She kissed me.

'Come back in one piece,' she said. 'A girl could get used to having you around.'

I checked my own watch. I had an hour, maximum. Everything would have to go as planned.

★

I followed the path through the gardens, past ornamental rhododendrons and azaleas, and great clumps of other bushes I couldn't name. I reached the fence at the bottom of Vaughn's lawn, where only days earlier the party had gathered to listen to the German transmission. I bent down to step between the strands of barbed wire, feeling the upper strand catch on my back as I stepped through.

'You want to watch yourself,' a voice said. 'You'll get a nasty scratch. Get lockjaw.'

I climbed out backwards and straightened up. One of the Blackshirts stood in front of me. The giant. I realised where I'd seen him before. Tommy Torson, East End boy turned boxing champion. He had his rifle slung over his shoulder, and he swung it down, slapping it into his palm. He levelled it at my head.

'You should have stuck with boxing,' I said. 'Leave the politics to the gentlemen.'

It was a test. One that could go one of two ways.

If he was an effective sentry, he'd shoot me. No witty repartee, no back and forth. He'd discovered me trying to sneak out. No innocent explanation. Only one way to deal with it. When I was on the rocky slopes overlooking the Khyber

Pass, and an enemy soldier stumbled on my post, I didn't stop to engage him in polite chitchat. Same in the trenches. Don't believe what they tell you about playing football at Christmas. When a man's been sent out to kill you, and you get the chance to pull the trigger first, you pull the trigger.

I was betting on him being an amateur. A sportsman. Queensberry Rules and all that. Clear rules of engagement, based on a Victorian attempt to impose order on man's baser instincts. If he said anything to me instead of shooting, he was a dead man.

77

'You're coming with me,' he said.

Five minutes gone.

'You fire that gun, you'll have every sentry at the facility on alert,' I said. 'It's goodbye, *Adler Tag*. I don't think Vaughn's going to thank you for that, do you?'

His eyes flicked to the house, up on the hill. I had no idea if what I'd said was true. In fact, it was highly doubtful. We were down in a hollow, where the noise of one shot from a rifle would be muffled by the topography.

But all that was beside the point. It's not what you say, it's how you say it. Put enough self-confidence into it and people will believe anything.

Better than that, tell somebody what they want to hear, and they'll believe you every time. Tommy Torson had made his name as a boxer. He'd been sent out with a gun, and I'd told him not to use it. That was music to his ears.

Torson grinned, and put the gun down, leaning it against a tree. A pleasurable interlude. Beat up the farmer, teach him a thing or two about boxing, pick up the gun again and report back to the house. They'd give him a prize, like in the good old days.

He strode towards me, rolling his sleeves up.

I ran.

★

I ran along the contour of the slope, along the fence, a grassy meadow on my right, with Vaughn's gardens and house in the distance. Torson followed me, as I knew he would. He left the gun behind, as I knew he would. I ran faster than he did, so eventually I stopped, to let him catch up.

He gained on me, breathing heavily. He was built for power, not for speed.

I ran back towards him, surprising him. He stopped and put his hands out, but I ducked around him, like a boy playing British Bulldog in the playground. Now I was closest to the gun, and I was the faster runner.

He chased me, his boots pounding the ground. He put on a burst of speed, but the race was a foregone conclusion. I beat him to the gun with seconds to spare. Not long enough to get it to my shoulder and cock the hammer, but that wasn't a problem. Sometimes you have to think outside the lines. The rifle was a multi-purpose weapon. Useful to fire small pieces of metal at speed, but it had other uses. I grabbed the barrel and swung it around like the Americans do with a baseball bat. Nice long steel barrel. Heavy oak stock. Beautifully weighted.

He ducked, thinking I was going for his head. It would have worked for him, but I was aiming lower. I'd been aiming for his knees, but him ducking brought his head into play. I adjusted the trajectory, like a batsman following a rising fast ball, and the oak stock hit the side of his head with a crack.

He slumped to the ground, and I swung the gun around for another blow, but it wasn't needed. He was already dead.

Ten minutes gone.

I looked up towards the house, looming in the distance, its chimneys visible over the slope of the lawns and gardens. No windows in sight. Nobody would have seen.

But I had a problem. We were directly on the route from Vaughn's house to the transmitter. In less than an hour, I'd be here again.

It would be dark, but they'd notice the body.

I grabbed it by the arms and dragged it along the line of the hill, following the route I'd run only a minute earlier. I kept my eyes on the woods below me, looking for a place I could leave the body. Suddenly, the woods looked a lot less wild than I'd expected. Tree trunks reached up to the canopy, but down below was a neat carpet of leaves. Nowhere to hide a body.

Worse still, I was leaving two gouges in the grass, where Torson's feet were digging into the soft ground. Probably not enough to raise suspicion, but probably wasn't good enough.

I bent down to shoulder the body, like putting on a heavy rucksack. I arched my back, stooping forwards, and I felt his feet lift off the ground behind me. An inch of clearance from the ground, but enough.

I staggered forwards, keeping my eyes on the far end of the grassy slope, fifty yards from me. The woods there looked thicker.

Torson's head lolled next to my cheek. I felt liquid on my face, and I smelt blood. I concentrated on each step, fifty yards shrinking to forty, thirty, then halfway there.

There was a fallen birch tree on my left. Blown down in a storm, pulling up a large root ball. A hole where the roots should have been. I shuffled over to the edge of the hole and tipped the body in.

It lay there at the bottom of the hole, a man-shaped silhouette against white sand.

I kicked in soil from the crumbling edge. There was a thin layer of soil and grass. Underneath that, sand and rock.

I kicked soil, sand and rock into the hole, working my way along the edge until the body was gone. It wasn't perfect, but it would do.

I checked my watch. Twenty to two.

Not enough time.

*

I'd left the window ajar but I needn't have worried. Margaret was leaning out, ready to help me in. She looked at me quizzically and I shook my head.

'What happened?' Margaret whispered.

'One of the Blackshirts was waiting for me,' I said. 'Are you all right to be in here?'

'Vaughn made his move,' she said. 'I couldn't do it. I told him I was going to make up with you, and if that meant I couldn't be part of his game then so be it.'

There was a creak from the corridor outside the room. Someone was up and about. Margaret froze.

'Get into bed,' she said.

We got under the covers and listened for more movement. Footsteps, walking away.

'Now what?' Margaret asked.

Fifteen minutes left.

'Wake me up at two,' I said.

78

The grandfather clock in the hall downstairs chimed two. A mournful sound, in the quiet old house. A few seconds later, a smaller clock, higher-pitched, further away, gave the same report.

There was a knock on the door. Vaughn must have been waiting for the clock. Probably been walking around the house in his camouflage warpaint, rucksack on, counting down the seconds.

'One minute,' I said loudly. Let him know who was in charge.

Vaughn left, clomping through the house, rousing the others.

I stroked Margaret's face.

'They'll use you as a hostage until it's all done and dusted,' I said to Margaret.

'I'll let them think that's what they're doing,' she said.

'If it all goes wrong . . .'

'I haven't seen you worried before,' she said.

'I'm not worried. I'm about to lead a badly trained team of Nazi sympathisers to infiltrate the country's most secret military installation. I'll either get killed in the process, or we'll succeed, and I'll have helped the Germans with their invasion. What's there to be worried about?'

'You'll figure it out,' she said, and kissed me on the lips. 'You're a good man, John Cook.'

Vaughn came back, boots heavy on the floor. The door opened and he peered in.

'Ready?' he asked.

'Ready,' I said.

Behind Vaughn, the remaining Blackshirt stood guard. He looked at Margaret and smiled. It wasn't a pleasant smile.

'If you touch her,' I said to him, 'I'll kill you.'

79

It was dark. Full cloud cover and no lights on the horizon.

Metal clinked on metal. Freddie hadn't taped down his buckles like I'd told him to. Freddie thought the rules didn't apply to him, and it was going to catch up with him sooner or later. In front, Vaughn scuffed through the low heather. He knew this landscape like the back of his hand, he'd said, so I'd put him in the lead. We walked quickly, the adrenaline rushing through our bodies, pushing us on.

The night air was strong with the smell of fox, out there somewhere, marking its territory.

The darkness, and the quiet, helped me think. And I had a lot to think about. Situation: I was leading three amateurs into a secret facility, presumably heavily guarded.

Complication one: I was meant to give advance warning of the attack, so Bunny and his guards could melt into the darkness and let us get in and out without confrontation, let Miriam see what she needed to see and get the word back to Berlin.

Complication two: instead of leading a sightseeing mission, I was now leading a demolition team.

Solution: give it my best shot, and hope that everything worked out like it was supposed to.

The more I thought it through, the less I liked it.

We reached a stream at the bottom of the long slope down from Vaughn's place. Until now we'd been on Vaughn's land.

His palatial house, his prize-winning gardens. Across the stream, the Forest was open to the horizon. No-man's-land.

We all felt it. We were crossing the Rubicon. Freddie wasted no time, wading into the fast-flowing water up to his knees. Vaughn followed, conspicuously showing how little he cared about a bit of cold water. Halfway across he reached back to take Miriam's hand and she skipped across, using two wet rocks as stepping stones.

My time in the trenches had given me a lifelong aversion to getting my feet wet, so I hurried along the bank until I found a rotten trunk, fallen across the stream. I stepped quickly across, and landed on the far side.

Back in no-man's-land, as if I never left.

Vaughn started up the slope, but I put my hand on his shoulder, halting him.

'Listen,' I said, keeping my voice low. They all crowded in around me. 'What we're doing is war. It's not a debate. It's not sticking leaflets on a lamppost. It's not leaving a rotten egg on the headmaster's chair. From here on out, we're the enemy, and once we go past their perimeter, they'll be shooting to kill.'

'If they start shooting, they're asking for trouble,' Freddie said.

'Remember, the dark is our friend,' I said. 'So we go slowly. Slow enough they don't see movement. Once we're in, we keep it dark, slow and silent. This mission is a success if we get in and out and they never knew we were there. The first thing they hear from us is our explosives going off, long after we've disappeared into the night.'

We'd been over this so many times it was second nature to everyone, but I wanted to drill it into them one last time. I wanted them focused on the idea of getting in and out without it turning into a gunfight.

'If it does go bad. Don't let them take you alive,' I continued. 'If they capture you, you'll be going into a dark hole where nobody will ever hear from you again. No rules. No crying uncle. They'll torture you until you tell them everything you can, about this mission, about the invasion. If you go down with a bullet wound, or with a broken leg from tripping in a rabbit hole in the dark, don't let them take you alive.'

80

The fence was as I remembered. No expense spared. Concrete posts, eight feet high, angled outwards towards the top. Holes drilled every six inches, so the wire could be threaded through. Every post firmly bedded into the ground with more concrete. I pushed a post, feeling for give. Nothing.

Cutting the wire would be easy, but keeping that fact secret wouldn't. The wire was tensioned somewhere along the boundary, pulled tight, like a guitar string. If we cut the wire, that strand would go slack all along the length of the fence. A good defence mechanism – instant feedback to anyone keeping an eye out for intruders.

Vaughn took off his rucksack and opened it. He pulled out two large wrenches, giving one to Freddie and one to me. We all knew our part. We'd practised this on a set-up on Vaughn's land. Freddie and I fastened our wrenches to the bottom wire, four feet apart from each other. I nodded to Vaughn, who took a large pair of wire cutters from his rucksack and cut the wire. The loose ends between me and Freddie sagged, but the rest of the length held taught as long as we kept the tension with our wrenches.

I walked in an arc back from the fence, back around the nearest concrete posts. I wrapped the wire around the post and tied it in a rough knot. It wasn't pretty, but it held the tension. Freddie did the same.

Now our section of fence had one less strand, near ground level. The next strand up was a foot off the ground.

We repeated the process, faster this time, now we had our technique. Soon we had eighteen inches of clearance between the ground and the lowest strand of wire.

There was a pause. A moment. Cutting the line had felt like a transgression but it was still only that. Crossing the line was different. Once you crossed the line you were committed.

Freddie took off his rucksack and casually threw it under the wire. I winced as it landed with a thump. The rational part of my brain knew the explosives it contained wouldn't go off without a detonating charge, but it's one thing to know something, another thing to bet your life on it.

I lay down and pushed my face into the grass. The soil smelt of year upon year of rotting leaves. If you'd asked the younger me, I'd have told you that no bad can come to a man in a world where the soil smells like that. Of course, that young man hadn't been to the front. Now I knew the full spectrum of things that can happen to a man when he puts himself in harm's way, but still the smell of the earth was a comfort.

I stood up, on the other side. Across the line.

'Time to move,' I said, using my command voice, no discussion. That broke the spell.

Miriam was the last under the fence. She pulled herself up from the grass and pulled a map from her pocket.

Vaughn opened his coat and spread it around the map, while Miriam shone her torch on it, covering the beam so it wouldn't give us away. She looked up, checking her bearings, then stood and walked to a large gorse bush in the middle of a patch of short, sheep-cropped grass.

I'd given Miriam the job of map-reader. She had a sharp mind and took things seriously. And it gave her a job to do, something to focus on.

'It should be here,' she said.

There was an edge of panic in her voice. That moment when reality intrudes on a well-laid plan. It's a moment that occurs, without fail, on every mission. No plan is perfect, and it's how you deal with the imperfection that separates the winners from the losers.

We kicked the long grass, hoping to find the access hatch. I'd seen it from inside the tunnel, the size of a manhole cover, set into concrete. My memory of how far along the tunnel it had been wasn't perfect.

'It's meant to be here,' she said.

I nodded at the gorse bush. Twenty feet across. Eight feet high. Thick foliage, dense with sharp thorns and the remnants of yellow flowers that would have been in full bloom a month earlier.

I reached into the bush and grabbed a branch, my arm complaining at the instant attack from hundreds of thorns. I pulled the branch, and the whole bush moved towards me easily. Too easily. No resistance from deep roots.

I walked backwards, pulling the bush with me. There was a certain weight to the whole thing, but not nearly enough. Most of the weight was from the two-foot diameter root ball, wrapped in hessian along with a clump of soil. Enough to keep the bush alive, the hessian acting as a barrier to stop the roots taking hold in the soil surrounding the access hatch. A neat disguise, straight out of a spy novel. It smacked of Bunny and his Elstree screenwriters.

Miriam was on her knees by the hatch, and the others hurried over, boots clomping on the ground. I held up my hand to them. They stopped, and I put my finger to my lips.

I knelt next to Miriam. The hatch was a simple manhole cover. A steel D-ring lying flat in the centre of a steel disc, stamped like a waffle with the imprint of its maker – Hancock Foundry, Leicester.

I pulled up the D-ring and got three fingers through it, then pulled the cover. It came away easily, a small shower of soil falling down into the darkness. I put the cover down on the grass and we all listened. There was nothing. No sirens. No running footsteps. No cries of alarm.

Miriam already had her rucksack off, ready to go in. We stood back, watching her. I pictured her sitting in the empty fuselage of a bomber as it flew across the Channel, steeling herself to jump out into the pitch-black sky, not knowing whether she'd land in a field or be impaled on a tree. Not many people would raise their hand for that mission.

Freddie was looking out into the darkness. Now our eyes were accustomed to the dark, we could make out the faintest outline of the clump of trees, with the secret transmitters hidden amongst them.

'Freddie,' I said. 'You're next.'

Freddie shook his head.

'No,' he said. 'I'll stay above ground. I'll meet you at the towers.'

Freddie was nervous. Nothing new there. From the moment I'd met him I couldn't think of a second when he'd been at peace. But this was different.

'You're coming with us,' I said. I still hadn't worked out how I was going to neutralise the threat of the explosives, but one thing was clear. If Freddie and the explosives weren't with us, I wouldn't stand a chance.

'I'll meet you there,' he said. 'Don't worry about me.'

He hurried off, into the dark.

I looked at Vaughn, but he looked away. Didn't want to meet my eye.

'What's going on?' I asked.

'Nothing,' he lied. 'Freddie being Freddie.'

I couldn't chase Freddie without giving the game away. As he disappeared into the night, my own illusions about keeping this night under control disappeared with him. I'd been a fool to think I could stage manage this whole thing. I'd been as naive as Bunny's Elstree screenwriters. Worse – I should have known better. I did know better.

Miriam was below us, in the tunnel. I handed her rucksack down, thinking furiously. It had been vanity to assume I could control this. But I still had a job to do. Get Miriam in, and then get her out. Then I could turn my attention to Freddie. Everything else was a distraction.

81

Miriam led the way along the concrete-lined tunnel. Vaughn followed and I brought up the rear. Our rubber soles had picked up sand and grit from the Forest, and every step was audible on the smooth concrete floor.

Just as when I'd come this way with Bunny, I noticed the upward slope. Soon we came to what Bunny had called the submarine door. I joined Miriam and we looked through the small window. It was dark. Nobody around. So far, so good. The last time I'd been here the whole place had been buzzing with technicians. That mental image had stuck with me, and I'd been expecting it again. But it looked like the operation shut down for the night. Perhaps this would work. Perhaps we'd get in and out without any problems.

Miriam took hold of the wheel on the door. It turned easily, a well-oiled mechanism, built and installed with the highest level of craftsmanship. When Bunny wanted to put on a show, he didn't mess around.

Miriam stopped on the other side of the door, experiencing the same awe I'd felt when Bunny had brought me here.

The cinema, Bunny had called it, a huge art deco lobby. A piece of whimsy from the designer and builders. Generous arches recessed into white plaster walls. There was even a wall of fake film posters, showing square-jawed heroes in army uniforms, swooning heroines, and dastardly villains with swastikas on their lapels.

'We deciphered radio transmissions talking about the picture house,' Miriam said, 'but we thought we must have got it wrong.'

'I suppose if you're building a facility where people are going to be underground all day, you may as well make it uplifting,' Vaughn said.

'Not in Germany you don't,' Miriam said.

She hurried to a heavy door next to a sign that read:

Strictly No Magnets

'In here,' she whispered.

*

The transmitter hummed with electricity, glowing from its rows and rows of dials. Miriam ran her hand lovingly along the Bakelite panels. She found a metal plaque embedded in the main console, and pulled out a notebook to take down details.

Vaughn pulled off his rucksack and delved inside. He pulled out a small pack, wrapped in brown cellophane. It was the size of a half-pound bag of flour.

I grabbed the TNT from his hand and shoved it back in his pack.

'If you want to blow it up,' I said, 'we'll do it when we know we're getting clear. We'll get through the hatch, and drop the explosive back down. All right?'

Vaughn glared at me. He knew I was right, but no man likes to be challenged, especially when his blood's up.

'Do as he says, Vaughn,' Miriam said. She was taking readings from a panel of glowing dials. He obeyed her. She outranked him, I realised. She was the special agent, sent by Berlin. He was just the local fixer.

'We need to go,' I said. 'We've been lucky. I don't want to push it.'

'I need more time,' Miriam said.

'There isn't more time,' I replied. Every second we spent here was a second longer than I liked.

'Two minutes,' Miriam said.

'One,' I countered.

It was arrogance, of course. Bickering gave us the illusion that either one of us was in control. But we were fooling ourselves. When you start thinking you've got the mission under control, that's when it shows you who's boss. This time was no exception.

I stepped out of the room and checked my watch. Five seconds gone. Fifty-five seconds left. The second hand crawled.

I heard a distant sound and froze. Nothing. Probably my imagination, senses amped up, hearing threats in the silence.

I could try to hurry Miriam, but I'd end up slowing things down. Best to leave her. Let her get the information she needed to take back to Berlin, convince them this was just a radio station.

I heard the sound again. Not my imagination. Not a drill. Rubber-soled boots on painted concrete, crunching over the dirt we'd brought in with us. Ten men at least. Maybe more.

Miriam wasn't ready. She was furiously copying down readings from a bank of dials in the transmitter room.

'Miriam,' I said. 'Time to go.'

'I need more time,' she said.

There was a shout from the long corridor, on the other side of the submarine door. No effort to hide their arrival. Why should they? They had right on their side, and twenty men, probably all armed with rifles. They'd been trained to defend this facility with their lives. Churchill had told them the invasion was about to take place. Now they got to play their part. Defend the homeland or go down trying.

'Miriam,' I said, as she ran to another panel of dials.

'Thirty seconds,' she said.

'We're out of time,' I said.

82

The submarine door was shut, but there was light coming through the small window. Light from the corridor beyond. Shadows played on the glass. Boots crunched on concrete. Men running into position. Metal on metal as guns were prepared.

I remembered what Bunny had said to me.

Nobody will know you're coming.

The men on the other side of the door weren't playing along with the scenario the Elstree scriptwriters had concocted. They didn't know I'd been invited in. They didn't care.

Vaughn and Miriam saw the light and knew its significance. Time to go.

The metal ladder that Bunny and I had climbed was on the far side of the foyer, painted white to blend in with the décor, leading upwards. In the high ceiling, twenty feet up, the hatch that would take us out to the clump, where Freddie would be waiting.

The submarine door opened and a soldier hurried into the cinema lobby. He was young, barely out of short trousers. He was a local lad. He'd been propping up the bar at The Cross for the past year. Hadn't been around for a while now. Must have signed up.

'You're not allowed to be here,' he said to Miriam.

Miriam raised her gun.

'Don't,' I said. But she didn't listen. She pulled the trigger. Deafening, in the concrete bunker. The young lad collapsed, dead before he hit the floor.

Another gunshot rang out, a rifle. Bolt-action. Single shot, from the corridor beyond the submarine door. Miriam's hand went to her shoulder and she pulled it away. It was red with blood.

A siren started up, the eerie wail rising steadily.

Miriam fainted, her body pulling blood to its core in a bid for survival.

The next sound was the crunch of the bolt as the man who'd shot Miriam loaded another round from his ten-shot magazine. I kicked the door shut. I looked for a lock, fantasising about a huge steel bar I could set across the whole door, but there was no way to secure the door from this side. The only thing stopping the sentries on the other side from opening it was the knowledge that we had guns, and that whoever opened it and stepped forwards would be dead within a second.

Above me, the round window in the door shattered and another shot hit the foyer wall.

I drew my Webley revolver from its holster, stood up, and put a round through the small window. I dropped my hand low and tried to angle it high, aiming for the top inch of the opening, but there wasn't much leeway. I hoped I hadn't taken anyone's head off.

I looked at the ladder. Twenty feet, straight up. Miriam was out cold on the floor. If I left her behind, this was all for nothing.

'Go,' I said to Vaughn, nodding at the ladder. 'Get that hatch open.'

Vaughn ran across the line of light from the submarine door, drawing a burst of fire. He reached the ladder unscathed and looked back at me.

'I'll bring her,' I said. 'Go!'

Vaughn's boots clanged on the ladder. They'd hear it in the corridor, on the other side of the submarine door. They'd be huddled there, on either side of the small window, working on a plan.

I put another round through the window, lower this time. I didn't *want* to hit any of them, but if it came to it, and I had to choose them or me going down in a firefight, I'd choose them. This wasn't a situation I'd created, I told myself. Everything that played out was on Bunny. This was his show.

First problem, Miriam was still in view of the window. I dragged her out of the shaft of light, into the darkness.

'You three!' I shouted. 'Keep your guns on that door and take out anyone that comes through it!'

If I was going to be an actor in Bunny's play, it was time to start playing the part well. If the men on the other side knew it was only me, with one revolver and five rounds in the barrel, and an unconscious woman, they might decide the odds were in their favour. Someone at the back would give the order to open the door and rush me. No skin off his nose if the first couple of men through the door didn't make it. That's what infantry were for, soaking up bullets.

'Use the Bren!' I shouted, over-egging it perhaps. The Bren gun, a two-man tripod-mounted machine-gun, was capable of firing five hundred rounds per minute. Eight rounds per second. Assuming a full unit of twenty men in that corridor, once the door was opened, a Bren would chew its way through all of them. Even the man at the back, giving orders, would think twice.

I put my shoulder to Miriam's waist, and pulled her upper body over mine in a fireman's lift, getting to my knees and then my feet, Miriam slung over my shoulder like a sack of feed.

I put two more rounds through the small window, ran across the shaft of light, and grabbed hold of the ladder.

83

The siren wailed from below, not loud enough to cover the sound of men running into the cinema, twenty feet below me. I heard confused shouts, then shots. I pulled my legs out of harm's way, just in time. Bullets clinked against the hatch as I closed it. I turned a circular handle to lock the mechanism and shoved an iron bar through the handle, wedging it tight against the concrete. Nobody would be coming through from below.

With the hatch closed, it was strangely quiet. Even the siren sounded muffled, like a radio playing in a distant room.

There was a thick mist. I could barely see Vaughn, four feet in front of me, kneeling by his sister, holding a compress to the wound on her shoulder.

There was the merest hint of purple morning light. Enough to give a dull illumination to the rising mist, but not enough to pierce it. The only discernible shapes in the blankness were looming columns. The trees, and the towers.

I pulled a compass from my jacket pocket and orientated myself. I was facing south. Taking a route to my left would get us out, in the direction of the Leckies' house.

I knelt by Vaughn. Miriam's skin was as pallid as the mist. She was in shock.

I showed Vaughn the compass.

'Head that way,' I said, making a chopping gesture towards the east, into the mist. 'Keep going until you're clear of the trees. You'll come to Palehouse Lane. Stay off it, but keep it on your right. I'll meet you at the Leckies' house.'

'Is she going to make it?' he asked. He was lost, on the verge of tears. Suddenly the war games and debates meant nothing. How different history would be, if all men had to confront the reality of failure as much as the excitement of victory, before they chose their path.

'Two possible outcomes,' I said. 'She either lives or dies.'

I pulled bandages from his rucksack. I wrapped a length of bandage around her, pulling it tight. With luck, it would hold the compress against the wound.

'If you stay here, she'll either die or end up in prison. They'll execute her for treason. If you take her, she'll either die, or she'll survive and there'll be a chance we can all evade capture.'

He picked her up.

I pressed the compass into his hand.

'Go to the Leckies' house,' I said. 'I'll catch up with you.'

He nodded, and stumbled forwards, into the mist.

'Where's Freddie?' I shouted after him, but he didn't turn around.

How far would he get, carrying her? What would he do when he realised his own chance of escape was vastly improved without his dying sister in his arms? Not a decision I'd wish on any man, even my enemy.

84

A muffled shot rang out. Impossible to tell where it came from. Another shot answered it. There was a dim flash in the gloomy haze. I set off in the direction of the flash, moving slowly. A tree loomed up at the last minute, and I pressed myself against its dark trunk.

A third shot. A rifle. A pistol shot replied. In the mist, it was impossible to tell who was who, and who was where. Like playing battleships against an unknown number of opponents.

A man ran towards me. I hid behind a tree, and he passed me by. It was Freddie. He had something in his hand. The same thing Vaughn had brought along. A small pack, the size of a bag of flour, wrapped in cellophane.

TNT.

Behind me, a rattle of machine-gun fire.

I gave chase, but was stopped by a jarring blow to my forehead. My fight-or-flight reflex kicked in, and I reached into the mist to engage with my assailant. But there was nobody there. I felt in the air in front of my throbbing forehead, and found my attacker. An angled steel bar. Solid. Cold. Dripping with moisture pulled out of the mist. I felt along the bar, it connected to an angled upright. I was at the base of one of the transmission towers.

What was Freddie up to? I had a bad feeling I knew the answer.

A breeze cleared the mist a few feet in front of me and my fears were confirmed. A small parcel, tied to one of the four corner struts of the transmission tower. I pulled a knife from my pocket and slit the rope tying the parcel to the tower, knowing what I'd see inside. A brown cellophane pack. Stuck into the pack, a detonator, and leading to the detonator, a short tail of fuse cord. The cord was burning. A slow fuse. Sixty seconds per foot, one foot left. He'd be aiming to have each of his explosives go off at the same time. Less chance of any defenders foiling the plan. I pulled the bomb apart and threw the fuse into the damp pine needles.

I'd got here in time, but how many others were out there?

The mist closed in again. A twig snapped to my right and I followed the sound, hoping it was Freddie and not a sentry. A silhouette in the mist caught my eye. His movement identified him, jerky, uncomfortable in his environment.

He saw me. Without hesitating, he drew his pistol and fired. A tree trunk behind me exploded in splinters. A miss.

'Freddie,' I said, 'time to go.'

He fired again. He'd made his choice. It wasn't one that was going to end well for him.

I drew my own revolver and got off a quick shot. Unlikely to hit him at thirty yards, more useful as a warning. He took the hint, turned and ran. And with that, the hunt was on.

I followed him, as quietly as I could, stopping to listen for him, and for sentries. A difficult environment for stealth, every footstep caused a whole symphony of cracks from dead branches. I gave up on quiet, and prioritised speed instead. I kept him in my sights, gaining on him. The mist was getting thinner, and the sky was getting lighter.

Freddie reached the base of another transmitter, pulling off his rucksack as he neared it, intent on getting the job done. In different circumstances, my kind of soldier.

I took up a position behind a pine, and peered round. A shot clipped the bark inches from my face, and I ducked back behind the tree, but I'd seen enough for an initial assessment.

He was thirty yards away, across open ground. Nothing to stop a bullet, just scrubby birch trees gaining a foothold in the clearing created to install the tower.

Cellophane crinkled as he unwrapped a pack of TNT.

He'd be focused on the task, locked into a process that had a definite number of steps, none of which could be hurried or skipped. One minute at most, but no less than forty seconds. Brave of him to stick to his mission, knowing I was trying to stop him.

I backed away from the tree, keeping its thick trunk between me and him. Ten yards back, I was invisible in the trees. I struck out to my left. If he was at the centre of a clock face, and I was at six, I wanted to get to ten. Once he realised I'd moved, he'd be expecting three or nine. A short cut in the ancient mind – if someone's not in front of me, they're about to pounce from my side. A right-handed man will turn to his left, a forehand shot. So I was going for a right hand turn, backhand for him, past the point of ninety degrees, somewhere over his right shoulder. His dead zone.

I hurried. I could picture what he was doing. Tying the fuse cord in a knot for increased effectiveness. Embedding the detonator in the soft putty of the TNT. Cutting the fuse cord the appropriate distance. Fast-burning fuse. Ten seconds per foot. He'd need time to get out of the blast zone. He'd be passing the cord through his hands, counting off the feet, three feet each time he spread his arms. Three . . . six . . .

He flicked his lighter. Right on schedule.

I aimed my revolver and fired, the bullet ricocheting off the steel tower behind him.

He swung around, wildly letting off a shot. It missed me by a comfortable margin. He was shooting blind, shooting to provide himself comfort, no hope of hitting his man.

He'd lit the fuse. Fast-burning. Ten seconds per foot. Six feet perhaps. He needed to move.

I put another two shots over his head, and he ducked down. He knew the timings. He'd be arguing with himself. Stay or go. Stay was only going to end one way, so he had to launch himself into a run, across the open ground.

He set off, and I fired again. I aimed low, and got him in the thigh. He went down, sprawled in the leaves.

Ten seconds per foot. One or two feet left.

I put another shot over his head, then it was time to move. I was in the blast radius. I rolled back, into a ditch, and flattened myself into the mud, pressing every inch of my body as far into the ground as I could. Back in the trench I'd spent my life trying to escape. Only this trench was barely a foot deep. Possibly enough to protect me. Possibly not. In any event, it was all I had, so it had to do.

I risked a look. Freddie had pulled himself to his feet. He took a step, but the injured leg failed him. He was out of time, and he knew it. We looked each other in the eye. He opened his mouth to curse me, as if that had some kind of power. There was a blinding flash as the fuse ignited the TNT, and in the next instant Freddie didn't exist.

I ducked back down into the ditch, pressing myself into the mud as the blast wave went over. It sucked the air out of my lungs and lifted me up, then dropped me back down.

A thick cloud of dust and leaves followed, everything that could be picked up and moved, thrown through the air by rolling waves of concussion. I kept my mouth shut. Some of that dust was Freddie, in particulate form.

I pulled myself up, ears ringing. The transmission tower still stood, untroubled. One corner of its base was destroyed, where Freddie had mounted the explosive, but the other three corners held fast.

85

The shed was a dark rectangle in the mist. Unremarkable. Just a low, single-storey building with a sheet-metal door painted dull green. No attempt at hiding it. No set dressing in the form of moveable gorse bushes. No pretence it was some kind of cinema. Just a concrete shed with a corrugated-metal roof.

The door swung open as I passed. Adams stepped out, the scar on his face emphasised as he drew on a cigarette.

'Job done?' he asked.

'Job done,' I answered.

He ground the cigarette out and gestured back inside the shed. I followed him.

I stepped inside and found myself looking down the barrel of an Enfield number two pistol. It was held by a young woman with a tight, pale face, dressed in the light blue uniform of the Women's Auxiliary Air Force. She was doing a good job of holding the gun steady, despite the adrenaline that must have been pumping through her body. She looked terrified, but there was a steely quality to her eyes that spoke of months of training and belief in the rightness of what she was about to do.

'It's all right,' Adams said, as he filled a kettle from a tap. 'He's with me.' The young woman lowered the gun, but kept alert.

We were in a small room, dark, with a greenish glow. Adams was at a sink on the left wall. In the middle of the room there was a metal desk with two chairs. Each chair was occupied. Two more WAAFs, both with headsets, wires trailing from a conduit that ran across the ceiling.

The woman with the gun put her finger to her lips. I nodded.

The WAAFs at the desk ignored us, intent on their work. They were focused on a glass dome, about the size of a dinner plate. It bowed out from the table, like a porthole on a ship. Some form of television. The screen glowed with a faint green light. A jagged line had been carefully drawn onto the screen with a white wax pencil. It was a shape recognisable to any Englishman – the south coast, from the Isle of Wight, along to Kent and up to the Thames Estuary. Below that line, a corresponding shape showing the coast of mainland Europe. A cloud of dots, too many to count, floated in what would be the English Channel.

The WAAF nearest the glass dome put a curved ruler over it and made a mark. She took a reading and relayed it to her partner.

'Bogies. Numerous. Forty miles out. One hundred and fifty-four degrees.'

Her partner wrote in a notebook, reading back the information as she did so.

'Forty miles, one hundred and fifty-four degrees.'

She pressed the side of her headset and spoke with a firmer voice, as if she were making a telephone call.

'Chain Home, this is Aspidistra. Bogies at forty miles, one hundred and fifty-four degrees.'

She listened.

'Too numerous to count,' she said.

She listened again.

'Copy Chain Home.'

The young woman with the pistol stepped between me and her colleagues at the desk, blocking my view.

Adams lit a match, igniting a gas ring under the kettle.

'Any messages for Bunny?' he asked.

I shook my head, then thought better of it.

'Tell him it had better be worth it,' I said, thinking of the young man lying dead thirty feet below us, and Miriam, probably bleeding to death in her brother's arms, somewhere out there in the mist.

'You know the answer to that,' Adams said.

I looked at the glowing screen in the middle of the table. The cloud of dots had crept closer to the jagged line that represented the coast, less than twenty miles south of us.

'Whatever it takes,' I said.

86

Vaughn's house was dark against the soft glow of the dawn sky. Red sky in the morning. A bad sign, if you believed in that kind of thing.

The front doors were unlocked. I took the stairs two at a time. No sign of the Blackshirt. He'd been left to guard Margaret. Keep her hostage, in case Vaughn or I decided not to follow Lord Howe's script.

I walked along the bedroom corridor. I wanted to run but I didn't give in to it. Don't give in, and it's not real.

I opened the door and stopped at the threshold. It was too much to take in: a collage of images telling a violent story. Blood dripped slowly down the wallpaper. Blood pooled on the floor. Blood smeared across the window. A chair lay in pieces, its legs broken.

There was something on the floor on the far side of the bed.

A shoe.

Margaret's shoe.

★

Spots of blood on the back stairs created a trail. I followed them, like Hansel and Gretel following breadcrumbs.

Since I'd come back from the war, I'd been empty. I'd gone through the motions. I'd found things that got me through the day, and through the year. Ploughing a hundred acres, row after row, day after day. Expanding the farm, letting the profits pile up in the bank. Sitting in the pub with Doc, letting the drink dull the edges. None of those things brought colour or feeling.

Margaret had changed things. I'd started to think about the future. The two of us. Getting through the war. Growing old. Children perhaps. Grandchildren.

Blakeney had taught me better. Planning is useful, he used to say, but only a simpleton expects things to go according to plan.

Another bloody handprint on the patio door beckoned me outside. I thought about ignoring it, staying inside. But my brief glimpse of a life worth living was over, so I had nothing to lose. Hard to shock a man whose light has gone out.

The trail of blood continued out on the patio, across the flagstones, to an ornamental pond. Stone steps led into the water, a peaceful spot for a swim. Wet footsteps told a story. Someone had walked into the water dripping blood, then emerged, dripping water.

The footsteps were smaller than mine. Considerably smaller.

'You took your time,' she said, from behind me.

Margaret sat on a deckchair, wrapped in a blanket, her hair wet.

'Got a bit messy,' she said.

'Looks like an abattoir up there.'

She nodded.

'Mission accomplished?' she asked.

'Difficult to say.'

87

We took Margaret's car to the Leckies'. Vaughn was sitting on a log in the back garden. Miriam lay on the ground by his feet, pale, her chest barely moving. He held her hand in his, but other than that he was doing a good job of ignoring her. I'd seen it before on the battlefield – dealing with the worst by pretending it was nothing, a voice inside his head telling him this was best for Miriam. Better not to upset her.

I crouched on the springy grass and listened to her breathing. Her lungs sounded fine, which gave me hope.

'We've got to go,' I said, thinking of the plan. A submarine half a mile off the coast.

'No,' Vaughn said.

'Say goodbye to your sister,' I said. I was angry with Vaughn. This whole exercise was his fault. Now he couldn't face the consequences.

'Freddie was right about you,' Vaughn said.

He knelt by her and took her hand.

'I messed it up,' she said.

'You were perfect,' he said. 'They'll give you a medal when you get back.'

Across the Forest, I could hear distant shouts.

Freddie was right about you, Vaughn had said. Quite possibly true. Freddie was a clever young man, entirely capable of weighing up the odds of someone being friend or foe. Easier for him than for Vaughn, who'd been blinded by his desire for Margaret. But in the final analysis, Freddie was dead, as were so many other men who'd been right about me.

★

Vaughn and I laid Miriam across the back seat of Margaret's car. Her face was waxy, and her lips were blue. The wound was wet with fresh blood. I met Margaret's eye. She knew.

There was a rattle from the back garden. Mrs Leckie's bird-scarers jangling as someone pushed past them.

'I'll delay them,' Vaughn said. 'You get Miriam away.' He kissed his sister on the lips.

He hurried around the side of the house. Margaret started the car.

'One minute,' I said. I followed Vaughn.

Adams was standing in the back garden, pointing a gun at Vaughn. Two more men joined him, grim-faced men in civilian suits, out of place in the rural setting.

'Lord Matheson,' Adams said. Vaughn held out his hand to shake. Adams didn't reciprocate.

'These gentlemen would like to have a word with you,' Adams said.

The mist had cleared, as had the clouds, the portentous orange sky replaced by a dome of deep blue. It would be another hot day.

Vaughn looked at the men, then at the sky. The southern horizon looked dark.

There was a sound. A distant rumbling, like thunder. We could see the South Downs in the distance. Above them, the blue was being overwritten by row upon row of black dots, with occasional bright flashes of light.

The sound grew louder, and the black dots multiplied. German bombers. Too numerous to count, like Nazi soldiers lined up at a Nuremberg rally. An immense force.

'Not much point talking today,' Vaughn said. 'We can talk tomorrow, depending on how things go.'

'We'll talk now,' Adams said. 'And tomorrow. And the day after that. Until you haven't got anything left to tell us.'

I watched the sky. One of the dots had left formation. I squinted. It was trailing smoke. Falling out of the sky. It came down ten or fifteen miles away, over the Kent border.

More winks of light flashed in the sky. The sun, catching on reflective surfaces. More bombers fell. Higher up, vapour trails etched themselves onto the blue. Ghostly white lines describing dogfights taking place miles above us.

'They were waiting for them,' Vaughn said. 'I wonder how they knew.'

88

'This woman's been shot,' Doc said. He looked at me and Margaret as if we were the culprits. 'What happened?'

'I can't tell you,' I said.

'For Christ's sake, Cook, this isn't the time. Hold her hand, this is going to hurt.'

Miriam squeezed my hand as Doc cut back her blouse around the wound. It was ugly, as all wounds are.

'She needs a hospital,' he said.

'Can't do that,' I said. 'She needs to be mobile.'

'You're gambling with her life, Cook,' he said. He bent close to Miriam, looked her in the eye.

'If you don't get to a hospital, there's a good chance you'll die,' he said. 'I can patch you up, but I don't know how much bleeding there is inside.'

'No hospital,' she said, giving my hand another squeeze.

Doc poured antiseptic onto a pad and pressed it against the wound. Miriam gasped in pain.

'This is a bad business, Cook,' Doc said.

★

I drove to the farm, trying to avoid potholes on the road, wincing every time we hit a bump. Miriam was spread out on the back seat, her head on Margaret's lap.

I didn't fancy Miriam's chances of walking across the fields, so I drove through the yard, and took the track down to the lower meadow. It was rutted from the tractor, and the under-carriage of the car scraped worryingly against the high ground between the ruts.

With a hundred yards to go to the river, I gave it up as a bad job, and stopped the car.

'We'll have to walk from here,' I said.

*

I carried Miriam like a child, holding her in my arms. She was deathly pale.

Margaret was standing in shallow water. She'd uncovered the rowing boat, and had it ready. The riverbank was muddy, and I slipped, almost going backwards and dropping Miriam. I held her, and fought to keep my balance.

I waded into the river and laid her in the boat, like a Viking princess ready for her last rites.

I climbed into the boat and took the oars from Margaret.

'If you see Doc before he leaves, tell him I said thanks,' I said.

'I'm coming with you,' Margaret said. 'You won't be able to make it through the lock by yourself.'

89

We let the current carry us, Miriam didn't have much time, but we needed the cover of dark to get through Lewes. We waited out the afternoon under a willow, south of Isfield, and navigated the lock at Barcombe as dusk was falling. We slipped through Lewes in the dark, thankful for the blackout.

After Lewes, we were south of the Downs, the country-side flattening out as we approached the sea. The tide was going out, and it pulled us along, the English Channel growing ever closer.

'They'll make Vaughn protector of Sussex,' Miriam said, at one point. Later, she asked if she was in India.

We pulled to the bank of the river with the docks at Newhaven in the distance. It was pitch-black, but I could hear the open sea ahead. My hands were raw from the oars. Even going with the flow of the river, it had been tough work.

'How's she doing?' I asked. Whatever the answer, there was no way Miriam was going to be able to row out to sea. I'd have to go with her. Get her to the rendezvous point then bail out before I was seen.

Margaret didn't reply.

'What is it?' I asked.

'She's gone,' Margaret said.

I felt Miriam's neck, sure Margaret was wrong. There'd be a faint pulse. Hard to detect, but there nonetheless. The slightest proof of life.

But Margaret was right. Miriam was gone.

All of Bunny's scheming had come to nothing. Morning would come, and again the skies would fill with German planes. The WAAFs in the shed, in the shadows of the transmission towers, would do their job, until someone in Berlin got fed up with waiting for Miriam's report, and sent a bomber to destroy the mysterious facility in the middle of the invasion zone. Better safe than sorry, they'd say to themselves, and they'd be right.

This wasn't the first time I'd known defeat, far from it, but that didn't make it any less bitter.

'We'll take her back,' I said.

'No,' Margaret said. 'There's a different plan.'

She pulled a sheaf of papers from inside Miriam's jacket, and stuffed them in her own pocket.

'What are you doing?' I asked.

But Margaret didn't answer. She didn't look at me. Didn't want me to see what she was thinking. She took Miriam's handbag, zipped it up, and put the strap over her head and shoulder.

'I told you,' she said, 'there's a lot you don't know about me.'

'Whatever it is,' I said, 'this isn't the answer.'

'Get out of the boat,' she said. I didn't like the tone of her voice. The lightness was gone. The Margaret I knew, pushed aside.

'I can't let you go,' I said.

'John,' she said.

There was a click in the darkness. A perfectly recognisable sound. Unmistakable, no matter how I tried to misinterpret it. The hammer of a Webley revolver, pulled back. Stage one of a two-stage firing process, ready for the finger on the trigger.

'You won't shoot me,' I said.

'What was it Bunny told you?' she asked.

'Margaret. This is insane.'

'Whatever it takes.'

'I'll row you out there,' I said, thinking frantically. As long as we were together, I'd have a chance to turn this around, regardless of what this turned out to be. Was it part of Bunny's plan? Or had Margaret been playing me for a fool the whole time?

'Margaret,' I said.

'Out of the boat,' she said.

'You can't go out there.'

'I'll shoot you,' she said. 'I don't want to, but I'll do it if I have to.'

'Is this Bunny?' I asked. 'Or them?'

I didn't get an answer. I didn't expect one. What was she going to do? Give me some kind of cock-and-bull story? Besides, she didn't need to say the words. The gun in her hand was speaking volumes.

'Swim to the far bank, and don't look back.'

Last chance, I realised. I looked down at the black water and made to put my hands on the side of the boat. I'd pivot from my waist, spinning back towards her, knock the gun from her hand.

But she was one step ahead of me. I felt the gun press against the back of my neck. My freedom of manoeuvre reduced. I froze.

'If you're on our side,' I said, 'and you get into trouble, send word. I'll come for you. Do whatever it takes.'

'Out of the boat,' she said.

I slipped out, and the tidal waters took me, pulling me down, grabbing at my clothes. I kicked for the surface, and when I felt air on my face, the boat was already ten yards away.

I swam for the bank, my clothes dragging like an anchor. Another ten yards from the boat, a sliding noise behind me, a splash. Miriam, consigned to the deep. Then the creak of oars.

'Say goodbye to the children,' she said, her voice carrying across the water.

I stopped swimming. I should follow her. Catch up. Stop her.

'Tell them I'm sorry,' she said.

Then all I heard was the rhythmic splash and pull of the oars, and the roar of the distant waves.

90

The report came through from the War Ag. We'd passed with flying colours. There'd been a few comments on areas for improvement which had Bill Taylor fuming, but it was an excuse for celebration, time to enjoy what we'd all achieved.

We set out a marquee in the meadow. A band, a barrel of beer. Pushed the boat out. Everyone who'd helped with the harvest was there.

Almost everyone.

Mum made a cake, one of many. The women brought sandwiches and the men brought jugs of home-brewed drinks. Doc, still waiting to receive his mobilisation orders, tended bar. We sat on picnic rugs on the grass, as the invasion took place above our heads.

The sky was an abstract painting of swirling white lines. The first day had been gripping. The second day a curiosity. Now, on day five, it was scenery. According to the papers, the bombers' targets had been our airfields at the start, as German High Command had sought to neutralise our air power, but yesterday the headlines had changed – civilian targets bombed. The horror we'd all been expecting since the first day of the war had finally arrived.

'There's another one,' Frankie said, pointing at a growing shape in the sky to the south, over the Downs. A parachute. A pilot, who'd bailed out before his plane hit the ground.

Frankie pulled out a notebook from his gas mask box. He kept score as best he could. He was up to eight parachutes and ten planes down, all within sight of our farm. How many more tally marks would go in his little book before the end? How many more years of war? Frankie was ten. Would we still be fighting by the time he was old enough to do his bit?

I stood up, brushing crumbs from my trousers, and shook hands with a new arrival. Milosz, the Polish soldier. He was wearing a crisp, new army uniform, and had a young lady on his arm.

'They took you on?' I asked.

'They said they could do with the manpower.' He looked up at the sky and spoke quietly. 'It's not going so good as they say on the BBC.'

I smiled at the young lady on his arm.

'Miss,' I said.

'This is Edith,' Milosz said. 'Edith, my friend John Cook. Edith's a barmaid. She says I'm her favourite customer.'

'What do *you* do, Mr Cook?' she asked.

'I'm a farmer,' I said.

'Don't you want to get more involved?' she asked. 'Do your bit?'

I squinted in the sun and smiled.

'I'll leave that to the young chaps,' I said, clapping Milosz on the arm. 'Anyway, us farmers are going to win this war, didn't you know?'

91

The art deco house was locked up. The lawn was bare, the garden furniture and games gone, like a stage after closing night, the set struck within hours of the performance.

There was no reason for me to expect Bunny to show up, but it was the last place I'd seen him. I'd followed the unconscious map my mind had laid out, hoping for the satisfaction of a debrief.

I had questions that I knew Bunny wouldn't answer.

I wanted to ask why he'd got me involved. It was like introducing a bull to a china shop. I knew the answer, but I wanted Bunny to say it out loud.

I gave it a couple of hours, watching the white lines in the sky. No sign of Bunny, but I hadn't expected any different. He and I were finished, one way or another.

Besides, I had a train to catch. A trip to Cornwall.

A loose end.

92

KING'S COUSIN DIES IN HUNTING ACCIDENT
Lord Lisl Howe, 4th Earl of Wessex, was found dead this morning after being reported missing on Sunday. The Earl had set out for his daily walk at his ancestral home in Cornwall. As was his habit, the Earl had taken his shotgun. The alarm was raised on Sunday night when it was discovered by his footman that he hadn't returned. An exhaustive search of the estate ended this morning with the discovery of the body. Lord Howe, who had recently been tipped as the next Commander in Chief, Home Forces, leaves behind an estranged wife and son, both of whom live in South Africa. A memorial service will be held at Westminster Abbey.

EPILOGUE

We sat in the kitchen, eating our tea and listening to the radio. Mabel, Kate's former housemaid, was washing up. Frankie wolfed down his bread and jam, eager to get outside before dark. Mabel had her eye on his plate, at the uneaten crusts. She'd have her own meal after us, but I knew she'd eat his scraps too. She'd been hungry every day of her life until she came to us, she'd told me. Not something you leave behind quickly or easily.

Elizabeth was quiet. Margaret had been a surrogate mother. She'd taken to spending hours alone, walking the fields.

Mabel liked listening to Lord Haw-Haw – a traitor who'd fled England and cast his lot in with Hitler, broadcasting from a secret location, deep in the Reich. He had better music than the BBC, in her opinion, and we found his propaganda so ludicrous it was comforting. Listening to his programme was illegal, but they'd have to arrest the whole country.

'This evening we have a special visitor to the studio,' Haw-Haw said in his exaggerated, Eton accent. 'Lady Miriam Matheson, a recent exile from her home in Great Britain. Lady Matheson, what prompted you to leave your ancestral home and settle in Germany?'

'Wasn't that the one we had doing our harvest?' Mum asked, excited to hear someone on the radio she might have met.

The door banged behind Frankie. I envied him, an evening of rabbits and sticks and all the fun a ten-year-old boy could have in the fields and the woods on a summer evening.

'Thank you for having me,' the guest speaker said, her voice rising and falling, fighting through static as it carried across the airwaves, hundreds of miles. 'I saw such poverty in England,' she said. 'Everyone's starving to death, and of course the harvests have all failed. I knew a farmer in England, and he said the game's about up, so I hopped on a boat and made my way over.'

Elizabeth glanced at me, a questioning look on her face.

'I understand the Luftwaffe will have control of the skies within the week, then we can launch the invasion proper. Hitler's given me his word I'll be back in London by the end of the month.'

I put a finger to my lips. Elizabeth did the same.

She smiled.

Author's note

This is a work of fiction. Many of the events and places have some basis in fact, but my first responsibility as a fiction writer is to write a compelling story, so please forgive me when I have taken liberties with historical or geographical facts. Uckfield and Ashdown Forest are real places, but most, if not all, of the details are not exactly what you'd find if you go looking for them. For instance, I spent a fun evening recently with the Uckfield Book Club, during which we all speculated exactly where John Cook's farm is. Everyone had slightly different opinions and, of course, nobody was right or wrong, because it's not real.

Nevertheless, a lot of what happens in this book has a basis in history.

Auxiliary Units, such as the one John Cook is encouraged to help set up, were a key feature of Britain's plans for defence against the predicted German invasion. There are a number of excellent books on the subject. For Sussex in particular, I found *The Secret Sussex Resistance*, by Stewart Angell, fascinating. Likewise, *With Britain in Mortal Danger*, by John Warwicker, and *The Last Ditch*, by David Lampe, have been very useful.

The secret underground radio installation, although seemingly outlandish, is based on a real facility, up on the high ground of Ashdown Forest. It really was built in secret by Canadian servicemen, and the transmission room really was called 'the cinema' because of its art deco architecture.

The radio transmitter was called Aspidistra (after the song, popular at the time – 'The Biggest Aspidistra in the World') because it was the biggest, and most powerful, radio transmitter in the world. It was installed, and used, to take over German radio broadcasts, just as in the book. Type 'Aspidistra transmitter' into a search engine and you will find some fascinating details and photos. In addition to the many online resources, I found *Truth Betrayed*, by W. J. West, a fascinating resource, as is *The Black Game*, by Ellic Howe.

The most outlandish departure from the truth is my suggestion that the Aspidistra station was in some way connected to Britain's secret radar capability, known as Chain Home. In reality, the radar stations were situated on the coast.

Coming from a rural town, I have a fascination for the kind of farming that shaped the countryside that I grew up in. Learning about the way that farmers worked their land in the first half of the twentieth century has been a true pleasure. I've become a firm fan of A. G. Street, a farmer-turned-writer from that period whose books are a joy to read. Many of them are available second-hand, and I've passed many a pleasant evening, reading up on minutiae such as how to harvest, how to build a stook, what kind of corn to plant, and so on, while holding in my hand a book written and printed in the 1930s (or earlier). If you enjoyed the harvest scene in this book, get hold of some A. G. Street – you won't regret it!

On the subject of corn, if you are reading this in the UK you are probably used to the idea that we use the term 'corn' to cover all cereal crops (mostly wheat, but not always). If you are American, you'll think that corn can only be used to describe one crop – maize. But now you know – British farmers in the first half of the twentieth century used corn as a general term, so I have too.

One story that Street tells, in his book *Shameful Harvest*, is based on the true story of a farmer who was killed by police when the War Ag determined he should have his farm taken from him. During wartime, the government had to step in to maintain food security, and a lot of good work was undoubtedly done by the men and women involved, but it wasn't all idyllic harvests, as the story of that poor farmer shows. I thought it a useful plot device to show that Cook is not always on the same side as the police, but I also wanted to draw attention to this forgotten part of Britain's history.

In the period immediately following Dunkirk, Britain was gripped by a terror of parachutists. As Cook observes, it was entirely logical to imagine that German agents and soldiers would be dropped into the country. A propaganda film from the time, available online – *Miss Grant Goes to the Door* – shows how worried people were, and how real the threat was perceived to be. It was a dangerous time, even for British pilots, many of whom floated to earth after being shot down only to find themselves at the sharp end of a farmer's bayonet.

One particularly dark chapter in the Dunkirk evacuation story is that some retreating British soldiers were told to look out for, and shoot on sight, enemy operatives who may have been parachuted behind their lines. Retreating in the face of the German advance, with conflicting information about who may or may not be a spy, it has been suggested that many soldiers suffered from a kind of mass hysteria whereby they saw German infiltrators everywhere they looked, including farmers, priests, and other innocent civilians. I found the article 'The "Fifth Column" and the British Experience of Retreat', by Glyn Prysor, published in *War in History*, Vol. 12, No. 4, a fascinating summary of this time.

Meanwhile, back in England, fear of the so-called fifth column was very real. There were many organisations that inspired Vaughn's fictional peace society. These organisations advocated for peace, but some of them received direct funding from Nazi Germany, and the British security services did their best to infiltrate and keep up with them. As the book suggests, there were indeed some very high-ranking members of society who supported these societies. *Hitler's British Traitors*, by Tim Tate, is an excellent overview.

Details of how to rig an explosive charge were taken from *The Partisan Leader's Handbook* and *The Countryman's Diary*, both government publications (the War Office) from 1939, which were distributed to men like John Cook who were to lead the fight back after the predicted invasion.

I learnt a lot about the Battle of Britain, as experienced by the people of Sussex, from *Battle Over Sussex 1940*, by Pat Burgess and Andy Saunders, as well as 'The War in East Sussex', printed by the *Sussex Express* in August 1945. In addition, I was kindly gifted an original copy of *The Battle of Britain, August–October 1940*, published in 1941 by His Majesty's Stationery Office. This fascinating document, written when the fate of the war was still very much unknown, gives a glimpse into the way that the story of the war was told, by the government, to the people of Britain.

All in all, I've tried to use the backdrop of the war to paint a convincing picture of life in Sussex in 1940, while remaining respectful to the men and women who served their country, either in the armed forces or on the Home Front, but if you go looking for historical inaccuracies you will certainly find them!

I hope you enjoyed spending time in wartime Sussex with John Cook and Lady Margaret as much as I did.

Look out for the next in the series – John Cook will return!

Acknowledgements

Jordan Lees is my agent, and has been John Cook's number one fan since the day we discussed my first draft of *The Last Line*. Jordan is a wonderful writer himself, and I couldn't have done this without him in my corner.

I've had the pleasure of working with a number of editors at Hodder & Stoughton. Thanks always to Morgan Springett, who bought the first book and took the leap of faith with me. Thanks to Phoebe Morgan, also a wonderful writer, for keeping an eye on things, and to Nick Sayers for taking me under his wing. This book has been edited by the awesome Cara Chimirri, whose ideas are always better than mine, and who I am very grateful to have on my team! Thanks also to Alara Delfosse for helping get word of the book out to the world, and thanks to the rest of the team at Hodder.

Launching a new, unknown author is a very tricky business. As a reader, how do you know to read someone unless you are recommended them by someone you trust? I have had the absolute pleasure and privilege to get to know a number of amazing people who took a chance on me, read my book even though they hadn't heard of me, and then took time and effort to write reviews, post pictures on social media, post on their blogs, and support me throughout the launch of *The Last Line*.

Thanks to Damien Lewis, Stephen Leather, Marion Todd, Robbie Morrison and Mason Cross, all of whom took valuable time away from their own writing to read *The Last Line* and provide fantastic quotes.

Special thanks go to my book blogger friends – too many to mention individually but you know who you are!

Finally, thanks as always to Danielle, Lauren and Charlotte, for everything.